NUMBERS

Dana Dane

NUMBERS

A NOVEL

One World | Ballantine Books | New York

A One World Books Trade Paperback Original

Copyright © 2009 by Dana Dane

Published in the United States by One World Books, an imprint of The Random House Publishing Group, a division of Random House, Inc., New York.

ONE WORLD is a registered trademark and the One World colophon is a trademark of Random House, Inc.

ISBN 978-0-345-50605-4

Printed in the United States of America

www.oneworldbooks.net

9 8 7 6 5 4 3 2 1

Book design by Laurie Jewell

*This book is dedicated to the memory
of my great friend Dupree "Du Me Babe" Wells.
You are never far from my thoughts.*

*In loving memory of my cousin
Shantel Shamik Gray-Robinson:
your strength was an inspiration
to every life you've touched.*

A Note from Nikki Turner

Dear Readers,

First and foremost: THANK YOU! THANK YOU! THANK YOU!

Friends, family, those who have read all my work, those that have read some, those who have been contemplating it, and even those who criticize my work: I want to say THANK YOU. My team and I couldn't do it without you.

Most of my tried-and-true readers have been keeping up with my Nikki Turner Presents novels *Gorilla Black* and *Against the Grain* and the Street Chronicles short-story collections (*Tales from da Hood,* *Girls in the Game, Christmas in the Hood*). I can't thank you enough for all of your undying support. You have helped me to help others share their stories with the world. I've been proud of each and every one of my authors' tales, but I am even more excited about working with the author of the latest book to be released in my line.

Among many other things, Dana Dane is a first-generation hip-hop icon, and now he adds published writer to the list. Congrats, Dana! Before I make all the formal introductions, let me take you on a trip down memory lane. One of my dearest passions besides writing is music, especially old-school music: Slick Rick, Dana Dane, Run-DMC, etc. (This is ironic, since I can't even hum in tune. Seriously! They kicked me out of the church choir. But that's another story altogether.) When Dana Dane's lawyer called and asked if I would be interested in doing a deal with his client, I could not pass up an opportunity to work with someone whose work I had loved and respected long before I ever picked up a pen to write a book.

After talking to the legendary artist, I found out that he had written a children's book and a few short stories but nothing, at the time, that would be a good fit for my line. Months later, after talking on the phone about everything from sneakers to hats, books, movies, politics, and the game called life, we both started to realize that though our industries (books and music) were two totally different animals of the entertainment jungle, we both had been through similar highs and lows as artists.

And then Dana Dane sent me the rough draft of *Numbers*.

This was it. I told him I loved it and thought that it would be an excellent way for him to enter into the book world, and he responded, "Cool! Let's make it do what it do." After slashing through all of the red tape with the lawyers, agents, and Ballantine, we worked it all out to make it happen. After the ink was dry I would tell people that Nikki Turner Presents had signed Dana Dane to do a book, and their first response was, "Is he going to write it or are you?" For the record, Dana was such a control freak (and I mean it in a good way) when it came to writing his book, he crossed every *T* and dotted every *I*. When it came to the editorial process, the man gave Melody (my right hand and big-city editor) and me hell. We found out that not only was the man smart and charismatic, he was stubborn. But at the end of the day I was very impressed by the pride Dana put into penning his novel. He was a joy to work with. With every round of edits, he would call me and say in his serious voice, "Nikki Turner, I have a newfound respect for you if this is what you do for all of the books you've written."

Through the entire process I soon realized that I liked the man behind the legendary songs "Nightmares" and "Cinderfella" more than I loved the artist. Often times, Dana thought that he was getting insight and jewels from me, but it was he who was passing so much of his expertise on the industry and life in general to me.

Dana is not only my author, he is my dear friend and my big brother. From the bottom of my heart, I really hope you enjoy his book as much as we enjoyed the crazy process of getting it to its finished product.

It gives me great pleasure, honor, and unbridled joy to unveil another Nikki Turner Presents . . . a Dana Dane classic . . . *Numbers.*

Prologue: A Hustler's Exit Plan

There are not enough . . . numbers.

Everyone in the hood wants more money, but there isn't enough to go around. There are endless excuses why financial freedom has bypassed most people. The truth of the matter is that more people spend their time working for money than working toward a goal.

Most think that they will get paid from get-rich-quick schemes or hitting the lottery—the fast-money myth. Many of the young men in the hood think they'll get rich from selling illegal substances. A majority of the inner-city youth feel they have no other recourse than the street hustle. This mindset is programmed into young people and set in motion by their environment. If I had a nickel for every time I heard somebody say, "I'm just getting into the street-hustle game to make x amount of dollars and then I'm out," I'd be financially set. It's rare that they follow their initial plan. This scenario is the one that has plagued street hustlers from the beginning. When is enough money enough? In the street hustle, just as in legitimate business, you have to develop an exit plan. I could tell you a thousand stories of street hustlers believing their own hype and getting caught up, but I won't. I will only tell you this one.

This is the tale of a young boy who goes by the moniker Numbers.

NUMBERS

The Beginning of the End

Numbers was putting on an Academy Award—winning performance, taking Jake through every emotion he could possibly think of: scared, confused, dumbfounded, flabbergasted, and victimized. Keyser Söze would have appreciated the level of game Numbers was laying down.

Eleven hours had passed since he'd been taken into custody, six of them under tough interrogation. Although the agents didn't know any more now than they did when they picked him up, Numbers knew that he was far from out of the fire. Crispy Carl had once told him, "When you stand in the flames, never let them see you sweat." And Numbers maintained his composure.

The holding room was painted a dull mint green. It was

cruel and unusual punishment just to have to look at it for too long. The only furnishings were four metal chairs and a rectangular table. A DEA agent sat on one side of the table with two empty chairs beside him, while Numbers sat on the opposite side. The fluorescent lights overhead seemed to beam only on him. Directly ahead of Numbers was a mirror five feet wide by three feet high. It was obvious that there were agents on the other side listening and watching everything that was said or done in the room. Every so often the agent who was with Numbers would turn around and act as if he was looking at himself, asking the same question again and again. This was his way of letting his superiors know he was getting nowhere fast.

"So where are the drugs and money?" Agent Smith asked for what seemed like the thousandth time. Smith had been at the agency for only a couple of years, but his supervisor liked to use him when they interrogated black suspects. They believed another black male could lure the black perps into a false sense of security and thus trick them into incriminating themselves.

Agent Smith fancied himself a good dresser. Today he was wearing a charcoal-gray suit with a light gray shirt and solid black tie. His top lip sported a well-trimmed pencil-thin mustache. "Don't make it worse for yourself than it already is," he said, as if he really cared. "If you play ball, we can knock some time off your sentence."

Numbers thought it was funny how the agent spoke to him as if they could have been friends under different circumstances. *But if he thinks that I'm gonna sit here and implicate myself, this nigger must be the one smoking hot monkey ass through a stem.* "I don't know how many ways I can tell you this, man, but I ain't done nothing. Y'all the ones that hauled me up in here, got me missing in action, my mom's probably worried sick. You tell me what's really good," Numbers challenged.

"Numbers," Agent Smith called him by his nickname, hoping to

get some type of reaction, "cut the crap. Yeah, we know what they call you in the streets; don't play dumb with us. We got you on tape with Coney setting up the whole drug transaction. Just tell us where the drugs are, and we'll make this a little easier on you." Agent Smith stood up and adjusted his shirt in his pants before walking around to the right side of the table and sitting on its edge. "Little brotha, you think I want to lock you up for the rest of your life? Nah, brotha, that's not what I want at all, but if you want me to be able to help you, you got to give me something to work with." This time he spoke in a hushed tone as if the conversation was just between him and Numbers.

Numbers looked straight ahead, his eyes defiant, at the two-way glass in front of him. He spoke, unfazed: "Drugs is not my thing, man! I say no to drugs like Nancy Reagan asked me to back in the day!"

"So you want to be a hard-ass?" Agent Smith hopped off the table. "We can be hard-asses too, you know." Right on cue Agent Smith's partner and two other suits Numbers recognized entered the room.

"Dupree Reginald Wallace, I am Agent Flask." Agent Flask was a tall, well-conditioned, clean-cut white dude, and he spoke with the arrogance of a man who knew something that he shouldn't. He didn't bother to introduce the two other suits. Just as well; they needed no introduction. Numbers knew these crooked cops, O'Doul and Lockhart, all too well from the projects. "You're in more trouble than you realize, kid." The two detectives smiled, looking sinister. "It would behoove you to cooperate with us. Do you know this person?" Agent Flask cracked a bedeviling smile when he tossed a picture of Coney on the table.

"What kind of rhetorical bullshit is this? You know I do. You just picked me up with him twelve hours ago."

"Then you should know he already gave you up. He told us about your whole operation. We've already cut a deal with him, but we may be able to help you help yourself if you give us your plug," Agent Flask said.

Numbers wasn't surprised that Coney had given him up, but that didn't mean that *he* was going out like a scrub. He kept his mouth shut.

"Okay," Flask said, "how about this guy?" He dropped a picture of Sanchez on the table. Sanchez was once Coney's drugs connect and was now one of the people who supplied Numbers. The agent held several other photos in his hand, waiting for Numbers's reply.

The stakes had just gone up, and the seat was getting hotter. Numbers had no idea whether or not they had pictures of him and Sanchez together. His next words could implicate him, but if Numbers was nothing else, he was a gambling man. "He looks sort of familiar, but the face doesn't ring a bell," Numbers said with an expression as serious as a death sentence. "Isn't he one of the original members of Menudo?"

Agent Flask frowned. He didn't think Numbers was funny, and he didn't like it when perps tried to play him. "Okay then, Mr. Funny Man, who is this . . . and this . . . and this . . . and this?" The agent tossed photo after photo on the steel table. Numbers took a few moments to look at them. It was like seeing a flashback of his entire life since becoming a street hustler, in colored glossy prints. The feds had provided a snapshot of almost everyone Numbers had dealt with in the underbelly of the street game, but what they were unable to do was provide any connection between them and Numbers. He was not in any of the photos, but somehow they knew he knew them—they just couldn't prove it, so Numbers believed. Why else would they still be digging?

"Come on, this is too much—all the games! I'm not that good at Pictionary, but I'm pretty good with music. Can we play Name That Tune next?" Numbers leaned back in his seat and crossed his arms, not showing his frustration, but he was getting vexed with the interrogation. He knew he could ask for his attorney at any time and put an end to the questioning, but he also knew they'd probably try to lose him in the system for who knows how long if he did.

"We've got all the time in the world," Agent Flask said, his square, chiseled face showing little reaction. He left the pictures spread out on the table and walked out of the interrogation room followed by the well-dressed agent. Detective Lockhart walked over calmly with a smirk on his face and abruptly slammed both of his fat hands down on the table, but Numbers did not react. O'Doul kicked one of the chairs toward Numbers, causing it to fall at his feet, and still Numbers did not flinch. O'Doul followed Lockhart out of the room, leaving Numbers alone with his thoughts.

Numbers began to reminisce about his childhood, recalling the many lessons his mentor, Crispy Carl, had taught him. One of the defining moments, a moment that shined like a beacon in his mind, was during one of the last times he'd seen Crispy Carl.

Numbers went to visit Carl at his one-bedroom hovel in 60 Carlton, right behind the building where he lived. Old Crispy Carl wasn't doing too well. He was very sick, with no money, no health benefits, and no family to take care of him. Except for Numbers's occasional visits, he was on his own in every sense of the word. But Crispy Carl never complained about his circumstances because he said his fate was his own doing. Although he never let on, he did look forward to the visits from Numbers; he loved the boy like a son.

"Who's that?" Crispy Carl called from his bed, alarm in his ailing voice.

"Who else did you give a key, old pimp?" Numbers strode through the door.

"That's you, Numbers? Where you been?"

"Getting my hustle on, of course. Somebody gotta feed your decrepit ass," he joked.

Crispy Carl wasn't offended by the remark—only a foolish man got upset by the truth. "You seen any of my hoes out there, Numbers?"

"They my hoes now, so stop sweating my bitches."

"Young pimpin', I taught you everything you know." Crispy Carl laughed himself into an uncontrollable coughing fit.

Numbers ran to the kitchen, got Carl a drink of water, and then helped him sit up to take a drink.

"Hey, young pimp, it's okay. We all gotta leave the game one way or another. But let me tell you this so you don't make the same mistake I made. When you leave the game, you want to roll out with C-Lo as your last number, you dig. See, if you go out with four-five-six, you can make the bank whatever you want it to be when you leave," making reference to the popular gambling game where three dice are used. "That's called having an exit plan. Crackers know how the game is played. They got 401(k) plans, pensions, and IRAs."

Crispy Carl paused to make sure Numbers understood what he was talking about and to gather his breath. "In the streets we ain't got none of that shit. Shit like that is foreign to cats like us that's hustling on the street every day. Still, that don't mean we can't set ourself up to live comfortable when it's time to put our cards down. You got to be smarter than the rest of these chumps out here. They think that quick money is gonna last forever, and ain't nothing lasting forever, feel me?" Crispy Carl sat up in his bed a little more. "See, the problem is these fools start believing their own hype like their shit don't stink. I'm guilty of that shit myself, young player, so believe me when I tell you, you got to get out when the time is right."

Numbers thought about what his mentor was saying. "How will

I know when it's that time? I've been hustling as long as you've known me, Crispy Carl."

"You'll know when to get out the game, but you have to start planning for your exit not now . . . but right now! You come a long way from the little runt I met at the number spot way back when. I'm proud of you for always being the man of your house."

The Man of the House

It could be said that Dupree Reginald Wallace was a natural-born hustler—he had to be. His father bailed out on him before Dupree was old enough to remember what the man looked like, and his two little sisters' father was kicked out by his mother when Dupree was eight, earning him the title of man of the house by default.

Dupree lived with his mother and twin sisters on the first floor of building 79 North Oxford Walk in the Fort Greene housing projects—one of the most frequented and notorious buildings in the hood. Building 79 bustled with activity; the stoop was always overflowing with people entering, exiting, or congregating.

Dupree was outside walking the fence the day his stepfather was banished from their lives. Walking the fence was one of the things the kids did to amuse themselves that summer. The challenge was to keep your balance and walk the length of the gray chain-link fence from the stoop—right under the kitchen window of Dupree's apartment—all the way around to the Park Avenue side of the building, a good 150 feet, give or take a few. Dupree had become one of the best at balancing himself and walking the fence like it was a tightrope. Even the blare of the boom box on the stoop blasting the sounds of Melle Mel and Grandmaster Flash & the Furious Five's new raw rap street gospel—*"It's like a jungle sometimes, it makes me wonder"*—could not distract him.

But Dupree's grace on the fence did not come without trial, error, and pain. Three years earlier, when he moved into the neighborhood at the innocent age of five, he attempted to follow after some of the older boys tightroping the gate. Chap, Marcus, and Raymond were eight or nine years old; only Marcus's little brother, Jarvis, was the same age as Dupree. Dupree wanted to show the boys he could keep up, so he mounted the fence. His first mistake was wearing hard-bottomed shoes, which made his task slippery at best, if not impossible for a novice. His second mistake was not having his shoelaces tied properly. And his third mistake was that he didn't know any of the boys he was mimicking.

As Dupree began attempting to walk a nearby fence not far from his new building, Chap grabbed the fence and started shaking it vigorously, shouting profanities and anything else he could think of to rattle Dupree's concentration. "You fuckhead . . . You gonna fall . . . You can't do it with them church shoes on and them big-ass feet."

It worked.

One of Dupree's shoelaces got caught in the fence, causing him to lose his balance and come crashing down on the hard cement, headfirst. Blood spurted out of his skull as if it were a split water hose. One of the boys, thinking Dupree was dying right before his eyes, screamed with fear, "His brain is leaking!"

Nearby, seventeen-year-old Big John was sitting on the stoop smoking a stogie when he heard one of the younger boys' screams. He had the physique of a full-grown man and was naturally muscular. Running toward the source of the noise, Big John acted quickly and untangled Dupree's shoelace from the fence. Then he ripped the tank top he was wearing off his back and placed it on Dupree's injured skull. "Are you okay, kid?" Dupree was unresponsive and groggy, sliding in and out of consciousness. Big John didn't know Dupree, but recognized him as the new kid that had just moved into the first floor. He scooped him up in his arms and rushed the boy to the steps of their building.

By this time another kid had run and told Dupree's mother what happened. Jenny was running out the door when she saw Big John flying up the six steps that led to her door with her child cradled in his arms.

"Bring him in the house and set him down right there." Big John followed her instructions and placed her baby boy on the couch. "Oh my God, how did this happen? My baby! Oh God, please don't let my baby die!" At first, she thought to call the ambulance. Although the Cumberland hospital was right across the street, maybe three-quarters of a football field's length away, she knew it would take the ambulance forty-five minutes to make a one-minute trip. The paramedics feared coming into the hood and gave less than a damn about servicing the underprivileged.

Jenny put cold, wet towels on his head and gently picked up her boy and prepared to walk him to the hospital. Big John offered to carry him, but Dupree's mother would have none of that—this was her firstborn, her baby. At the emergency ward, the medics tended to him immediately at Jenny's insistence.

Dupree ended up being okay, and Jenny was forever grateful to Big John. He became one of the first friends they made in the PJs.

The aftermath of Dupree's injury was twenty-two stitches, a bald spot on the right side of his noggin, and a scar for life.

Now Dupree was being cheered on as he approached the point of the fence near the stoop and his kitchen window.

"Man, I don't think anyone has walked it that fast before!" Jarvis gushed in approval. Jarvis and Dupree were now best friends.

"Get outta here," Chap hated. "He ain't do it faster than me."

"Yes he did," Jarvis rebutted, now in Chap's face.

"No way."

"Way." They continued to argue.

Dupree was not paying them any attention. He was still up on the fence, but instead of walking he was looking through his kitchen window.

"You don't do nothing around here anyway! You a liar and a cheat! You can pack your shit and get out!" his mother screamed at his stepfather. Her toned body was coiled and ready to strike, and her big almond eyes appeared to be even larger than usual.

"Bitch, who you think you mouthing off to?" Elroy lashed back. He was six foot one, with flawless brown skin. Most of the women in the projects thought he was very good-looking, but it was hard to see that now, with his face all contorted. Elroy stepped into Jenny's face, invading her space. Although she stood barely five feet tall, she was a fireball and refused to take any mess from anyone—especially a man.

"Elroy, I don't have time for this shit. Go on chasing them hoochies, I'm done. You out there fucking whatever'll get naked for you and ain't even taking care of your daughters." She turned around to walk away when Elroy grabbed her by the back of the neck.

"Ah!" she gasped, pain mixed with anger. *If I get free of his clutches, he gonna wish he never put his hands on me,* Jenny promised herself.

Dupree jumped off the fence and raced up the stairs. He wouldn't have been able to run any faster if he had on a red body-suit with a lightning bolt on the chest.

Big John was perched at his usual spot on the stoop talking with some other people, puffing on a cigarette and listening to his music. "Easy, little man," he warned lightly.

Dupree paid Big John no mind, flying right past him and through the open lobby door. His little husky frame blasted through his apartment front door as he yelled, "Don't hit my mommy!" He was furious. This was the first and last time he would ever see a man physically abuse his mother.

Their two-bedroom apartment was small, sparsely furnished, but neat. The living room contained one long daybed that sat up against the left wall, and on the right there was a dining table with a black-and-white thirteen-inch TV on top. Elroy was in between the kitchen entrance and the dining table shaking Jenny by the back of her neck. She struggled to escape his grip, to no avail.

"Bitch, don't ever turn your back on me."

Dupree ran at his stepfather swinging with all his might and was greeted by a backhand to his left cheek. He had heard people say they would slap fire out of a person's face before, and now he knew what they meant. His cheek was ablaze as he lay sprawled out on the floor near the refrigerator, crying in pain.

Realizing what he'd done, Elroy froze for a moment, letting up slightly. But that moment was all Jenny needed to slip from his grasp. In an instant she made it to the kitchen and snatched up the black cast iron frying pan that lived atop the stove. In her best imitation of Billie Jean King, she swung the pan until it connected with her target.

In a fit of rage, she continued to practice following through with her forehand. "Don't—you—ever—put—your—hands—on—me—or—my—son—ever—again—in—your—life," punctuating every word with a crack from the frying pan until she had beat him down to the dull brown project-tiled floor.

Hearing what sounded like someone in a world of hurt, Big John rushed up to the apartment. The door was open. When he saw what was going down, he grabbed the pan from Jenny.

"Ms. Jenny! That's enough—you're gonna kill 'im."

"Dupree," Jenny called to her son, "come here, I need you to go to the store for me."

Dupree came out of the back room that he shared with his two younger sisters. He was wearing his favorite light-blue Lee jeans, a striped navy, light blue, and white crewneck shirt, and a pair of navy blue Pro-Keds 69ers on his feet. Although Jenny didn't have much money, she always made sure her children looked well kept, except for that black Brillo for hair Dupree's deadbeat dad cursed him with. For that, there was nothing she could do but keep it cut, and most of the time three dollars for the barber was not in the budget.

In the two weeks since the unpleasant incident with his

stepfather, the swelling on Dupree's caramel-brown face had vanished. Physically, he looked as if it had never happened. Jenny was grateful that her daughters had not been present to see the fight. Fortunately, they had spent that night with Jenny's girl-friend Sandy and her two daughters, who lived in the Farragut housing projects. When they returned the next day, Jenny made it her business to tell her four-year-old twin daughters that their father would not be living with them any longer. Jenny wasn't normally the type to mince words, but she spared her daughters the full details. The girls would miss their father, but she knew getting rid of Elroy was best for them all in the long run.

"Did you make up your bed?" Jenny asked Dupree when he walked into the kitchen.

"Yes, Mommy." Dupree was a momma's boy.

"That's my little man." She smiled. "I need you to go get me a pack of Newports, a pound of salt pork, a quart of milk, and a stick of butter from the store." She held out four dollar bills. "And don't be running out in that street without looking both ways!" she cautioned.

"Yes, Mommy," Dupree replied. "Can I keep the change?"

"Yes, baby, but hurry back. I want to cook breakfast for y'all this morning."

Dupree stepped off the stoop into a clear Saturday morning. A soft summer breeze brushed his skin as he thought about how much change he'd saved up to this point and how much would be left over after purchasing the groceries for his mother. He was saving up for a Duncan yo-yo and a spinning top; he needed about a dollar more. Knowing there would only be about twenty to forty cents change, he wondered how he was going to get the rest.

"Ms. Jenny's son!" a voice screamed out. "Yoo-hoo! Ms. Jenny's son!" Everyone in the neighborhood addressed the other adults with a *Ms.* or *Mr.* tagged to their first name. "Ms. Jenny's son," the voice repeated.

Dupree looked up to see who it was that was so desperately trying to get his attention.

"Right here." The voice belonged to a graying older lady, somewhere in her late forties. She was leaning out her seventh-floor window waving frantically. "Are you going to the store, young man?"

"Yes, Ms. Margaret," Dupree yelled back up to her. Ms. Margaret was a cafeteria worker at his elementary school, P.S. 67. Given all the kids she served over the twenty-odd years she was employed there, he wasn't surprised that she didn't remember his name.

"Okay. Hold on, honey." She disappeared inside her window and within moments was back with a brown paper bag, which she tossed to Dupree. It contained money and a list of the items that she wanted from the store. "Thank you, sweetie, and take fifty cents for yourself."

Dupree's face lit up when he heard he would be making another fifty cents on one trip to the store. "Thank you, Ms. Margaret." He snatched up the bag and scurried off across Park Avenue to the store.

Dupree's sister Takeisha, the oldest of the twin girls by three minutes and almost the spitting image of her mother, with her round cheeks and almond eyes, could not care less about her breakfast. Her attention was on a bootleg Barbie doll her daddy had bought for her fourth birthday. The younger, Lakeisha, had the same doll but opted to sit with her eyes affixed to the Saturday-morning cartoons on the small black-and-white TV. It didn't have an antenna, but the metal coat hanger their mother stuffed in its place worked just fine. Lakeisha resembled her father and Takeisha her mother.

Dupree sat at the dining table with his back to the refrigerator, barely eating, preoccupied with his thoughts. He had gotten ninety cents just by going to the store for his mother and a neighbor. *What if I went to the store for more people? I could make even more money.*

"I don't know what you daydreaming 'bout, boy, but you better not waste my food," his mother snapped.

"Yes, Mommy." Dupree smiled and began eating with gusto. The salt pork and grits with toast and jelly disappeared off his plate. Then he jumped up and darted out the front door, leaving the empty plate on the table before his mother could protest. There were people to see, errands to run, and money to make.

For the rest of the summer Dupree knocked on his neighbors' doors asking if they needed anything from the store. Eventually he had regular customers he made store runs for, including Ms. Margaret, who never gave him less than fifty cents for his efforts.

Everything was going as smooth as Asian silk until Dupree got robbed by the dirty twins—Bo-Bo and Go-Go—who lived in 56 Monument Walk, the building diagonally across from his. No longer feeling safe going to the store by himself, he got Jarvis to start running errands with him. It cut into his profits, but some money was better than no money.

Dupree and Jarvis were like Laurel and Hardy or Abbott and Costello—an odd couple. Jarvis lived on the fourth floor in a three-bedroom apartment with his mother, two sisters, and two brothers; he was the middle child. Like most families in the projects, their main source of income was welfare. Jarvis was slimmer and taller than Dupree, with a long head. People teased him all the time, calling him names like Jarhead. Because of the constant teasing, Jar, as Dupree called him, would get into fights on the regular. After a while, Dupree came to the conclusion that Jarvis just got a kick out of fighting. The two of them got into a few tussles but never anything serious.

"Jar, you seen the new skateboard they got out? It's made of some type of plastic, and when you get on it, it bends, but it won't break. And it has big, clear wheels, too." Dupree spoke enthusiastically.

Jarvis, struggling to eat a candy bar and carry a bag of groceries at the same time, spoke with his mouth full. "Yeah, Calvin from building 102 got that skateboard. He said he paid fifteen dollars for it."

"For real? I got twenty-eight dollars and seventy-two cents saved up. How much you got?" Dupree looked at Jarvis.

"About nine or ten dollars," he said with a little less enthusiasm than Dupree.

"That's okay! I'll chip in the rest and help you get yours."

Jarvis smiled at his friend. That was one of the things he liked about Dupree. No matter what, Dupree was always willing to share what he had or help him out in some way. Jarvis would do anything for Dupree as well.

After they dropped all the packages off to their respective customers, they headed to Fulton Street, downtown. Of course they were going without the permission of their mothers. Going to the store across Park Avenue and going downtown were different things entirely. If their mothers found out, it would cost them an ass whipping for sure. But it was too nice out to worry about consequences.

Everyone was out enjoying the beautiful midsummer day. Some kids were riding bikes or playing basketball on the court in front of the building, and others were playing skellys. Young girls were jumping rope. The older kids and adults sat on benches. Hip-hop music was on the come up, and the teenagers on the bench were jamming to *Planet Rock* by Afrika Bambaataa and the Soulsonic Force—pop locking and dancing.

Dupree and Jarvis walked through the projects past the benches in back of building 99, past the nursery up North Portland Avenue, where they stopped at Sarjay's candy store and bought some goodies. Then they continued across Myrtle Avenue into Fort Greene Park, walking and talking. They were now approaching the fence that separated the playground from the rest of the park.

"I think I'ma get a red one. How 'bout you, Jar?" Dupree was imagining the skateboard he would be buying shortly. He fingered the change in his shorts pockets.

"I don't know yet," Jarvis said. He held out his bag of Cheez Doodles to Dupree. "Want some?"

Dupree reached in and took a handful.

"Yo! Little dudes, where y'all going?" The voice came from directly behind them. Dupree looked back.

It was the dirty twins, sitting on the bench finishing off some pizza. Fear ran up Dupree's spine. He quickly turned his head and picked up his pace, nudging Jarvis to do the same. He knew the little thugs were nothing but trouble.

Jarvis was unfazed, but he could tell his friend was scared.

The eleven-year-old identical dirtballs were always tore up, and today was no different. Their clothes were soiled and tattered, their hair unkempt, their faces filthy, and they reeked of urine. The twins' mother was a dope fiend, and their father, when he was around, was a drunk. Other than beating the twins' asses whenever they felt like it, neither parent paid any attention to them. Well, at least that's what Dupree heard the grown-ups say. He used to feel sorry for them—until they jumped him and took his change. Now he wasn't sure what he felt.

"Yo, par . . . you with the big head," Go-Go shouted toward the boys, using language he overheard from the teenagers. "Hold up!"

Dupree tried to ignore them by walking even faster, but his friend had a different idea.

Jarvis stopped.

"Come on, Jar!" Dupree exclaimed, but he knew he was wasting his breath, because Jarvis had no intentions of avoiding a good fight.

"Ya momma," Jarvis retorted. Although the twins were three years older than they were, Jarvis was almost their height. "That's right—I said 'Ya momma'!"

Steaming mad, the twins moved in on Jarvis like he had been the one that started trouble with them. Bo-Bo circled to the left, while Go-Go circled to the right. Bo-Bo reached out first, touching Jarvis's pocket, making his change jingle. Go-Go smirked before taking a wild swing that grazed Jarvis's ear.

Dupree wanted no part of the twins. He took off running past the water sprinkler toward one of the park's exits, but something made him stop. What, he had no idea. Being that his feet were no longer obeying the commands of his brain, he looked back. Jarvis was fighting off both of the boys as hard as he could and losing. Dupree thought about the time when Elroy slapped him and compared it to the punches the twins had landed when they jumped him. What he felt from their young punches was nowhere near the pain he'd felt from his stepfather.

Dupree had made up his mind, and this time his feet were listening. He was going to war alongside his friend: win, lose, or draw. *That's what friends did for each other.* With those thoughts fresh in his head, he charged back to aid Jarvis, the change in his pocket jingling more vigorously with every step.

When Dupree made it back to the action, he didn't waste any more time. His first punch connected with Bo-Bo's eye socket, catching him off guard. Bo-Bo was supposed to be the tougher of the two. He doubled over in pain, clutching his face.

Go-Go was shocked when he heard his brother scream. He looked up to see what had happened, but that proved to be the wrong move. Jarvis caught him with two well-placed punches to the face.

The blows dropped him. Blood gushed from his nose as he lay crumpled next to his brother.

Figuring that he'd had enough, Dupree began pulling Jarvis by the arm, away from the twins. "Come on, Jar!"

"No!" Jarvis pulled away from Dupree and kicked each boy one time hard in the abdomen for good measure. The twins moaned in anguish.

Now it was over.

Dupree and Jarvis took off running, looking back occasionally to see if they were being followed.

They weren't.

They ran across Willoughby Street, turning left down Ashland Place on the side of Brooklyn Hospital, holding their pockets so the change wouldn't dance around too crazily. They didn't stop running until they were halfway up the block. That's when they looked at each other. Panting and out of breath, they began to laugh uncontrollably.

Jarvis never said anything about his friend running away; Dupree had told him how scared he was of the twins. He was just happy his best friend overcame his fear and decided to come back to his aid—that's what counted.

Now the dirty twins would think twice before messing with them again.

"Jarvis," Dupree said, beckoning to his best friend as he skateboarded across the grounds between the project buildings, "watch this trick." He continued pushing off with his left foot, picking up momentum as he headed straight for the cardboard box in his path. When Dupree was a foot away from the box he applied pressure to the back of his skateboard with his left heel, then he raised his right foot and slid it up the base, causing himself and the board to become airborne, and launched clear over the cardboard box. The landing was perfect; his arms were extended like the wings of a bird as he skidded to a halt.

"Man, that was nice," Jarvis admitted.

Over the last three summers, Dupree and Jarvis had become pretty good on their skateboards. Though Jarvis was fearless when it came to fighting, Dupree was the daredevil on the skateboard and the more athletic of the two.

"Come on, Jar, you can do it. Just make sure you push off hard enough," Dupree encouraged.

Jarvis wasn't as confident as his friend, but he was determined not to let Dupree show him up, even if he broke his neck in the process.

"Dupree!"

Jarvis stopped in his tracks, thinking he heard someone call his friend's name—it sounded like Dupree's mother.

"Come on, Jar, I know you not a chicken." Dupree egged his friend on, apparently not aware that someone had called him.

"Dee!" his mother called again, but the boys were far enough from the apartment window that her voice was barely audible by the time it reached them. "Deeeee!" she repeated. "Come here! Hurry up." Jenny could see Jarvis but not Dupree from the window. But she knew Dee was out playing with his friend nearby.

"Ya mom is calling you, Du. I know you heard her that time."

"Stop stalling and do the stunt," Dupree badgered, thinking that Jarvis was trying to pull his leg.

"Nah, fo' real—ya mom did call you," Jarvis said with an I'm-dead-serious expression on his face.

Dupree kicked off on his skateboard toward his first-floor window. Sure enough, she had been searching for him. "Yes, Mommy?" he called up to her.

"Come in the house. I need you to run to the store for me real quick. Hurry up." She disappeared into the apartment.

Dupree stomped on the back of his skateboard; when it popped up into the air, he grabbed it with his right hand and bounded up the stoop and into the building. "I'll be right back, Jar," he said over his shoulder.

"Cool." Jarvis waited at the foot of the stairs, balancing on his board.

Even with the institution of the New York State Lottery in '82, most people continued to bet with the underground number holes they were familiar with. One of the most popular spots in the neighborhood was located on the corner of Park Avenue and Cumberland Street—basically a storefront, no sign on the outside—just two big windows covered with a gray coat so no one was able to look inside. It was run by an overweight thirty-something Guido named Louie Provolone. That wasn't his real last name, but most people called him Provolone or Big Cheese because they said he always smelled like cheese. Dupree thought Louie smelled more like stale milk and the cigar he kept clamped between his tight lips.

Not too many kids had ever seen the inside of Provolone's number hole—not because it was off limits, it just wasn't really kid-friendly. There was an excessive amount of drinking, sex talk, and swearing, especially when someone *almost* hit their number. That was cause to curse the sun, moon, and stars. Provolone's was a home away from home for a lot of its patrons—their second job, for the few who had a job.

Crispy Carl was a regular at the spot. He was dark, but his complexion wasn't the reason they called him Crispy. Crispy Carl was a forty-six-year-old ex-pimp, and everything he wore—from his fried-and-dyed hair to his tailor-fit zoot suits—was always crisp and sharp. He might not have been as fly as he was in his prime, and he might have lost most of his hair, but in his age bracket he was still by far the smoothest, slickest-dressing man in the hood.

Crispy Carl lost his whores and money during the Frank Lucas era, when he got hooked on heroin. He was clean now, but the pimp game had passed him by. Now he spent countless hours sipping Jack Daniels and reading the Big Mack number sheet. If anybody was looking, most of the time he could be found perched on the bench in front of the spot, or inside if the weather was foul.

A lot of people fancied hitting him up for predictions on the number of the day, and he was more than willing to oblige them. He always volunteered a tale to validate the reasoning why he liked a certain number. The funny thing was, Crispy Carl didn't hit his number any more than anyone else—people just got a kick out of the stories he told.

Dupree came barreling across the street with Jarvis on his tail. With only ten minutes or so to get his mother's bet in, he was in a hurry—so much so that he nearly ran over Crispy Carl's foot with his skateboard.

"Okay, watch it, young grasshopper!" Crispy Carl exclaimed. "The fastest way to get to ya destination, more often than not, is to be steady and consistent." He held Dupree by the arm, preventing him from entering the store.

Dupree looked at him, puzzled. "I'm sorry," he offered.

"Little man, where you think you going?"

"I got to put a number in for my mother," Dupree answered politely, even though he wasn't feeling the fact that the man was hindering him from completing his mother's errand.

"Okay, little player, but be careful with that skateboard. Us old-timers' bones don't heal as quickly as they used to." Crispy Carl released the young man's arm so that he and his friend could go on about their business.

"You got that right, Crispy Carl," one of his cronies chimed in.

The main room of the number hole was about fifteen by fifteen feet and filled with smoke. On both sides were wooden counters that took up the entire length of the walls. They were used to lean on and fill out number slips. The once light-gray walls were now mostly covered with scribbled numbers, names, and so forth, written in pen, pencil, and markers. There were metal and wooden chairs scattered about the room, and a wooden bench to the right of the entrance. The five trash cans must have been for decoration, because discarded number slips littered the floor. Straight ahead was a large window; behind that window were two women, one black and one Puerto Rican, whose job was to take the bets. Both were in their late twenties or early thirties and fairly attractive. Hanging on the wall over that window was a large, black-framed, circular clock with a white face and black hands.

The time was 2:45 P.M.

Dupree hesitantly made his way to the opening in the wall, while Jarvis stayed near the entrance looking around. Dupree was the third person in the Hispanic lady's line. When it was his turn, he removed the number slip his mother had scribbled on and the twenty-five cents from his pocket and placed them on the counter.

"A little young to be betting?" the Hispanic lady said to Dupree through a mouth full of food. Provolone didn't give his workers lunch breaks.

"It's for my mother."

"Then let's make sure we get it right, baby." She separated the top white sheet from the bottom yellow copy and then passed the yellow one back to Dupree. With a smile, she placed the white sheet in a box beneath the counter and the quarter in a drawer.

On Dupree's way out the man who had detained him earlier called, "Come here, little player."

Dupree walked over to him.

"Do me a solid and take a look at these." Crispy Carl showed him a list of numbers that had come out over the past week in the Big Mack. Crispy Carl hadn't hit the number in a while and hoped a fresh perspective would change his luck.

Dupree studied all the three-digit numbers on the list, not sure what he was looking for.

"Well, little dude, what do you think?"

"What do I think about what?" Dupree answered, baffled.

"What do you think is a good number to play today?" Crispy Carl specified.

"How would I know?" Dupree shrugged.

"Come on, little man, just give me three numbers."

"Two five eight," Dupree blurted out.

"Two fifty-eight. That sounds like a good one." Crispy Carl popped off his perch and briskly stepped into the number spot to place his bet.

Dupree was thoroughly confused but didn't question what had taken place. Instead, he just laid out his skateboard, pushed off, and headed home, with Jarvis in tow.

Although Jenny rarely hit the numbers, she played them religiously. The next day she sent Dupree back across Park to play her numbers again, and when he showed up in front of the store, Crispy Carl was excited to see him.

"Numbers! My little man, what's going on?" Dupree had no idea who Numbers was, so he didn't respond. "Yeah, I'm talking to you! That's your new handle from now on: Numbers!" Crispy Carl told him. "Do you know why I'm gonna call you Numbers?"

Dupree shook his head.

"Then I'll tell you why." Crispy Carl gave him a wide smile while removing some bills from his pocket. "My boy, Numbers, this is for you." He passed Dupree a crisp fifty-dollar bill. Dupree's eyes grew to twice their normal size.

Crispy Carl read the confusion in his new friend's eyes. "Remember the number you gave me yesterday afternoon?" he asked.

"Uh-uh," Dupree said.

"Little partner, the number you gave me, two fifty-eight, it came out straight like that, and that's your share." Crispy Carl put his hands on Dupree's shoulder, giving him a huge congratulatory shake.

Dupree smiled back at his new partner and mentor.

Over the next couple of weeks, 40 percent of the picks Dupree provided Crispy Carl with turned out to be winners. Hitting the number at that rate was exceptional; the average gambler hit the number—at best—10 to 20 percent of the time.

Numbers had been born.

The Knack

Numbers was sitting at his desk doodling in his math textbook when he felt someone hovering over him. It was Mr. Greenstein, his sixth-grade math teacher.

"Come with me," Mr. Greenstein ordered, looking over his bifocals.

Some of the children snickered and oohed, believing Numbers was in trouble. Jarvis looked at him with an expression that asked, What happened? Numbers gestured with his shoulders and hands to let him know he didn't know what was going on.

"Children, stay in your seats, complete your assignments, and remain quiet! I'll be right back." Then Mr. Greenstein led Numbers out of the classroom. Numbers knew once the teacher left the classroom his fellow classmates would go bonkers. He followed Mr. Greenstein through the school corridors, wondering what he had been caught doing.

Mr. Greenstein and Numbers walked down the stairs to the principal's office. Numbers felt his heart race a little. He knew he was in trouble for sure, he just didn't know why.

When he followed his teacher into the office he saw Principal Gordon Mathews sitting behind his desk wearing a navy suit with a blue striped tie. Then he noticed the person sitting across from his principal: his mother. Numbers almost stopped breathing.

Oh, damn, he thought. *The last thing I need is for Mom to lay those heavy hands of hers on me.* Numbers looked at his mother, trying to read her thoughts, but her expression gave away nothing.

"Have a seat, young man," Mr. Mathews said; it came out more like a command than a polite suggestion.

Numbers took a seat by his mother, who smiled at him wryly.

"Do you know why we brought you in here?" Mr. Mathews asked.

Numbers shook his head. Mr. Greenstein stood over his shoulder like a sentry assigned to make sure he wouldn't bolt out of the room.

"Well, it has come to my attention that you may have falsified your tests." However respectful Mr. Mathews was attempting to sound, there was no nice way to call a person a cheat.

"Dee, you can tell me." His mother looked him square in the eyes. "It's okay if you made a mistake. Did you cheat on your math test?"

Is this what this is all about? Numbers breathed a sigh of relief, trying to regain his normal breathing pattern. *They think I cheated on my math test.*

"No, Mommy, I didn't cheat."

"If you didn't cheat, young man, how do you account for getting a hundred on your last three math tests?" the principal asked in a condescending manner.

Numbers shrugged. "I don't know, but I didn't cheat!" He spoke with a little more confidence now.

"Well, there must be some explanation, because Mr. Greenstein informs me that the highest grade you ever scored previously on one of his tests was a seventy-seven. So either you're a genius all of a sudden, or you're a cheat," Mr. Mathews stated bluntly.

Jenny took offense at the principal's accusations. She believed her son when he said he didn't cheat—plus, she knew that he knew the consequences of lying to her would be far worse than anything the principal could ever do.

"Hold it now, Mr. Mathews. If my son said he didn't cheat, he didn't cheat!" she shot back. "If you don't believe him, Mr. Greenstein, you can give him some more problems to solve right here and now and we can settle it." Jenny felt confident her son wasn't lying but hoped she hadn't put her foot in her mouth.

Numbers was a bit nervous being put on the spot, but what could he do? It was time to put up or shut up.

"Well, Mr. Greenstein?" Mr. Mathews looked to him for affirmation.

"I guess we can have him answer a few questions," Mr. Greenstein replied, taking a pencil from behind his ear and walking over to the principal's desk. He began writing problems on a sheet of paper.

Numbers stole a look at his mother and couldn't help but smile a little inside. It felt good to have his mother standing up for him. He could see how his sudden abilities in math were puzzling, but he was just never interested in the class. He knew it was only a case of him applying himself.

Mr. Greenstein placed the sheet of paper on a hardcover book and then passed it to Numbers.

Numbers looked over the problems for a moment before glancing up toward the ceiling. He went into a daze for about thirty seconds, something he did when he was in deep thought. Then, with a slight smirk, he began writing. Sixty seconds later he was finished, and he handed the book and the sheet of paper back to Mr. Greenstein.

Mr. Greenstein looked over the problems for five minutes or so, mumbling to himself.

"Is there a problem, Mr. Greenstein?" the principal inquired.

"Well, no, I mean, yes," Mr. Greenstein replied with his forehead scrunched up, looking through his bifocals intently at the paper.

"So I guess someone wasn't telling the truth after all," Mr. Mathews said matter-of-factly, giving Numbers a stern stare.

"No, Gordon, that's not the problem. The answers are all correct." Mr. Greenstein was baffled.

Jenny smiled at her son proudly.

"Well then?" Mr. Mathews asked again. "What?"

"Uh, well, uh," Mr. Greenstein stammered, "they are correct, but I don't know how he figured them out. He didn't write anything on the paper. It's like he figured the answers out in his head. I can't even do that!" he confessed.

The principal and teacher apologized profusely to Ms. Jenny and would later make arrangements for Numbers to be placed in an advanced program in junior high school.

Over the years of running numbers and errands to the stores for people, Numbers had always been able to keep everyone's money accounted for in his head without writing it down. It was a knack he'd acquired, and somehow it had carried over into his schoolwork. He didn't understand where his gift for numbers had come from, but Jenny did. She had encountered this uncanny talent for numbers once before. Jenny had thought that other than donating his sperm and his coarse mane, Numbers's father hadn't given him anything, but happily, she realized now she was wrong.

When Jenny told her son of his father's abilities with numbers, Numbers grew curious to meet him. He had only seen his father in a picture his mother had of them when they both attended Sumter High School in South Carolina. He'd always wondered about the man in that picture.

Jenny was downtown meeting with her social worker, and then she was going to look for work. She was tired of collecting welfare and working odd jobs off the books at the dry cleaners, the local bar, and at the supermarket. None of them paid much, nor did they offer any benefits. She was determined to find something substantial.

Numbers was now twelve years old, and Jenny left him in charge of babysitting his sisters. He would've had Jarvis come down and keep him company today, but his friend was on punishment again, for fighting. Jarvis was more of a reactor than a thinker; for that reason he always got into scuffles.

Numbers decided he would pull out a deck of cards and

play a game of solitaire. His sisters were in the back, as usual, playing, and he hoped they would stay there. He loved them, but sometimes they could be real pests.

Sitting at the table in his usual seat with his back to the refrigerator, Numbers started shuffling and flipping over cards. He'd developed an uncanny ability to predict what the next card in the deck would be before he turned it up. It was like he had a sixth sense when it came to cards and numbers in general. When he was focused, he could foretell the correct card 80 to 90 percent of the time. As he sat there calling out numbers to himself, then flipping up the exact card he'd called, his rhythm was interrupted by his sister's voice.

"When is Mommy coming back?" Takeisha asked.

"Can I have some juice?" Lakeisha followed.

"I don't know, okay," he answered both of them in one breath.

"What are you doing?" Takeisha asked, holding a doll.

"What does it look like I'm doing? Playing cards," he snapped, as if she had interrupted him from doing something very important.

"Can we play?" Lakeisha asked, getting her juice out of the refrigerator.

At first Numbers thought to say no, but his annoyance dissolved when he looked at them. He loved them dearly.

"Okay, the game is—"

"Go Fish!" the girls interjected before he could finish his statement.

"Go Fish it is."

Jenny sat in the waiting area in a long-sleeved, white ruffled blouse with a brown knee-length skirt and a pair of brown shoes, her coat draped across her legs. She wore her hair in an Afro and had on little makeup. Though she wasn't a supermodel, she was an attractive female.

The waiting area was packed with single mothers and their screaming children. It was a madhouse. It took all of Jenny's strength not to pull her hair out; she hated coming to this godforsaken place. It smelled like dirty diapers and cigarette smoke. Still, it was better than the social worker coming to her house trying to account for every nickel and dime she spent.

"Brian, get over here," a mother yelled at her kid. "You're just like your father. His dumb ass never listened either, that's why the fool is in prison now. You remind me of him so much it makes me sick to look at you. Now, get your ass over here." The boy paid her no attention and continued romping around the room along with the other bad-ass kids.

"Ms. Johnson," the caseworker called out as she walked from behind the glass. The young girl who was just screaming at her son stood up.

"Brian, get your ass over here right now!" she yelled. When the boy ignored her she got infuriated, marched over to him, and snatched the six-year-old up by his armpit. "I'm Johnson," she replied, dragging her son toward the caseworker.

Thank God! Jenny thought, glad the loudmouth girl was leaving the area. Jenny had been coming to this social services office for the last nine years. It wasn't what she'd planned for her life; none of this had been in her plans. She hadn't planned on getting pregnant and having to move to New York City. Nor had she planned to move out of her brother's place abruptly and have to get on welfare.

Even after her sister practically disowned her for getting pregnant at seventeen, Jenny still hadn't believed her situation was as grave as it was. Indignantly she lashed out as if none of what had happened to her was her doing. "You've always been jealous of me. You never loved me. You just put up with me 'cuz you had to," she raged at her sister Anna Beth.

Anna Beth was fifteen years Jenny's senior, the oldest of the seven siblings. Since their mother and father had died seventeen years earlier, Anna Beth had taken on the role of head of the household. And as the head, she made one of the hardest decisions she ever had to make in her life: she put her youngest sister out the family house.

At two o'clock that afternoon Jenny packed up what she was able to carry in a duffle bag and left. She was ordered by Anna Beth to be out of the house before her two nieces came home from school. Only her brother Greggor was home when she left, and he hated to see Jenny go; they were the closest of the seven, but he also knew that once the eldest made up her mind, that was that.

Anna Beth never looked up from washing clothes in the big tub in the kitchen when Jenny walked by to leave. She couldn't bear to see her baby sister—she was afraid she might change her mind.

Jenny walked out into the brisk fall afternoon on Bradford Street with all of $18.34 to her name. She wore bell-bottom jeans, a wool tweed coat, brown shoes, and a brown knit cap that covered her ears. She was seventeen years old, homeless and pregnant. Any other time she would have thought it was a beautiful day to take a walk, but today the twenty-minute walk to Purdy Street where her boyfriend lived felt like a marathon. But she was certain that once she was there, Lewis—her future baby's father—would know what to do.

Lewis lived with his mother and little sister. He wasn't exceptionally handsome, but girls liked his flawless bronzed brown skin. He said that most girls thought his family was part Cherokee, but all that was needed to dispel that claim was to look at his coarse hair. It was plain ol' nappy.

Given his five-foot-nine, slim build, it would be a safe bet to think Lewis was athletic, but it would've been a losing bet. What Lewis did have going for him was an uncanny way with digits. He could calculate numbers better than most high school teachers. It was truly a gift. And it landed him a job at Coughlin's General Store managing the books. It also gave him access to some of the prettier girls who needed help with their math.

His tutoring ability was how he got to meet and get close to Jenny. He was a year older, and she found him mildly attractive. At first it was just friendly, but that changed on the day Jenny was able to manipulate Lewis into cutting class with her. She liked the fact that he was older than she was, yet still a virgin. Now she was the teacher. She taught him everything he knew about sex—but now she wished she would have taught him to pull out.

Jenny slowly approached the two-bedroom, one-level house sitting on cinder blocks. The grass was cut, but the paint was peeling from years of wear. At first she thought to turn around and walk away, but she had nowhere to go. Jenny knocked on the door tentatively and waited. There was no answer.

She turned to leave, unsure what she would do next, when someone walked up.

"Jenny May, hey there, baby, what you doing here?" Lewis asked in his southern drawl as he came up the walkway. He seemed surprised but pleased to see her.

"I need to talk to you, Lewis."

"What's with the bag?" he asked, tugging at it playfully.

"Can we go in the house? I walked here all the way from my house. I'm thirsty."

Lewis walked into the house, followed by Jenny.

Once inside, Jenny dropped her bag on the floor, thankful to be giving her shoulder a rest. She sat down in the living room on a couch covered with a light green floral sheet. Lewis was at the kitchen sink directly across from the couch fetching a glass of water.

They were in the house alone. Lewis's mother was working at one of her two jobs, and his little sister was at Ms. Pearl's house.

Ms. Pearl watched most of the single mothers' kids in the neighborhood. It was as close to a day-care center as they could come to in this poor area of town.

"Here you go." Lewis sat next to Jenny, handing her the glass of water.

She took a long sip, then stared down at the glass trying to figure out how she would break the news.

Lewis could tell she was somewhat uneasy. He placed his right arm around her shoulder and took the glass of water away with his left. "Don't worry, my mother won't be home for hours," he said in his sexiest voice, placing the glass of water on the old wooden coffee table in front of the couch.

Jenny folded her arms and began to tremble slightly. Lewis used the opportunity to make his move, sliding his hand up her leg. "Stop," Jenny said softly.

Lewis ignored her request and moved his other hand toward her breast, caressing her over the coat she wore.

"I didn't come here for that," Jenny erupted, standing up.

"So what you come here for?" he shot back. Tears welled up in Jenny's eyes, and her trembling increased. Lewis was confused. "What? What? What did I do?" he pleaded, sitting on the couch with his palms in the air.

Jenny managed to get the words past the lump in her throat, "I'm pregnant."

"Huh?"

"I'm pregnant." The words made their way out more freely this time.

"So why you telling me?" he asked coldly, jumping up from his seat.

"You know why I'm telling you," she retorted, trying with no luck to hold back the tears that were streaming effortlessly down her cheeks. "Please don't be like that, Lewis."

"I'm not being like nothing. How you gonna come up in here trying to pin a baby on me, knowing you've been having sex way before me," he rationalized, avoiding eye contact.

It was true, Jenny wasn't a virgin like Lewis when they got together, nor was she promiscuous like her sister Anna Beth and Lewis suggested. She had had sex with only one boy before Lewis. She'd thought she was in love with him but soon found out he was having sex with one of her so-called friends. She ended it right then and there.

"How dare you say that to me?" she cried. "You know I'm not like that, Lewis."

"All I know is you better go find the father of that bastard you're carrying," Lewis spat.

Before Jenny knew what she had done, she hauled off and punched him square in the mouth. His mouth filled with blood instantly—Muhammad Ali would have been proud of her right cross.

Lewis stood there in shock and fear, holding his mouth. He saw the anger and hatred in her eyes and made the correct decision to not say another word. Jenny was ready to swing on him again, but when Lewis cowed she turned on her heels, grabbed her duffle bag, and stormed out.

When she moved in with her oldest brother, Samuel, and his wife and kids in New York, she thought it was her chance to start over. She lived with them for almost three years after Dupree was born but couldn't endure the constant fighting in the household. She didn't want her son raised in such a volatile environment. When Jenny left she wished she had the means to take her niece and nephew with her, but she could barely take care of Dupree and herself.

The first couple of years after leaving Samuel's house, she bounced around from shelter to shelter waiting for a vacancy to open up in one of the subsidized housing developments social services would provide. In the meantime, she met her daughters' father.

Elroy hadn't come around much since Jenny had beat him with the frying pan. He reappeared on the girls' birthday and like Houdini disappeared, never to be heard from until their next birthday or whenever he felt like it, which wasn't often. He had the deadbeat-dad disease, too.

When he did come around, he was more concerned with getting back with Jenny than their well-being or spending time with his daughters. Once Jenny let him know she wasn't interested in having sex with him, he'd catch an attitude and storm out until he felt it was time to try his luck again. *Screw him,* she thought.

"Jenny May Wallace," a squatty, light-brown-complexioned man with salt-and-pepper hair read from his clipboard.

"Right here, Mr. Sampson." Jenny stood up.

"Good to see you, Jenny. Come this way," Mr. Sampson said. "How are the children? Are they in school today?"

"Thank you, Mr. Sampson. They're good, and yes, they're in school," she lied. The twins were supposed to go on a school trip, but Jenny didn't have the money to send them. She had Numbers stay home with them.

Jenny followed Mr. Sampson into a small office, where he took a seat behind his desk. She sat in the one metal chair in front of the desk and rested her coat on her lap.

"Have you been working? Is there a man living in your house? Anything you want to declare to me?" he interrogated.

"No," she lied.

"Jenny, did you think about what we discussed last time you were here?"

"Yes."

"Then are you going to take the high school equivalency test? You're a very intelligent young lady, I'm sure you would pass it," he pressed.

"Yes, Mr. Sampson, I'm ready. . . . I need this to better my life for me and my children."

Mr. Sampson was pleased with her response. He genuinely cared about her well-being. He had only been her caseworker for the last year and five months. The change was the best thing that could've happened to Jenny. He was much different from the Caucasian lady, Mrs. Whiter, who had been her caseworker for the previous seven years. Mrs. Whiter was condescending, intrusive, rude, and did not care one bit about Jenny's welfare. Mr. Sampson was more like a father figure than a caseworker.

"Okay then, Jenny, take these papers to Bayard Rustin High School and set up a date to take the test. Once you've passed the test I'll set you up with some job interviews. I'm very pleased that you've decided to do this for yourself, and I promise you, you won't regret it." Mr. Sampson wrote some information on a sheet of paper and passed it to Jenny. "Next time we talk I want to hear that you have a high school diploma."

"I won't let you or myself down," Jenny said confidently, giving Mr. Sampson a daughterly hug.

A month later, at the age of thirty, Jenny received her high school diploma. A month after that, she secured a job with the city doing clerical work at the health department. City jobs didn't pay much, but the medical benefits were good for her and her three children. Money was still tight, but at least it was money she was earning herself. This was the first time she truly felt independent.

The Game Changes

It was the fall of '87, and Numbers's birthday was right around the corner. On October 8 he'd be turning thirteen. Although he still enjoyed riding his skateboard, his interests were changing. He was paying more attention to the way he dressed, and to girls. And he was beginning to grow out of his baby fat, slimming down and looking more like his father every day. Jenny wished he looked more like her, although he did have her lips and eyes. Overall, she was pleased at how handsome her son was becoming.

The previous month, Numbers had spent all the money he earned in the summer from running errands and playing numbers on helping his mother get school clothes for him and his sisters. His birthday was in seven days, and he was broke. He and Jarvis wanted to take two neighborhood girls to the movies. The one Numbers liked was named Rosa-Marie Vasquez. She was Puerto Rican, and she liked Numbers also, but her mother forbade her to go out with black boys.

One day, when Numbers went to Rosa-Marie's house to get her to come out, Ms. Vasquez pulled him aside to speak to him. In an almost unintelligible Spanish accent, she said, "Dup'ee, you good boy. I like you. My daughter . . . you okay to be friends. But you no date her! Latino and Negro no good together, *comprendo*?" She nodded.

Numbers mimicked her nod but he really didn't mean it. Ms. Vasquez believed a black man was not as good as a Puerto Rican man for her daughter. Numbers didn't understand this logic. After all, her husband had left her to be a single parent just like Numbers's dad did to his mother. He and Rosa-Marie would just have to sneak to the movies.

Numbers figured if he could hit a bolita (two-number betting) or the Brooklyn (three numbers), he'd have enough for his movie date with Rosa-Marie. Over the course of the next four days, he did errands and made number runs, but he didn't hit any of the numbers he played. School was in session, so he was unable to play in the afternoons and could only play the late number.

After school on Thursday, Numbers walked across the street toward the number spot. Park Avenue's traffic flowed east close to the projects side, then he had to walk under the Brooklyn-Queens Expressway, or the El, where people parked their cars. Crispy Carl always kept his light-blue Ford Thunderbird under the El. It wasn't the latest model, but he kept it detailed. Numbers loved to walk by the car and admire it.

He crossed the street and saw Crispy Carl holding court on the bench outside the number joint.

"If that ain't the truth, my name ain't Crispy Motherfuckin'

Carl." He always said that. When Numbers first met Crispy Carl, he actually thought Motherfuckin' was his middle name for a while, until he said the name to his mother and she popped him in the mouth. Everyone in the vicinity reacted with a hearty laugh at what Crispy Carl had to say.

"Hey, Mr. Carl." Numbers nodded as he walked up.

"Numbers, get over here and give your man Crispy Carl some skin." He beamed, slapping Numbers's hand. "So, what's the number for this evening, li'l man? I know you got a fix on it."

"No clue," Numbers said softly, unsure of himself. "Haven't been feeling lucky lately."

Crispy Carl took a swig of his Jack. "Is that right? Well, let's see what we can do to make some greenbacks." He got up from his post, placing the half-pint bottle of Jack Daniels in his inside jacket pocket.

He walked into the number spot with his arm draped across Numbers's shoulder. The room was smoky with the usual activity. He directed Numbers to one of the nearest counters and joined him with his Big Mack number sheet, pen, and number slip. Carl gazed at the sheet as if in deep concentration. Numbers had grown to recognize that look on Mr. Carl's face. He knew a story would soon follow.

"You know, Numbers," Crispy Carl began, "most of the time when it comes to making decisions, the first thing that comes to mind is the right decision. When you think about stuff too long, you end up making the wrong call. I 'member when I was pimping down by the navy yard back in the days. One of my hoes came to me with a proposition. She told me this punk-ass pimp named Smalley had a sweet lick with some cadets on shore leave. My bitch, Lola, and one of Smalley's bitches would work three cadets and in one night pull in four thousand dollars. My gut told me all money wasn't good money, not to go in with the arrangement. But my little grimy bitch was like 'Please, Daddy, let's get this money, please.' " He made a bad attempt to speak in a female's tone. He abruptly ended the story. "So what was the first number you thought of today, Numbers?"

"Eight."

"Why eight?"

"My birthday is in two days, October eighth, and the number was on my mind earlier." Numbers looked at the clock on the wall. It read 2:55.

"How old you gonna be—twenty-one?" Crispy Carl joked.

"No, thirteen." Numbers smiled. Crispy Carl always made him laugh. Numbers often wondered how it would be to have Mr. Carl as his father.

"Are you gonna have a blackmitzvah? You're a man now." He was laughing at the confused expression on Numbers's face. "Okay, that's the number we gonna play today: 108." Crispy Carl wrote the numbers on the slip for fifty cents straight. "We playing the one-oh because October is the tenth month," Carl explained, "and eight is your b-day. Here, take this up to the window." He handed Numbers some change and the slip.

Numbers went to the window and placed the bet. By now the ladies at the window were used to seeing him.

"Hello, honey, how are you today?" Sally, the black lady, asked.

"Fine, thank you. Have a good day," Numbers replied.

"You too, sweetie." She'd already begun taking the next person's bet.

"NOBODY MOVE. EVERYBODY STAY WHERE YOU'RE AT!" a chubby white man commanded. He wore black shoes, blue pants, and a dingy white dress shirt under an old beige-and-brown-plaid suit jacket. The detective was flanked by several uniformed officers.

A man tried to scoot out the door, only to be hemmed up violently by one of the officers.

"Didn't you hear the detective, scumbag?" The white officer pushed the man's face up against the closest wall.

The two women behind the window had already gone into action, throwing slips and money into a stash box in a hole in the floor as covertly as possible.

Lawry, the plainclothes detective, peeped the activity and quickly started making his way to the window. "Didn't I tell you cunts not to move?" His path was deterred by Louie running interference for his workers.

"Hey, Detective Lawry," Louie smiled. "We took care of the powers that be. Why you's coming up in here busting up my spot? This is the second time this month." Louie talked with a thick Italian accent.

"Louie, we've got to shut you down. Your time's running out. The administration is cracking down on these illegal number holes now that the lottery is in place." Detective Lawry spoke to Louie like an old acquaintance. "The game is changing. I told you last year it was coming to this." Then something else caught Lawry's attention.

Numbers was frozen by the window with the number slip in hand.

"See, this is exactly what I'm talking about." He pointed at Numbers. "You got these underage monkeys running around here like they're at the city zoo or something. Come here, little blackie. You ready to go to jail like the rest of your tribe?" he barked at Numbers.

Numbers didn't budge.

"Come on, Detective Lawry, easy on the boy," Louie offered.

"I said, come here, little darkie, right now," Lawry demanded again. This time Numbers slowly took a step forward.

All eyes were on Detective Lawry, fearing what he had planned for the youngest person in the spot. Crispy Carl knew Detective

Lawry was as low as they came. In terms of dirty cops, he was landfill.

"Hold on now, Detective Lawry, he's with me," Crispy Carl said, said stepping up.

Lawry swung around without warning, catching Crispy Carl off guard—directly in the abdomen—with his fat fist. Numbers and the other regulars gasped as Crispy Carl crumbled to the floor with the wind knocked out of him.

"Did anybody ask you anything, nigger?" Lawry fumed, looking at Crispy Carl at his feet.

"That ain't right. That's totally uncalled for," an older lady spoke out.

"You made your point, Detective," Louie conceded, holding his hands up, signaling that he'd given up. "What do you want?"

"Louie, you know I don't want to do this to you, but I got a job to do. Shut it down right now. The next time I have to come back here it's going to be real problems." He glared at the patrons as he made his way out of the spot. He stopped when he got to the door and studied Numbers. "Stay out of my path, little blackie."

"Mommy, Numbers is bothering us," the twins called out in unison. "Stop, doo-doo head! Get out of here, poopy face!" Lakeisha and Takeisha screamed at him.

Numbers was interfering with their teatime. The girls sat on the floor playing between the full-sized bed they shared and the twin-sized bed their mother slept on. They had dolls, doll accessories, and play dishes everywhere—all or most compliments of Numbers's winnings.

"Boy, leave La-La and Ta-Ta alone and get from out my room before I have to come back there," Jenny threatened. Numbers was not finished messing with the girls quite yet. He playfully pulled each of their ponytails before dashing out of the room.

"Maaaa!" the girls cried out.

Numbers was bored out of his skull. His mother had put him on punishment, again, after hearing about what happened at the number spot. She told him that she wanted him to stay away from that place, which was ironic because she was the one who sent him there in the first place.

Crispy Carl and Numbers did hit the number they put in that evening: 108 came out just like that. Straight. Louie didn't want to pay out at first, but when all the other customers started demanding their money back, he figured it would be cheaper to pay up. Crispy Carl and Numbers were the only winners.

For the last month and a half, Numbers had followed his mother's orders and stayed out of the spot, but with Christmas approaching he decided to try his luck. When Jenny sent him to the store across Park Avenue to get her a pack of Newports, Numbers thought he'd be slick and put in a quick number. He could have had Crispy Carl place the bet for him but decided it would be quicker to do it himself. He didn't have time to listen to one of Carl's stories.

Lady Luck, Numbers would find out, was not on his side. Not only did he miss his number by one digit, but one of his mother's friends saw him in the spot and wasted no time ratting him out. Now he had been on punishment for the last four days and was going stir-crazy. No TV. No skateboarding. No company. No outside. No fun. His routine for the last four days was school and straight to the house. This time Mom said the punishment was until she said otherwise. While on punishment, he heard that the number spot had been raided again.

Numbers retreated to his room. He had been given his own room right before he turned thirteen.

Bright and early one morning, Numbers came into his mother's room in a near panic. Jenny woke up to find Numbers standing over her looking confused.

"What's wrong with you, boy?" she asked, still groggy.

"I don't know, Mommy, I'm scared."

"Scared of what?" She opened her eyes wider.

"I'm bleeding white cream from my ding-a-ling," Numbers answered. He held out his hand wiggling his fingers to show her the sticky goo.

Jenny giggled. "Oh, my baby."

She'd never really cared much if her son's father was around or not, but when it came to situations like this, when a boy needed male guidance, she couldn't help but loathe Lewis for abandoning him. That morning Jenny explained to her son about the birds and the bees, which, Numbers would find out, had nothing to do with birds or bees.

"Dee, come here. I need you to run to the store for me," Jenny called.

Freedom at last, Numbers thought, even if it was only for the time it would take to run his errand and back. He glanced at the little clock on his dresser; it showed 5:30 P.M. He jumped out of the bed and made his way to the tiny bathroom. His mother's stockings were hanging all over the shower-curtain rod. He gazed in the mirror, picked up the hairbrush that rested on the toilet-tank lid, ran water over the bristles, then evenly stroked his low-cut Caesar do several times from the crown of his head downward. This had been his daily regimen since the barber told him it was the way to train his hair into a beehive of waves. Slowly but surely, he noticed his nappiness was starting to respond. He didn't quite have the beehive yet, but a few waves were forming. Once he was satisfied with his hair, he dressed in a denim shirt, a pair of Wrangler jeans, and his Li'l Abner boots.

The smell of macaroni and cheese and corn bread filled the apartment by the time Numbers emerged out of the bathroom. His mother was in the kitchen talking to Ms. Lindsay from the tenth floor. She was one of the lucky ones. She lived in a three-bedroom apartment with her son, Maxwell, and daughter, Tabitha. They each had their own room. Ms. Lindsay was a pure-bred gossipmonger, always talking about someone or giving advice on someone else's kids even though her kids were the worst. Numbers often wondered why his mother was even friends with the woman. He didn't care for her much, but she was an adult so he respected her. His mother always told him that he didn't have to like an adult, but he better respect them.

Ms. Lindsay was about five years older than Jenny. She was dark-complexioned, five-seven in height, with bushy eyebrows and a mustache she sometimes attempted to shave. Most of the time she wore her hair in a bouffant. She looked liked she might have had a shape before the kids, but now she was more square than anything.

"Hey, Numbers," Ms. Lindsay called. She was sitting at the dining table smoking a cigarette. "Got yourself in a little trouble, huh?" She asked a question she already knew the answer to, because Ms. Lindsay was the fat pig who squealed on him. Fearing he might say the wrong thing, Numbers said nothing.

Jenny was cleaning fish in the kitchen sink. She was an exceptional cook. Anna Beth always kept her in the kitchen cooking something when she was growing up in Sumter, South Carolina. "Dee, take the five dollars out of my back pocket." She poked her right hip out so Numbers could remove the money while she continued to clean the whitings. "I need some cornmeal, the big thing of lard, and hot sauce from the supermarket on Myrtle Avenue."

"Ma, what's all the fish for?" Numbers asked.

"I'm having a card game, so hurry up back from the store. People gonna start getting here about seven."

"Can you get me a beer, being that you're going to the store anyway?" Ms. Lindsay extended seventy cents to him. "Keep the change."

Numbers wanted to say no, but his mother would surely think he was being rude and scold him for doing so. Well, at least she was tipping him, Numbers rationalized before bringing his attention back to what his mother had just said.

A card game?

What kind of cards would they be playing: Go Fish, I Declare War, or maybe Crazy Eights? Numbers grabbed his heavy red-and-black lumber jacket from the couch next to the door and his Walkman and headed out. He thought about running upstairs to get Jarvis but decided against it.

The usually crowded stoop was empty. Only a crazy old man named Shakespeare lingered by the building talking to God, himself, or his imaginary friend. Numbers never knew what was wrong with Shakespeare; he just stayed clear of him.

The temperature had dropped considerably on this late afternoon. He zipped his coat all the way up to his chin. The leaves on the trees were all but gone, and even though it was Friday, not too many people were out. Numbers made his way through the projects listening to his *Dana Dane with Fame* album, the song "Nightmares." Dana Dane lived right above him in apartment 2E. Numbers was ecstatic when Dana Dane gave him a signed copy of his cassette tape.

Numbers walked hurriedly past the back of building 102, past the buildings and nursery on the right-hand side, then past the front of building 117. In the middle of the buildings up ahead was a play structure, monkey bars and a slide, but the kids rarely played there. Mostly the thugs, players, and drug dealers hung out there if they weren't in front of building 79. Today was no exception. The usual suspects were congregated there, rolling dice, shooting the breeze, drinking quarts of beer, and smoking. Numbers walked on, making a mental note that on the way back he would take another route.

At the supermarket he picked up the items his mother wanted and waited in line. It was a little busy, and almost twenty minutes passed before he finally paid for his groceries.

"Young man, would you pack my bags?" an older lady behind Numbers requested as he was picking up his package to leave.

Numbers thought about it for a second. "Okay." He set his bag down on the floor at the end of the counter and began packing her bags. For his trouble he was given fifty cents. Numbers decided to pack a few more people's bags. Twenty minutes later he'd accumulated $3.85. He wished he could stay until the supermarket closed, but he knew if he didn't get home, his ass was grass, as his mother would put it. He wondered why he'd never thought about bagging groceries for money before.

The twins were asleep in the room with the door closed. They usually slept through the night uninterrupted, and despite all the noise from the card game taking place in the front, that was still the case.

There were ten cardplayers not including his mother in the smoke-clustered front room of the apartment. The room smelled of fish, marijuana, cigarettes, liquor, and musk. It seemed like everyone was chain-smoking and/or drinking some type of alcohol. Marvin Gaye tunes played in the background, but you could barely hear the lyrics over all the loud talking. To cool the apartment down, the old pull-latch windows were open as wide as they could be, but the temperature inside was still above eighty degrees. The old metal heaters and pipes that were installed in all of the projects put out a lot of heat when the boiler was on.

Jenny had set up two card tables and borrowed folding chairs from various neighbors to accommodate her guests. Five players sat at each table, and the game was poker. Numbers was surprised to see Crispy Carl among them, dressed in a red suit with black pinstripes, a matching red hat and shoes, looking like the old pimp he was.

"Come on and deal," Crispy Carl taunted Mr. Mac, taking a swig from his personal bottle of Jack Daniels.

"Numbers, my little man, come over here," Crispy Carl requested after catching sight of Numbers. Numbers slid his way toward the living room behind the seat of Mr. Simon, who was sitting closest to the kitchen.

"Where you think you're going?" Jenny inquired matter-of-factly, looking up from her plate. She was standing near the kitchen counter.

"Mr. Carl called me," Numbers answered.

Mac dealt the cards.

"Jenny, let Numbers come over here and talk to his daddy," Crispy Carl said, looking at the queen of clubs he had been dealt for his faceup card and shielding the facedown card with his hand. He lifted it just enough to take a peek. Those who weren't enthralled by the hand they were playing, like nosy Ms. Lindsay at the other table, laughed lightly.

"You wish, you old fart," Jenny countered. More chuckles followed.

Mr. Mac dealt each player two cards; one facedown and the other faceup.

"I'll bet three dollars," Crispy Carl said, leading off the bet with the high card.

"What you got down there, another queen?" Wayne asked. He folded and tossed his hand away. Carl took a swig of his Jack and smiled at Numbers.

"I'ma fold, too. Yeah, he probably do got a pair of queens." Pearl was the oldest player at the table. She tossed her hand as well.

There were two players left in the hand other than Crispy

Carl—the dealer, Mac, who was studying his hand, and Sybil. Sybil was a very attractive brown-skinned lady, thirty-something, with streaks of gray hair on the front of her head. "Yeah, I'll call that three dollars, he ain't got nothing," Sybil taunted, looking at Carl through her Yves Saint Laurent prescription eyewear.

"I'll call, too." Mac tossed his three dollars to the middle of the table.

Numbers stood over Crispy Carl's shoulder watching the game, not quite understanding what was going on, but Crispy Carl was always willing to school him.

"The name of the game is five-card stud," he began to teach Numbers. "You can win the hand with the best cards or, like Sybil always likes to try and do, bluff your way through." He saw the confused look on Numbers's face. "That means to try to scare the rest of the table into folding their hands by betting big."

"Whatever," Sybil scoffed.

Mac dealt the third card to Crispy Carl faceup. It was a 10 of clubs. Now Crispy Carl had a queen and a 10 showing. Sybil's next card was a queen of spades.

"I could use that queen," Crispy Carl joked, even though he was serious as high blood pressure.

"I bet you could, Mr. Pimp No More." Sybil laughed, and the rest of the table laughed right along with her. She now had a queen and an 8 showing.

Mac turned up his second card: an ace of diamonds, to go with his jack of diamonds. The bet was now on Mac with the ace high.

"Okay, that's what I'm talking 'bout," Mac gushed with confidence. "The bet is six dollars."

Crispy Carl slowly tossed a five-dollar bill and a single into the pot, seeming unsure of his bet.

"I'm not bluffing now." Sybil quickly counted off six singles and another six dollars from her pile of money and threw the whole twelve dollars into the pot. Crispy Carl explained that the pot is what they called the money in the middle of the table. The bet was now an additional six dollars to Mac and Crispy Carl to stay in the hand. "Let's see who's bluffing now," Sybil said, taunting the two men with a stoic face.

"I wasn't bluffing either, when I told you I would give you what you deserved," Crispy Carl shot back at her.

"Shut ya ol' black ass up," she countered.

"You like this ol' black thing," he said.

Most of the players there knew Carl and Sybil once had a little thing going.

"See there, Numbers, Sybil has a pair of eights, but Mac's aces can beat those." Carl was talking as if he was a psychic and knew what Sybil's and Mac's facedown cards were, but he didn't. He was just making a gambler's speculation. Numbers stood there soaking it all up. Crispy Carl did not react; he just waited to see if Mac would call the bet.

"I'll call." Mac smiled, wagering his six bills. Crispy Carl called as well.

Mac turned up Crispy Carl's fourth card. It was a king of clubs. Sybil's card was a king of hearts. Mac flipped over a four of spades for himself. Now he had an ace high, jack, and four. The bet was still on him. It was turning out to be a good hand for the house.

Jenny peered on, watching the outcome. The house took one dollar off every ten dollars in the pot. Jenny had already accumulated a good amount of proceeds in a big pickle jar she had in the kitchen. She just hoped she could keep enough players at each table so she wouldn't have to play and bet back her earnings.

Mac hesitated for a brief moment, then called out and put up twenty dollars. Now Sybil lifted her hole card (the facedown card) slightly, peeking at it, tilting her head almost to table level, contemplating her next move as she waited on Carl. She looked around the table at Mac's cards and Carl's cards briefly, then back at hers with no expression. Crispy Carl didn't say a word, just pitched his twenty dollars into the pot.

Sybil still didn't give anything away by way of expression. "I call," she said, following Crispy Carl.

"It's getting good now," said Crispy Carl adjusting himself in his seat, crossing his left leg over his right. The move caused his pants leg to rise up, showing his black, red, and white argyle socks.

All the time the hand was taking place, Numbers did not count cards as he would usually do when he played other card games. The game had him entranced. He did attempt to guess what everyone's fifth card would be. Numbers drifted off in his mind. He could hear the grown-ups talking, laughing, and taunting one another, but it was all background noise. He started going over in his mind what cards were played, less the cards that were face-down that he couldn't see. When he snapped back to the here and now, he had an idea of what cards might play. He speculated that the next three cards would be a 10, a 7, and a 4.

Mac was eager to deal. He was finished counting the money he had left in front of him and was ready for the fifth card. Counting out his money was a tactic to pilfer some confidence from the other players. It was in vain.

"Ya dumb blind ass can't count, but whatever you have there is mine after this," Crispy Carl said, clowning him.

"Uh-uh, that's my cash," Sybil joined in.

Numbers giggled at their banter; so did his mother and a few others.

"Here we go." Mac ignored them and prepared to deal the fifth and final card.

There was a big ruckus going on at the other table, but no one at this table cared. This was the payoff card.

Mac dealt to Crispy Carl; it was a 10. His final hand minus the hole card was a pair of 10's high, a king, and a queen. Before he caught the additional 10, he had a straight working.

Numbers was one for one on his guess.

The next card went to Sybil. It was an 8. She now had a pair of 8s, a queen, and a jack faceup. She smirked.

Numbers was one for two.

Mac dealt himself a 4 of hearts. He now displayed a pair of 4's, an ace, and a jack.

Numbers was two for three. *Not bad,* he thought to himself.

The bid was on Crispy Carl with the pair of 10s leading. Crispy Carl took a look at his bottom card, then calmly sipped his elixir, fingered his money, and said, "Check"; he didn't bet any money. "Now you know that shit's not gonna fly over here," Sybil said, betting twenty dollars.

Mac was eager; Sybil barely got her money into the pot before he raised the bet ten dollars. Crispy Carl called the thirty dollars. Sybil smirked even more, her face saying, *I got them.* She raised the bet twenty. Mac called the bet and then Crispy Carl. Each player had bet fifty on this card alone. It was surely a hefty pot, the best one of the night, Jenny calculated.

"Well, Sybil, we paid to see your hand, let's see it," Crispy Carl directed.

Sybil had a pair of 8's, a queen, and a jack, and she turned up her hole card, which was an 8. "Three eights, three of a kind, you tricks!" she shouted, slapping the card on the table.

"Fuck!" Mac screamed, revealing his hole card: an ace. He had a pair of aces and a pair of 4's. Two pair couldn't beat three of a kind on its best day.

Sybil celebrated with a swallow of her beer. "Well, that's it, Jenny, count up my winnings for me and take the house cut," she bragged. "Crispy's ass probably got a pair of queens to go with the tens, he finished, too."

"Not quite, Cruella De Vil. Hold your horses," Crispy Carl said, making fun of the gray streaks in her hair. "Numbers, come and turn this card up for me," he requested. Numbers moved in, reached and picked up the card. Before he touched it, he knew what it was. He turned it up slowly so all could see, and it was just what he'd guessed it would be: a 10. Crispy Carl won the hand with a higher three of a kind than Sybil's.

"Come to Daddy." Crispy Carl swept the money toward him after Jenny took the house cut.

Sybil sulked in her chair, pissed off.

Wow, I need to learn how to play this game, Numbers thought.

How to Finish

Crispy Carl taught Numbers how to hustle Pitty Pat, poker, Tunk, and craps, but there was something about the game of C-Lo that drew Numbers in. Though he knew he didn't have any real control of the dice, he felt comfortable in this element. This game was more about confidence, your gift for gab and beating the odds. Numbers loved to listen to the rollers talk smack, as Mr. Carl called it. When he watched Crispy Carl shoot dice, Numbers would soak up all of his lyrics.

Crispy Carl and Numbers emerged from the number spot that had since been converted into the corner bodega divvying up the money from the bolita they hit straight for two dollars. The bet netted them $128. People were still betting numbers in the back of the store. This business was too lucrative for Louie to give up, so he camouflaged it with the grocery store out front and continued to pay off the powers that be.

A dice game was just getting started on the Cumberland side of the store. Archie, a six-foot-four brown brother from the projects, had the bank. Archie was once an NBA prospect, but he never went to class when he was in college and eventually fell victim to the streets.

"The bank is thirty dollars," he called out, shaking the three dice in his right hand above his head near his ear. "What you got, old man?" he asked Silver, a brown-skinned old-school cat whose hair had turned white in his teens due to some type of gene disorder.

"I got five of that, young'un," Silver shouted, placing a five dollar bill under his left foot.

"Ten," a younger guy called.

"I got the bank stopped," Crispy Carl said.

"Okay. Bet goes to the bank stopper. All other bets are dead! I done caught me a sucker." Archie beamed a picture-perfect smile.

Carl leaned over to Numbers. "Numbers, give me fifteen and go half with me on the bank."

Numbers was still new to the game, but he trusted Crispy Carl's hustle.

"Crispy, you finished already? You bumming money off shorty doo-wop? Pay up," Archie taunted, rolling the dice onto the uneven concrete pavement. The dice came to a stop: 4-3-4.

"Oh, that lady Tracy is hard to beat." *Tracy* was slang for "three." "She got you quaking in them fake gators." Archie tried his hand at intimidating Crispy Carl.

Before Crispy Carl moved toward the dice, he unbuttoned his single-breasted olive-green gabardine jacket. Then he kneeled down, raising his left pant leg to reveal beige, olive, and brown argyle socks. His shoes weren't new, but they shined like they were fresh out the box. He'd barely picked up all three dice off the ground when he let them slide back out of his hand proclaiming, "Show 'em how a bottom bitch roll."

The dice fell into line: 4 . . . 4 . . . 4. Trips—instant winner.

"Yeah, baby, pimpin' ain't easy, but it's a living," he said while taking the money from Archie's hand. "My bank. The bank is sixty dollars. You see, Numbers, you gotta talk to ya dice and let 'em know you in control, that's the key. If you don't mean it"—he fingered the dice—"ya dice will know and they'll break you!"

Archie peeled some bills from his pocket, "That's some bull-shit, Crispy. I just broke your ass right here last week." He laughed. "I got the bank stopped. Now what?"

Carl squatted down, this time schooling the dice (flipping them over in front of him without really rolling them). "That's another thing," he said, finally picking up the dice and shaking them. "You gotta have a short memory for your losses and disap-pointments." He tossed out the dice. "Make that money for your pimp, bitches!" he hollered as if he was preaching a sermon. 1 . . . 6 . . .

"Ace, motherfucker!" Archie screamed, waiting for the last chuck to stop spinning. Archie needed it to fall on 6 to give him the win without having to shoot. Crispy Carl, on the other hand, needed the rock to stop on an ace. The last cube spun for a long time before finally coming to a halt.

. . . 1. "Head-crack baby, pay up." Crispy Carl showed no ex-pression waiting for Archie to pay.

Archie was huffing, puffing, and cursing under his breath as he flung the money into Crispy Carl's hand. With his back to everyone so no one would know what his stash looked like, he pulled out his wallet and peeled off a few more bills.

"This is the final lesson, Numbers," Crispy Carl said, grinning. "The bank's a buck twenty." Carl called out what the bank was worth to whoever was listening.

The cipher began calling out their bets. Silver bet twenty, the other young dude wagered fifty, and another young dude in the cipher put down thirty.

"That's what I'm talking 'bout . . . twenty dollars open. Who want it?" Crispy asked, schooling the dice again.

"I got the whole one hundred and twenty dollars right here." Archie slammed the money down at his feet.

"Like I said, Numbers"—Crispy Carl stopped schooling the dice for a moment and turned to Numbers from his squatting position—"the last thing you need to know, when you got 'em down, is to keep 'em there." With a smile, he started shaking the dice extra elaborately before letting them roll from his fingers. "Bitches, get that trick!" he shouted at the dice.

They landed: 4 . . . 6 . . . and 5.

"That's right, four, five, and six. C-Lo, baby, the name of the game!" Crispy Carl yelled excitedly to everyone in earshot.

"Damn!" Archie kicked the money at his feet. It was evident it was his last. He stood there mumbling to himself, pissed off and broke. Not a good combination.

"Now we cut the bank," he told Numbers, schooling him on the finer points of the game. "When you roll C-Lo you can do that."

Numbers watched Crispy Carl make the bank forty. He passed the other two hundred off to Numbers to hold. By the time Crispy Carl was finished ten minutes later, he'd made an additional three hundred bucks. When all was said and done, Numbers and Crispy Carl walked away with $250 each.

"That's how you finish," Crispy Carl instructed.

Numbers ran home and gave most of the money to his mother.

Hallway Games

Broz, Numbers, Jayquan, Tee, Jarvis, and Waketta were huddled on the rooftop staircase landing in building 79 playing Pitty Pat. Broz sat on the top step closest to the handrail; Waketta sat on the other side closest to the wall. Tee stood on the stairs in between them. Jayquan and Numbers kneeled and squatted on the landing. Jarvis leaned on the wall behind Numbers, eating junk food, as usual waiting for his opportunity to get into the game.

Tee was up about fifteen to twenty dollars, but to hear him tell it he was on the verge of pawning his baby brother just to stay in the game for the next hand. That's how Tee was—he'd lie about his winnings and exaggerate his losses because he didn't want anyone trying to bum off him. The funny thing was, every time he went broke, he'd be the first one with his hand out asking for a loan. He was always begging, but when he had it, you couldn't get a red nickel out of him.

Fat Boy Broz, on the other hand, loved to brag and boast if he was winning. He didn't care if he broke one of them or not, he wouldn't take the chance of lending anyone money to stay in the game and possibly turn the tables and leave him broke.

Waketta was one of the few girls who hung around the boys and gambled. She was fifteen years old, like the rest of them. Well developed up top, with a nice round booty, Waketta was loud and ghetto, just like her momma. She lived on the ninth floor with her mother and little sister. Her mother, Dixie, was always getting into it with some man's girlfriend or wife. Dixie was promiscuous. She drank too much and talked even more. Waketta had two things in common with her mother: a killer body and a loud mouth.

Jayquan was, for the most part, the quiet type. The one to avoid confrontation, he was more of a diplomat.

"Whose deal is it?" Waketta snapped. She was pissed that Tee had won his fourth consecutive hand and high spades.

"Don't you see me shuffling?" Broz snapped back.

"I know you not mad because Tee is winning." Numbers laughed. "This the first time he won in how long?"

"I don't care! I hate when his broke, yellow-teeth ass win," Waketta bellowed.

"You'll be asking me to borrow two bucks in a minute. Now watch," Tee said. Tee had a way of getting on everyone's nerves.

"What? You owe me four dollars, and if you don't give me my money, I'ma kick your ass," Waketta threatened.

"Later for you," Tee said, trying to make light of it, knowing Waketta meant what she said.

"Deal, Broz! How many times you got to shuffle the freaking cards?" Numbers was growing impatient with the banter. He was losing money today. For some reason, he was off his game. Every time he discarded, it seemed to be the one Tee needed to win the hand. Broz dealt out five cards to each player and turned up an ace of spades.

"Nobody's got the ace-of-spades high card, so who's got the king?" Broz inquired to no one in particular while picking up his hand.

"Tee, it's on you, you need the ace?" Waketta asked.

Tee did not respond.

"My pluck," Waketta said, reaching for the deck.

"Hold up, I need that," Numbers said, throwing out a matching ace of hearts.

"Nah, I need that." Tee threw out an ace of diamonds before Numbers could complete his turn.

"Why you playing like that, stupid?" Numbers was upset that Tee had gotten him to reveal his card.

"Your mother's stupid," Tee lashed out.

"What? Ya mother's a whore. Too bad. I feel sorry for you!" Numbers reversed Tee's snap.

Everyone except Tee laughed.

"Fuck you, bitch! That's why you don't know your daddy." Tee's attempts to belittle Numbers worked. His comment struck a nerve. Numbers was boiling.

Seeing that Numbers was mad, Jayquan tried to intervene: "Come on, y'all, let's just play cards."

"Numbers, you gonna let him talk about you and your daddy like that?" Waketta said. The instigation worked.

"I'll punch you in your mouth," Numbers threatened.

"Do it," Tee said, stepping up the stairs through the game to the landing where Numbers stood.

It wasn't really the comment about his father that bothered Numbers; Tee had just gotten on his last nerve. He was always try-ing to act like he was tough, and Numbers wanted to put him in his place once and for all. Everyone else started talking loud, trying to get Tee and Numbers back to the game. They'd been loud for the last hour, and now the noise had climbed to its peak.

Numbers balled up his fist, ready to make right on his promise to punch Tee in the face. Jarvis was standing up against the wall, finishing up his last Twinkie, amused that someone made his friend so heated that he was ready to fight. Numbers knew that was why his friend was smiling, but he didn't care. All he cared about right then was putting a whipping on Tee.

Face-to-face, Tee and Numbers stood about an inch apart.

"What?" Numbers challenged.

"What you wanna do?" Tee replied.

"What you wanna do?"

They began to bump and push each other, going around in a circle, neither wanting to throw the first blow.

Bam!

"STAY WHERE YOU AT, DON'T RUN!" an authoritative voice commanded. Someone was busting through the thirteenth-floor hallway door.

Numbers and Tee did the opposite; they dispatched their tiff and sprinted behind Jarvis, who had kicked open the roof door and bolted out onto the roof and into the sunset. Jayquan was fresh on their heels, and after Waketta grabbed up her money, she followed in their tracks. Broz's fat ass didn't even bother to run, he just sat there conceding his capture. The uniformed officer hurried up the stairs after the delinquent kids—straight past Broz. "Don't move!" he said, heading to the roof.

No sooner had the pink-faced officer stepped onto the roof than Broz wobbled his chubby ass down to his twelfth-floor apartment.

Jarvis, Numbers, and Tee darted across the graveled rooftop toward the attached building, 68 Cumberland Walk, with Jayquan and Waketta not far behind. The distance between the roof-access doors was about 250 feet, give or take. Jarvis was starting to slow down. He had put on some extra weight eating all the junk food.

"Keep running, Jar, don't slow down!" Numbers shouted. He was about to pass Jarvis.

As they approached the 68 roof access, the door swung open. It was another uniformed cop. He was taller than the other, and overweight. He was breathing heavy and his white face was blushing red.

"Oh, shit!" Jarvis cried out, sliding to a halt on the gravel. Numbers almost ran into his back. The police had them sandwiched in. There was no place to run—they were caught. Numbers knew if his mother found out about this, he would get the ass whipping to eclipse all ass whippings. She had warned him to stay out of the stairwell gambling, but of course he was hardheaded and didn't listen. Now he'd have to pay the piper.

The taller officer, Lockhart, still breathing deeply, said, "See, Tommy, I told you these little monkeys always run."

His nightstick drawn, Officer O'Doul was breathing heavily as well. "Okay, you little monkeys—over there." He pointed to the roof's edge.

Numbers and his friends were led to the wall with a few nudges from the cops' nightsticks. Left to right, they were lined up: Jayquan, Waketta, Jarvis, Numbers, and then Tee. Numbers looked at each of his friends' faces. Fear was evident on all of them. *And rightfully so*, he thought. Numbers knew cops were grimy. He'd learned it firsthand with the Crispy Carl incident.

Officer O'Doul stood back watching while Officer Lockhart paced in front of the kids, twirling his nightstick. He was finally getting his original pink-white color back in his face. "Well, we have a dilemma here," he spoke with a heavy Irish accent. "We only have two pairs of cuffs, and five of you. So two of you are coming with us, and the other three are getting tossed off the roof." Numbers looked at the officers defiantly. Jayquan, Jarvis, and Waketta looked frightened, but nothing like Tee. Tee was trembling so uncontrollably he looked as though he was ready to throw up or pass out.

"How 'bout you, Sambo?" Lockhart walked up to Jayquan and slapped him, squeezing his jaw roughly between his fingers. Moisture welled up in Jayquan's eyes, but he did not shed a tear. Lockhart shoved Jayquan backward by the face almost into the roof ledge. Then he moved on to Waketta.

"Wow, this jungle bunny's going to be something when she gets older," Lockhart said, looking back at Officer O'Doul. "How old are you?" Waketta didn't answer. He strolled by her and winked. "I'll get back to you, doll." Waketta sucked her teeth at him. O'Doul looked on, smirking devilishly.

"Are you eyeballing me, Big Head?" Officer Lockhart ridiculed Jarvis. Goddamn, boy, you got a big-ass head! Your mother has to be a mare to give birth to a horse head like you." He grabbed Jarvis by the collar and began batting him in the head. Jarvis cowed. Hoping for more of a fight, Lockhart lost interest in Jarvis and let his eyes continue down to Numbers and Tee. Then he backtracked to Waketta.

"Now, where were we, sweetheart?" He grabbed his baton, which was hanging from his left wrist, held it horizontally with both hands out in front of him. He approached Waketta and pressed the stick against her stomach. "You better not move," he threatened. Slowly he moved the nightstick up her abdomen like he was rolling out pastry dough until it was under her breasts. Tears began to roll down Waketta's face from the humiliation. Lockhart raised the baton higher until her young, firm breasts were propped up.

Numbers couldn't take it anymore. "Leave her alone, pig."

"Oh, your little boyfriend can't wait his turn, huh? Okay." He removed the stick from Waketta's breasts, slowly letting them fall to their natural position. She sobbed. He moved toward Numbers. Numbers stood tall, with his chest out and head up. Officer Lockhart stood in front of him. "What's your name, boy?" he asked, pretending to be polite.

"Dupree," Numbers answered, remembering one of the rules Crispy Carl had taught him. Never give out your street name.

"Dupree," Lockhart snickered. "You must be a descendant of kings or something." He looked back at his partner, laughing.

In an instant, Lockhart's face had turned as red and evil as Satan's. He shoved the round butt of his nightstick into Numbers's gut. Numbers let out a gasp and then folded over toward the ground. Lockhart reached out his large white hands, snatched Numbers by the throat, and stood him up straight. Numbers pulled at the big white officer's hands and arms, gasping for air.

Jarvis wanted to help his friend—they all did, except Tee, who was crying and shaking like a fall leaf. But no one dared to make a move, as Officer O'Doul stood watchful with his hand on his .38 revolver.

"This dirty little raisin wants to go off the rooftop," Lockhart threatened, his choke hold forcing Numbers back against the roof ledge. Numbers's head and shoulders were over the ledge, and his feet were off the ground. All he could think about was his mother and sisters. He was the man of the house. What would they do without him? His mother would be devastated. Then all he saw were black spots as he felt himself slipping out of consciousness.

The only thing he could hear was Tee praying, "Lord, please help us, mighty God; you have the power to save us. Please help your faithful servants, Lord, please."

Just when Numbers thought he was on his last breath and was going to be tossed off the roof, Officer Lockhart released him. Numbers slumped to his knees, coughing for air.

"Deacon Darkie, done pissed all over himself." Officer Lockhart laughed once again with his partner. Tee had lost all control of his bladder. The two cops continued to laugh heartily at Tee, whom Numbers believed probably saved his life with his prayers or his pissing on himself or both.

"Let's go," O'Doul called to his partner. "Take this as a warning, you little niggers! The next time I won't be so nice." He put his nightstick away and walked toward 68's roof access.

Crispy Carl had once told Numbers that he didn't need to exact revenge on bad people because karma would take care of their negative deeds. Now as he lay on the ground struggling to catch his breath, Numbers wasn't sure if he could wait for karma.

As far as Numbers knew, the only other person from the projects who attended his high school was Rosa-Marie—who was now his girlfriend, as long as her mother didn't find out. Even though the majority of students who attended Brooklyn Tech were white or Asian, it was still one of the most ethnically diverse schools in the borough. When Numbers first entered the school, he experienced culture shock. He was used to being around only blacks and Latinos. He hadn't ventured out of the Fort Greene projects much other than to downtown Brooklyn, his two trips to Virginia to visit his Aunt Camille and her family, his rare visits to the Bronx to see his uncle, and his frequent trips to Delancey Street to shop for gear.

After his math gift was discovered at P.S. 67 elementary school, Numbers's mother had enrolled him in the SAMM program (Science, Art, Music, and Math) at Junior High School 258, on the corner of Macon and Marcy. From there he was admitted to Brooklyn Technical, a high school for academic achievers. His mother was so proud of him.

Now in his junior year, Numbers was growing up to be quite handsome. At five ten and about 140 pounds, he'd lost all of his baby fat. He was one of the best-dressed guys in his grade—in the school for that matter.

Jenny was always at work. She worked at the health department during the day and A&S department store at night. Numbers had the run of the apartment until his sisters came home from the after-school program, if they didn't stay with Ms. Sandy, in Farragut.

Numbers, Jarvis, Waketta, and a girl named Sharon, who lived in building 81, sometimes cut class and rendezvoused at Numbers's crib. Today they were in his room on his full-sized bed getting drunk off Cisco and playing High Card. The person with the lowest card plucked from the deck had to take off an article of clothing. The girls were down to their panties and bras. Jarvis had on his Fruit of the Looms and a pair of socks. Numbers still had on his pants. Sharon was okay-looking, but she was skinny with no shape compared with Waketta. Waketta, with her nice round 34B titties and plump ass, was a young thoroughbred. Grown men wanted to give her the business. Jarvis had been trying to get into her pants since his first boner. Now seeing Waketta in her bra and panties had his penis Iron Mike Tyson hard. If everything went as planned, he'd get some of that today. Numbers was going to help his friend crack that. The plan was for Numbers to take Sharon into his mother's room while Jarvis stayed with Waketta. Numbers had no problem with the arrangement. He wasn't too particular on which one he got, as long as he got some. When the girls were down to just their panties, Numbers changed the rules.

"The girl and guy with the highest cards have to give each other some tongue." Numbers picked first: a deuce of hearts. Waketta plucked a 5 of spades, Jarvis pulled a 3 of diamonds, and Sharon got a 4 of spades.

"Jar, Ketta, Jar, Ketta, Jar, Ketta," Numbers chanted, egging them on. They moved closer together and began slobbering each other down. Jarvis was really starting to get into it and sneaked some feels on her breast. Waketta wasn't as enthusiastic. She pushed him off, wiped her mouth with the back of her hand, and took a long swig from one of the bottles of Cisco, blushing a little. Sharon looked on, smiling.

"Yeah, boy! That's how you do it," Numbers congratulated his friend. "Y'all ready for the next round? This time whichever guy and girl get the highest card kiss and the guy and girl with the lowest card kiss, too." Without waiting for an answer, Numbers plucked his card. King. Jarvis drew a 7. Waketta turned up a jack, and Sharon's card was a 9. Now Numbers and Waketta were paired up, and so were Jarvis and Sharon. Waketta slid across the bed toward Numbers. As they got closer, they both began to giggle at the thought of kissing each other. Jarvis and Sharon looked on, waiting for the other two to start it off. Jarvis wished he was kissing Waketta again. Waketta took Numbers's hands and placed them on her young tender breasts, and Numbers's penis got stiff instantly as she placed her lips on his. They tongued, slobbered, sucked, and slurped each other's faces for five minutes. Jarvis and Sharon had become unlocked and were just watching the two of them go at it.

"Damn, y'all not coming up for air," Jarvis interjected jealously.

"For real," Sharon added with a giggle.

Numbers and Waketta started laughing in each other's mouths. They would have kept going if the peanut gallery hadn't said anything. Waketta wasn't quite finished. She stood up and grabbed Numbers by the hand, then led him out of the room. Numbers looked back at his friend, who he could tell was pissed off, but Numbers believed Jarvis knew the rules of the game. Don't hate the player, hate the game. Waketta had chosen him. There was nothing he could do about that.

Waketta led him to his mother's room. That was the day they had sex, losing their virginity together. Even though Waketta knew Rosa-Marie was Numbers's girl, she didn't care. She wanted what she wanted.

Rosa, in only her panties, lay on the bed next to Numbers with her brownish tan body partly covered by the sheet. With her light brown flawless complexion and features, she resembled Dorothy Dandridge in *Carmen Jones.* But it was her hazel eyes that really took Numbers's breath away. He had adored her since they were kids. He felt like he had waited the entire seventeen years of his life for this moment. He couldn't believe it as he stared up at the ceiling. *They were about to do it.* They were in their senior year, and this would be the perfect graduation gift. They had fooled around and made out numerous times before, but Rosa-Marie was never ready to go all the way and Numbers never pressed her. He was nervous, like it was his first time. As far as Rosa-Marie would ever know, it would be.

"You okay?" Numbers asked, attempting to make small talk.

"Uh-huh. You?" Rosa-Marie replied softly. She paused for a long moment. "Do you have a condom?"

When Jenny found out her son had a sperm count she educated

him on the use of protection—and not just that one time. She felt if it was important enough to say once, it was important enough to say several times to make sure her point got across. She didn't want Numbers to burden himself with children at a very young age like she had.

"Yes. You ready?"

"Are you?"

"Yes." Numbers turned to her and gently cupped her soft, delicate breast. Rosa-Marie closed her eyes and enjoyed his tender caress. He kissed her lips slowly at first. Their breathing and movements grew hot and heavy. Numbers moved his hands off her breast down her abdomen to her small bush. He rubbed her there as their breathing quickened. He pushed his middle finger into her tight, wet vagina.

"Hmmmm," she moaned, her mouth opened just enough to let her tongue glide across her perfect white teeth.

Numbers stared at her features, mesmerized. Her beauty was undeniable. He played with her wet spot, making her chest heave as he fingered her clit. Their nervousness subsided. Numbers reached over to his pants on the floor next to his bed and removed a condom from his pocket. He anxiously rolled the latex down over his young hard muscle. Rosa-Marie waited patiently, watching him get ready for her. Numbers rolled over on top of her, and they kissed, grinding their bodies together. Although he'd had a couple of previous sexual encounters with Waketta, he was still inexperienced. He fumbled to insert his dick into her virgin slit. Rosa couldn't wait for him to find it and reached down to guide him.

"Ooh, yes baby, I love you," she cooed, speaking in Spanish, as she felt his dick move deeper inside her, breaking her hymen. They humped each other slowly and deliberately, until her pussy fully accepted him. Then they bumped and humped like dogs in heat. Rosa wasn't sure how her first time was supposed to be, but she was pleased. She knew there was a lot to learn, and she was looking forward to learning it with Numbers. And Numbers imagined that this was what it felt like to make love to an angel.

Make 'Em Pay

Numbers was endowed with a hustler's spirit. Throughout high school, he indulged in various hustles. The first summer after freshman year, he and Jarvis worked at Pratt Institute as camp counselors, earning minimum wage. From eight in the morning till three in the afternoon, they were in charge of children ages five to eleven. They had boo-koo fun. The only setback was that they had to wait three weeks to get their first check. It seemed like the whole summer passed before they got it. As soon as their boss called them into the office to collect their earnings, they hightailed it to the check-cashing spot and then to lower Manhattan—Delancey Street—to buy some wears. Delancey Street was a nucleus for inexpensive fashions. Numbers's mom had been taking him there for as long as he could remember. After shopping, Numbers was damn near broke. But not for long: the summer youth program was his second hustle; gambling was his first.

Working the summer camp was a great experience, but the following summer Numbers opted not to sign up again—it was too time-consuming and didn't pay enough. Instead he worked another money-making scheme Crispy Carl put him up on. It was a game called Chuck-A-Luck. With start-off capital as low as ten or twenty dollars, he could rake in five to ten times that amount in a few hours. All he needed to skin his vics was a board, three dice, and a cup. He numbered a flat board from 1 to 6. The gamblers would place their bets on their desired number. Numbers would then shake the dice in the cup and slam it down on the board, calling out, "Chuck-A-Luck, Chuck-A-Luck, put down a quarter, win a buck." The bettor could win up to three times his wager. Numbers hustled hard during his sophomore summer with his Chuck-A-Luck board and rolling dice.

During the summer after his junior year, Numbers met a brother named Muhammad Saleem, a street peddler who hustled down on Fulton Street, selling sundresses, sandals, handbags, and other accessories. Numbers came across his setup on the corner of Fulton Street and Nostrand Avenue and stopped after seeing a very attractive dress he wanted to buy for his mother. While he was there, Numbers convinced a young lady that one of Saleem's dresses would look fantastic on her. She purchased the sundress, a bag, and a silk scarf. Saleem was impressed by Numbers's sales spirit and gave him a job.

Selling sundresses, hats, scarves, and other accessories would train Numbers for what lay ahead; he learned he could sell just about anything. Numbers was a natural, but his street-vendor career was cut short after 5-o confiscated his product multiple times in one week.

Throughout the school year, Numbers made cash playing cards during his lunch period. He received satisfactory grades and was somewhat popular, known for being the fly-dressing hustler from Fort Greene with the prettiest girl in the school.

All was cool until his mother was called up to the school during his senior year because of his excessive gambling. Jenny hated to have to take a day off from work for nonsense. She forbade Numbers from hustling in the school. His gambling and other antics had been okay with her as long as they didn't interfere with his schooling, but now they did. Numbers respected his mother's wishes for the most part, so that was the end of that. He only gambled occasionally for the next year or so.

What now? Numbers pondered. What would he do to keep getting cash? He decided during the middle of his senior year to try his hand at a regular gig. He got a part-time job at Mickey D's. Other than the summer youth program, this was his first real employment.

Numbers had planned to go to college in the fall with Rosa-Marie, but he never followed up. Instead he worked at McDonald's full-time.

Crispy Carl once told Numbers, "When you start taking what you do or what you have in your life for granted, you're sure to lose it." Now that Numbers was picking up his last paycheck from McDonald's, he understood what that meant. After working at Mickey D's for more than two years, he got fired. He had to admit, it was his own fault, and stupid! He knew he shouldn't have been smoking blunts while he was still on the clock. That was some dumb-nigger shit, and he chastised himself repeatedly while walking across Fulton Street.

"FUCK!" he yelled out into the warm summer air, swinging his fist at no one. People looked at him like he was crazy, but he didn't notice.

Numbers took his check out of his pocket and looked at it again, hoping the amount would have somehow miraculously changed into more. But $463.32 was all it was and all it would be. This was two weeks' worth of pay, including overtime. He went to the check-cashing place downtown on Willoughby Street. They took five dollars and change for their fee. *At this rate I'll be broke before I get home,* Numbers thought cynically. He bought a Pepsi and headed home. Fort Greene was one of the biggest project developments in BK. It consisted of the Raymond Ingersoll Houses and the Walt Whitman Houses, where Numbers lived. The people in the Ingersoll section called the Whitman section the far side. The people in the Whitman section called the Ingersoll section the third side. It was crazy how the sides had so much animosity toward each other even though they were, in essence, part of the same projects.

Numbers crossed the Flatbush Avenue Extension onto Myrtle Avenue and the third side. He continued on Myrtle until he crossed Navy Street, called the middle side, since it divided the two. Once he crossed St. Edwards, he was in the area they called the island. And that's exactly what it was—an island between Whitman and Ingersoll. While each one of the other three sections had more than fifteen buildings, each either six, eleven, or thirteen stories high, the island only had eight buildings, each six stories. On the corner of North Portland and Myrtle were Sarjay's candy store, Johnny's grocery store, and the dry cleaners, as well as the rent office for the Walt Whitman Houses.

Numbers often walked through the island because it was a shortcut to his building. It was about four o' clock in the afternoon on a clear Friday. A big dice game was going on in the middle of the attached buildings at 157 and 158 North Elliott Place. Numbers knew a few of the dudes who lived on the island but seldom hung out with them. The island boys usually ran in their own clique. There were about a dozen steps leading to the stoop landing and about ten dudes in the cipher, but not all of them were gambling. There was one fine-ass chick named Suki, who was half black and half Asian. By the way the dude Coney kept looking to Suki for approval, it was evident that they were together. It was hard to believe that a specimen as fine as she could find solace in a nigger who looked like Grape Ape. But if it was true that money made a nigger look better to chicks, this nigger's paper was long enough to make him look like Billy Dee Williams. Most of the guys there didn't know that Suki was a ride-or-die bitch. She would bust her gun for her nigger Coney if directed to do so.

Numbers recognized a few of the locals from his side in the cipher. A couple were there betting grips of loot. One up-and-coming hustler, Crush, from the third side, had just lost a grip, and he was pissed. The bank was being controlled by Coney. Coney was loud and flashy and craved being the center of attention. He had everyone afraid to bet on his line, since he'd just rolled C-Lo then head crack five times in a row before that. When Numbers walked up on the game, Coney had just cut the bank to five hundred dollars. That was more than Numbers's whole paycheck, which was all he had. Numbers hadn't rolled dice in a minute, but he wasn't planning on losing. He always found a way to step up when the pressure was on.

"Shoot four hundred fifty of the bank, player," Numbers called out to Coney.

"Aiight, it's a bet, little man, the bank is four-fifty, since nobody else is on the line," Coney shot back before rolling the dice.

Ace! Just like that, Numbers was up $450. It was now his bank, because he stopped the bank head up. Numbers made the whole $900 bank. Crispy Carl had schooled him long ago: scared money don't make money.

"Shoot that chump change," Coney hollered confidently.

"That's a bet. Yeah, baby, you ain't ready for this lick right here. These are my freaks, and they love giving me head. Come on, ladies, suck it good!" Numbers yelled, rolling the dice. The dice stopped spinning on 4 . . . 4 . . . 6. "Head crack! I told you how my ladies do!" Numbers had thrown a winner, doubling his bank. As he walked up to Coney to collect his cash, he spared a glance over at Suki. She was beaming at him.

Coney waved him off. "Shoot the eighteen hundred." He dropped the loot at Numbers's feet and yelled more assertively this time, "Shoot it again!"

Numbers shook the squares, then released the two green and one red clear dice. They danced and rotated over the cracks in the pavement, and when the first one stopped the number was . . . 6!

Afterward he rolled two more 6's—four automatic wins in succession. The dice were on fire for him. Each time Numbers rolled a 6, the onlookers reacted—some in disbelief, some in awe, and others in envy. He accumulated over $7,200 in the bank. He needed to roll C-Lo in order to cut the bank down or hope Coney didn't stop the bank. That was the problem: Coney had long dough. He looked at Numbers and gave him a smile like he approved of his moxie. Numbers thought Coney was done.

"Aiight, taking all bets!" Numbers exclaimed confidently, looking to the cipher of gamblers standing around.

But Coney wasn't finished yet. "Little man, shoot whatever's in the bank."

"Word, no doubt," Numbers replied cockily. "I got you now! He done fell into my trap! I'm 'bout to double this money up!" He pumped himself up. "My females bigger and better. Make 'em pay!" he hollered, letting the cubes twirl out of his palm.

At the same time, trying to rattle Numbers, Coney screamed out, *"Ace!"* The first green stone was a 4, the next one to stop was the red die, a 5. The last spun on the cement like a top for what seemed like forever as everyone seemed to hold their breath. If it landed on a 6 it would be C-Lo. Numbers would be able to cut the bank down or even walk away with all the loot he won. The last square finally came to rest on . . . 2.

Nothing.

Numbers's heart was pumping. That was the lick he needed. He doubted if Coney would be able to stop the bank again for more than fourteen thou. Numbers corralled the dice, kneeled down, and schooled them in front of him.

"You still got time to save yourself. We won't think bad of you if you want to change your mind." He smiled at Coney, hoping he would take him up on his offer, but knowing he wouldn't.

"Son, this is nothing. You gonna have to roll eight more autos to break me," Coney said and smiled, revealing a row of gold fronts. Coney did have more money on him but not nearly enough to stop a fourteen-thousand-dollar bank. "Come on, you scared rabbit, school is out. What you gonna do?" Coney said, mocking him.

Numbers nodded at him, as if to say, *"Okay, you want it, you got it!* All he could think of was what Crispy Carl had taught him about how to finish. This was another opportunity to show he had learned his lessons well. He set up the dice on the ground with 4's faceup. Then he picked them up, shook them lightly, and tossed them in Coney's direction.

"My females bigger and better. Ladies, make 'em pay," Numbers encouraged the dice.

They bounced off across the cement, landing right in front of Coney's foot: 6 . . . 6 . . . 1! *An ace!*

It was over. Numbers had lost everything. Almost everyone there had their two cents to offer.

"Oh shit, he sold out."

"Damn, Numbs, you almost got that."

"Ooh, that hurts."

"His money ain't long enough to fuck with Coney Island."

"That's all she wrote, burger flipper," Crush added. "Get the fuck up outta here!"

For some reason this chump Crush had it in for him. Every time they crossed paths, he had something to say. This time Numbers let it go, because that was all she wrote. He was flat broke, but he kept his head up. "That's it, I'm done," Numbers said, trying not to sound dejected.

Coney was impressed by Numbers's heart and hustle. He said out loud to all who could hear him, "That's how you gamble. Little man got heart!"

"Fuck him," Crush chimed in, not trying to hide his contempt.

Numbers ignored him, turned around, and started walking away down the stairs. He didn't care about the haters or the kudos; he needed the cash.

"Yo! Shorty Doo-Wop, let me holla at you." Numbers waited for Coney to walk over to him. Although Coney called him Shorty, Numbers was at least two to three inches taller than him. "What's ya name?" Coney asked.

"Numbers."

"Aiight, Numbers, how would you like to make some real numbers?" Coney inquired.

"How?" Numbers asked.

"Hustling, little man, the best hustle there is."

"Aiight," Numbers replied, curious. "What's that?"

"Meet me tomorrow by the Fort Greene Park wall, and I'll put you up on e'rything." Coney beamed as he turned and made his way back to the dice game. "Who want some of this?" he said, waving the greenbacks.

Soldier

"I'm telling you, Jar, all I needed to throw was one more lick or C-Lo, and I had his ass," Numbers said enthusiastically about his dice-game antics the day before. The sky was slightly overcast this Saturday afternoon. He and Jarvis were sitting on the three-foot-high wall in Fort Greene Park, across the street from the dry cleaners on Myrtle Avenue.

"Numb, you a gambling fool; I can't believe you bet all ya money. Then again, yes I can. Your ass is crazy, son." Jarvis shook his head, laughing, while cracking open a bag of Wise onion and garlic potato chips.

"Man, I shoulda finished him," Numbers said, thinking back to his earlier schooling from Crispy Carl.

"So why he want you to meet him over here?" Jarvis asked in between handfuls of chips.

"Dude said he liked my style and I could make some real money if I rolled with him. That's all he told me." And that was enough. "I need cash. I'm down for whatever, short of killin' a nigger," Numbers said seriously.

A red BMW M5 rolled up and beeped the horn. It was kitted up to the maximum with gold BBS rims. Neither Numbers nor Jarvis was familiar with the ride. When the door opened, Coney raised himself up out of the car just enough to get his head over the roof and call out, "Yo, Numbers, let's roll, son."

"I'll catch you on the full circle," Numbers said, using some of Crispy Carl's lyrics, meaning he would see his friend later. He gave Jarvis a pound, pushed off the wall, and jumped into the passenger seat.

"So, you a hustling little motherfucker, huh?" Coney said knowingly.

Numbers peered at him. "I always be up in seventy-nine. I know this little freak bitch on the seventh floor." Coney smiled, seeing he'd caught Numbers off guard with his information on him. Numbers wondered what else Coney knew about him. "Yeah, I did my homework. I'm not just gonna let any nigger up in my ride without knowing the four-one-one on 'im," Coney said. Numbers was at a disadvantage; he didn't know anything about Coney except that he had long dough and had beat him for his little cash in the dice game.

"So, you ready to get some real numbers, Numbers?" Coney chuckled at his play on words.

"Yeah," Numbers answered, figuring that was the answer Coney wanted. He could tell Coney was the kind of nigger who always had to be right.

"Bet. So let's ride."

Coney and Numbers pulled off heading east on Myrtle Avenue,

leaving Jar sitting on the park wall still chomping on his chips. Coney drove to Adelphi and made a right down that block to DeKalb Avenue. He pulled across the light to the south corner of Adelphi and DeKalb-Rothschild Park, which was still considered Fort Greene. A young black dude about Numbers's age exited the park and headed toward the car when he saw the red M5 roll up. He walked around the front of the car, not paying any real attention to Numbers, and greeted Coney with his hand and a brown paper bag. The transaction was so smooth, if Numbers hadn't been staring, he would have missed it.

"What's this?" Coney said.

"It's the whole thing, C. I'm done," dude said.

"Bet, Gravy will be through here in about the next hour or so to hit you off. I'll be back tomorrow."

"I got you, par," the young black dude replied, and then walked around the back of the car. Coney pulled off quickly.

"This game is supply and demand." Coney was speaking in riddles and code for all Numbers knew, but he still logged all the info. "Whoever on the streets is the most consistent, with quality product, gets the spoils. Once you create a clientele, you got to make sure you deliver. If you can't supply, you're in jeopardy of losing ya customers, you dig?" He looked directly at Numbers to make sure he was paying attention, not seeming to care that he was driving on a busy street in the middle of the day.

Numbers nodded, having an idea of what Coney was talking about but not caring at the moment. He just hoped the nigger would turn around and pay attention to the road.

Coney made similar stops throughout Kings County. He stopped at the Lafayette Gardens, Marcy, Tompkins, and Sumner projects, at Nostrand Avenue, and at various spots in Bed-Stuy and East New York—Numbers counted upward of fifteen stops, not including the times he stopped at a pay phone to answer his beeper. At each spot he was presented with a brown paper bag.

Numbers guessed money was in the bags but was unsure what illegal substance they were selling to get the money.

Now they were back on their side of town. Coney pulled up on York Street and made a U-turn near a johnny pump in the Farragut projects in front of building 111 Bridge. He looked up the block, not seeing who he was searching for. They sat in the ride quiet for about two minutes. Then a fresh-dressed twenty-something light-skinned pretty boy strolled out of building 111 with a bad chick at his side. The broad looked like a young Jayne Kennedy—complexion and all. Numbers thought it was her; he couldn't keep his eyes off her tight, sexy body. Coney's facial expression turned menacing. *Is the dude creeping with Coney's girl-friend or something?* Numbers wondered. Coney abruptly got out of the car without a word. Pretty Boy was so busy laughing and talking with the dime piece, he never even noticed Coney approaching. By the time he got hip, Coney was two feet away from him. Too late—Pretty Boy had no time to react.

Coney dead-armed him with a right to the chin, and Pretty Boy's eyes rolled back in his head. His body went limp, like someone had snatched the bones out of it, and he crashed to the pavement. The chick screamed, but didn't run. "Oh shit," Numbers said out loud, happy Coney was too far away to hear. Numbers was just as stunned as the girl. Coney reached down and removed the gold chain and diamond-encrusted Jesus piece from the dude's neck, then dug his pockets out. Still he wasn't finished. He leaned down again and slapped Pretty Boy in his face several times until he regained consciousness.

"Tony," he addressed the dazed soldier, "when I come back you better have all my loot, or the next time you won't be getting woke up." Coney rose and winked at the hottie. "Baby, you need to get with a real nigga." He turned and walked away, leaving her to attend to Tony.

Coney got back in the car and placed the chain and piece

around his rearview mirror. "That bitch is bad. I think she wants me," he exclaimed like he'd just came back from spitting some game to her. He was acting like nothing happened; they pulled off and headed back to the Fort.

"So, young 'un, you wanna get some of this money? I'm moving the boy and the snowman. I got most of BK locked, baby." Coney spoke proudly of his illegal dealings. *So that's what Coney was distributing throughout the borough.* Now that he knew what Coney was hustling, it didn't sound like his cup of tea. Selling death to the hood wasn't something he felt comfortable with. He'd seen how drugs had ruined people's lives.

Later on that evening Numbers hooked up with Jarvis and Waketta, his two running partners. He wanted to fill them in on his day with Coney. They went to the corner store on Park Avenue and bought a few quarts of Olde E and a couple of White Owls to roll up their cheba. Then they went right up the block to Flushing Avenue to the Sands Junior High School Park to drink and puff. This was another playground that kids barely came to. Most of the time ex-cons would frequent the park to do their upper-body workout. Everyone else used it as their get-high spot when school was out.

"Roll the next blunt, Ketta. I like the way you lick it," Jarvis quipped. Numbers laughed.

"Homo, you'll never know how it feel, Little Dick," she snapped back.

Jarvis was tipsy to say the least. He was sipping on his second quart, and they were about to light up their third blunt. Every time he got too buzzed, he had the tendency to become a jabber-jaws.

"That's all right, Numbs told me you suck a good one," he said, turning the quart up to his lips.

Numbers looked at Jarvis scathingly, wondering why he would put him out there like that.

"I ain't never sucked Numbers's or nobody else's dick," Waketta lied. She wasn't surprised Numbers would tell Jarvis, but still she gave Numbers a dirty look.

Waketta knew Rosa-Marie was Numbers's girl, but she didn't care. Ever since he took up for her on the roof that time with the dirty cops, they had become very close, and she would do anything for Numbers. He always had her back and made her feel special. She loved him and Numbers felt the same for her. If not for Rosa, Waketta would have been his main chick. She had become just as close to him as Jarvis was.

"You just mad nobody want your big-head ass," she said, wetting the cigar with her tongue, then wrapping her juicy lips around it. The sucking motion she performed on the blunt was her way of teasing Jarvis, showing him what he would never experience from her.

"Fuck you, ho!" he belted out, although he knew the only one who ever penetrated her sexy, chocolate sweet spot was Numbers.

"So are you gonna pump drugs for Coney?" Jarvis asked, changing the subject, turning his attention away from Waketta.

"I don't know. I don't think so, that's not my thing," Numbers replied after accepting the blunt Waketta passed his way. "Most likely not." He leaned back on the bench, taking in the cool night breeze, and exhaled a circular puff of smoke.

"Numbs, you should do it. If I was you, I would. Later for that money is money," Jarvis proclaimed.

After unsuccessfully attempting to hustle up some cash, Numbers entered his apartment to find his mother crying hysterically, doubled over the dining room table. He couldn't remember the last time he'd seen her cry. It was Monday afternoon. She was supposed to be at work.

"Mommy, what's wrong?" Pause. "What's going on? What are you doing home? Did you lose your job?"

She said nothing.

He walked up and put his arms around her, attempting to console her. She forced her head up from the table but sobbed for several moments more before she could utter two words: "It's Ta-Ta."

"What about her? What happened to her? Where is she?" Numbers's heart raced, his eyes watering. Jenny wiped away the steady stream of tears from her face, her almond eyes bloodshot.

"Ta-Ta might have cancer," she said, finally able to push the words from her throat.

"What?" Numbers was stunned. All at once, as if someone had turned on a faucet, tears cascaded down Numbers's face. He wrapped his arms more tightly around his mother and leaned his face on the top of her permed head. She held his arms close to her heart and they cried together for a long while.

"I took Ta-Ta and La-La to their first OB/GYN visit, and the doctor found a lump under her left breast near her lung. They sent us to an oncologist at Brooklyn Hospital to run tests. The doctor said it might be cancer, but they aren't sure.

"Where are Ta-Ta and La-La, Mommy?" Numbers asked, now sitting in a chair across from his mother.

"They went to the store and then were going upstairs to get their hair braided by Ms. Lindsay's daughter," she said.

"Does she know?"

"She knows she has a lump, but she doesn't know the full extent of what it means. I didn't want to scare her. I'm going to wait until they do more tests."

"They're hoping that it's benign, but either way they may still have to operate. They have to do a biopsy of the lump, Dupree. They said my benefits may not cover everything they have to do. I will still have to come up with some money." Her round young face drooped with sadness as she spoke.

"When will they know? How much extra money will we need?" Numbers asked, staring off into space, his mind working. He wanted to kick himself for losing his job.

"The test results won't be back for a couple of weeks. Don't worry, Dee, it will be okay," she said, trying to sound positive. She knew he felt it was his duty to take care of them, and he always did.

That night Numbers lay in his bed, restlessly devising ways to hustle up loot. He would just have to start gambling and hustling every day, all day. Chuck-A-Luck, cards, selling dresses, getting another job, it didn't matter, he would do whatever he needed to do to get money.

His family needed him. He had no choice.

Coney's M.O.

Numbers needed to get the 411 on Coney, and he knew exactly who to talk to. Big John ran with all the thugs in the hood. He'd been locked down with some of the projects' most infamous characters, so he had the skinny on most of the official and wannabe thugs.

He told Numbers that Coney wasn't originally from Fort Greene and that he was transplanted from the Marlboro projects in Coney Island, thus his handle. Coney and his mother and two brothers had moved into the hood after their apartment went up in flames because of a defective space heater or something like that. They lived in a shelter until an apartment became available, and that's how they ended up here in Fort Greene in building 117 up by Little

Harlem. Coney's two older brothers were serving fifteen- and twenty-year bids for various robberies.

"Coney's brothers' rap sheets got him his juice, that and the fact that he looks like a gorilla," Big John laughed.

"That nigger ain't hard, but he act the part. He be walking hunched over bowlegged and shit trying to look muscular and tough." Big John mimicked the way Coney walked.

"He's just a flashy dude who keeps young boys round him, manipulating them with a few dollars or by letting them wear his dookie gold chains to do his dirt. That nigger ain't no killer," Big John said to Numbers. "But me, myself, I'd whip his ass if he got outta line with me. He know who to fuck with. He a shystie-ass nigger, Numbers, believe me. You know Archie got shot a while back, right?"

Numbers nodded.

"That shit happened over a basketball game. Coney, Gravy, and this big young boy named Slade were playing Archie, Archie's boy Greg, and a little dribbling motherfucker named Hands for a hundred bucks each. Slade was good, but not nearly as nice as Archie. They about the same height, like six-something, and Hands didn't shoot good, but he can handle the rock and pass his ass off. Archie was the scorer," Big John recalled.

"Y'all niggers can't hold me," Coney said, walking back behind the foul line after scoring. "What's that, Gravy? Twenty-eight up? Game's thirty, right? Come on, college boy, D up," Coney taunted Archie, bouncing the ball to him to check up.

"Next basket wins," Gravy called out.

"Son, I be serving scrubs like you for fun, so you know I'ma crack that ass for loot," Archie lashed back.

Archie handed the ball over to Greg, who was matched up with Coney. Coney was good, but Greg could stop him if he wasn't intimidated.

"Get up in Coney's ass!" Big John screamed to Greg.

"Yo! Greg, stop his ass. He can't do shit with you, don't let him house you!" Archie yelled at Greg, trying to motivate him too.

"I got 'im," Greg shouted back.

Coney passed the ball to Slade. "Run it back, big man," Coney ordered. Slade passed the ball right back to Coney, who was at the foul line. He pivoted left, holding the pill in both hands, waving it over his head in front of Greg, who was in his defensive stand.

"Yeah, boy, I'm about to take that ass to the barhar." Coney started backing him down into the hole.

Greg tried to hold Coney off with his forearm in his back. Gravy was on Coney's left side, and Slade on the right. Archie's squad was playing like a man-to-man zone type D. Coney faked left and spun right, leaving Greg frozen, then drove down the middle about to lay the ball up strong. He had a clear path to the hoop—the ball came off his fingers and it looked like game. Then, out of nowhere, Archie came soaring into the picture, booyah—rejected Coney's shot. Niggers watching went crazy and Big John could be heard laughing his ass off from the sidelines. Coney was pissed. Hands picked up the loose rock and took it back out above the key. Greg and Archie cleared out the middle.

"It's over, y'all bitches!" Archie screamed at Coney's squad.

"I got ya bitch," Coney said, pushing up on Greg, denying him the ball. He didn't want Greg to score the winning bucket on him.

Hands was at the key, dribbling between his legs and behind his back. Gravy swiped at the ball, but there was no way in hell he was going to steal it from Hands. Now Archie was on the left wing near the three-point mark. He faked right toward the middle, spun off, and ran down the baseline pointing upward toward the hoop. Hands saw Archie in his peripheral vision and heaved the ball up in the air toward the basket. Now Coney got ups like Kevin Johnson. He went up after the ball, and that was a mistake. Archie caught it on the way up and flushed it in his face. The crowd went nuts.

Coney was heated, and to add insult to injury, Archie wouldn't shut the fuck up. He was walking behind Coney, taunting him, steady screaming in his ear. "Yeah, baby, that how you do it! You bitch-ass niggers can't stop the Arch. Fuck outta here."

Coney couldn't take it. He turned around and swung on Archie, catching his jawbone. Archie took it and let off his own blows.

Big John jumped in the middle of the fight, trying to help control it before it got outta hand. Just then the beat cops showed up, causing everyone to scatter.

"I told that nigger Archie to watch his back 'cuz Coney was a sneaky fuck, but he was like, 'Fuck that nigger,' " Big John said to Numbers.

"So did Coney pay up?" Numbers asked, wondering what happened next.

"Hell no!" Big John answered. "And he wasn't satisfied stiffing them for the money either. Later that night, Archie was coming out the back of his building. Some little nigger rolled up and busted a cap in his knee. The little nigger said some slick shit like 'Let me see you dunk that' or some shit like that. On the real I know it was Suki who put the hot one in Archie. All I'm saying is watch that fool Coney, aiight, Numbers?"

"No doubt," Numbers replied, satisfied with the 411 he'd received.

The siren from the po-po's squad car sounded like it was right on their heels as they ran like their asses were on fire the hundred or so yards down the Washington Park Place side of Fort Greene Park toward the PJs. In hindsight, Numbers thought this was the dumbest shit he'd ever done.

The merchant at the deli on Washington Park Place and DeKalb Avenue closed up by himself every Friday and always carried large amounts of cash in his bag to be deposited in the bank the next day—at least that's what Chap had told him. Chap had turned out to be a two-bit thug and thief who couldn't be trusted. Desperation has a way of making an otherwise sane man do dumb shit, but Numbers would have to work that out with himself later; right now he was running for his freedom like Toby in *Roots*. If he could just make it to the projects, he could get lost in one of the buildings. The cops put their squad car in reverse and tried to maneuver through traffic on a one-way street to get at him and Chap. Numbers heard another cop car up ahead. They were about to be trapped.

Numbers was fast, Carl Lewis fast, and tonight he was not going to jail with Chap's dumb ass. He had made it to the park entrance at Willoughby when he broke away from Chap. He prayed the cops didn't see him turn in to the park. He didn't want to split with Chap, but that was his only alternative if he didn't want to get knocked. After sprinting up Dead Man's Hill, Numbers hid under some bushes that smelled like dog shit. Blue and red lights were jumping and sirens wailed as he mumbled a small prayer that if Chap got pinched he wouldn't snitch.

Chap and Numbers weren't enemies, but they weren't friends either. For the most part they tolerated each other because they lived in the same building. Chap was twenty-three years old and a little shorter than Numbers at five-ten, but stockier, weighing about 180. His hair was done in corn rows, and he was missing a front tooth, which had been knocked out in a jailhouse brawl. Chap had served time on Rikers Island and carried those jail stints like a badge of honor; he'd been released not even three weeks prior.

On this night Numbers hadn't been able to find any of his usual suspects to hang out with; he'd run into Chap at the bodega on Washington Park Place and Myrtle, right across the street from Fort Greene Park.

"What up, Du?" Chap said.

"I go by Numbers, Chap," he said, giving him a halfhearted pound with an As-if-you-didn't-know attitude.

"No doubt, they call me Barsheik now," Chap replied with a

You-know-what-time-it-is attitude. He was one of those asshole niggers giving the 5 Percent Nation a bad name. "I see you just copped some Els. What up with that? I'm down?"

Numbers figured, *What the fuck, it's better than drinking and smoking alone.* They both bought three 40s of Olde E and walked along Myrtle Avenue to the park entrance leading to the chess/checker tables near St. Edwards Street. They sat in the park reminiscing about when they were kids. It seemed both like a long time ago and like yesterday when they used to walk the fences. Maybe it was the talk of the childhood or maybe it was just the high, but they somehow reconnected.

"Yo! Numbers, you wanna get some bank tonight?" As Chap spoke, smoke escaped from the spot where his tooth was missing.

Numbers was sitting on the back of a wooden bench, one foot on the seat, the other on the stone checkers table, rubbing his headful of waves with both hands. "You bugging," he said seriously.

"Nah, check it," Chap said, and passed the blunt to Numbers. "It's this old Korean that always leaves the store by himself. I been scopin' him out for 'bout a week. No lie, the other day—like Tuesday—he had more than a thousand dollars in the register. Today is Friday. I'm telling you, he's gotta have triple that now."

The more Numbers drank, the more Chap's plan seemed like it could work.

"Aiight, Cha . . . Barsheik, let's get this money," Numbers agreed, popping off the bench, feeling the effects of the alcohol and weed.

In the cover of darkness, Numbers and Chap crept up behind a tree across the street from the store in the park and waited for the owner to close up.

"So how we gonna do this?" Numbers asked. "I don't want to hurt dude or nothing."

"Nah, I'm gonna go up behind him and yoke him off his feet. You rip his pockets and take the dough."

An hour passed before the owner exited and began rolling down the steel security gate in front of the store. Numbers had just turned his back to take a leak, and as soon as the gate descended Chap sprang into action, not waiting for Numbers to finish pissing.

"Come on, Numbs."

The streetlight at the corner was busted—perfect for a mugging. Chap quickly skulked from behind the park wall across the street, leaving Numbers behind. For a cool Friday night, the streets were nearly barren of pedestrians, but there was a moderate amount of car traffic. Numbers was just coming out of the park when he saw Chap run up behind the merchant, yoke him up by the neck, and stab him multiple times. Numbers stood frozen, not believing what he was seeing. He knew he shouldn't have been fucking with this stupid-ass fool.

As luck would have it, a cop car was rushing across DeKalb Avenue on its way to another call when the merchant screamed in anguish. Numbers stood there watching Chap dig in the man's pockets and pull out a brown paper bag. Numbers figured the bag was filled with money. The cop car came to a screeching halt, nearly getting rammed by the bus behind it. Instantly its lights flashed and sirens squealed. The driver attempted to back up but was blocked by the B38 bus and other cars. Chap dashed across the street toward Numbers, who was standing there stuck, looking at the man squirming in pain across the street. His high was blown.

"Come on, nigger." Chap tugged Numbers's arm as he jetted down the block toward the projects.

Numbers almost didn't run because he didn't think he could be connected to the crime, but he didn't want to chance it, so he fled.

. . . .

Two weeks had passed since Takeisha went in for her biopsy. She waited nervously in the oncologist's office with her twin, her mother, Numbers, and her Aunt Camille, who'd come up from Virginia for moral support. Dr. Cavalha came into his office. He was an average height and of Middle Eastern descent and spoke with a slight accent. "I apologize, but only the immediate family can be in here," he said.

"This is my immediate family," Takeisha notified the doctor apprehensively.

"Okay then." Dr. Cavalha accepted her answer hesitantly. He made his way behind his desk and stared into a chart for a long moment. It seemed as though no one else in the room took a breath. He looked up and let his eyes bounce off each face before resting on Takeisha's. "Please hear me out before you jump to any conclusions. I'm sorry to inform you, but the lump is malignant."

Tears began to well up in the eyes of everyone except Numbers. He wanted to stay strong for his sisters and mother. Lakeisha wrapped her arms around her sister, and Jenny wrapped herself around both of them. Aunt Camille rubbed her sister's back and wept.

"But I think we caught it in its early stages," the doctor contin- ued. "It can be overcome with aggressive treatment. I suggest we remove the tumor and then follow the surgery with radiation. It won't be easy, but I'm confident we can beat this." He smiled in hopes of providing the family with assurance.

It was a staggering blow. The twins' father was nowhere to be found, as usual, when they needed him. Jenny would have to take off work to tend to her daughter. She was not about to let Takeisha go through this traumatic time without her by her side. Her ben- efits would cover most of the medical bills, but she wouldn't be paid while she was out on leave.

Numbers needed cash and needed it now. He made up his

mind. He would take Coney up on his offer. Messing around with Chap a couple of weeks back had almost landed him in the clink, and Chap only came off with a hundred-odd dollars for all his troubles. If he was going to risk everything, Numbers thought, it would be trying to make some real bank.

The following day, Numbers met up with Coney in Little Harlem. Coney had another dude with him who Numbers had never seen before but had heard his name mentioned by Big John.

"Yo! Gravy, little man right here"—Coney gestured to Numbers—"he's under your wing. Show him how to get that paper out here."

"I hope he's mo' thorough than that other booty-ass nigga. He ain't worth the paper I wipe my ass with. I'm about to duff his ass out." Gravy laughed.

Numbers noticed that Gravy had big lips and little teeth; the teeth were better suited for a baby than a six-foot-two cock-diesel thug with beady eyes and a unibrow. He had a face only a mother could love. His physique was a different story. Gravy looked as though he spent all day in the gym, but he actually got his muscles while serving time for beating up his baby's mother. He caught the broad going down on a square-ass accountant nig-ger in the Mustang Gravy had bought for her. He beat her ass like a man and then beat the dude's ass like a bitch. Gravy almost killed old boy, but his lawyer played the heat-of-passion card. If it wasn't for his record, Gravy wouldn't even have gotten the two years. He was as close to being Coney's right-hand man as there was, since Coney trusted no one. Gravy was a thug, but he was a likeable thug.

"Aiight, Gravy, don't worry about young. I'll take care of him, dun." Then Coney got back into his ride and sped off down the av-enue.

"Numbers, huh?" Gravy said, sizing his new worker up. "I'm feeling that hot shit, let's get some digits." Gravy smiled, showing the two rolls of Chiclets he called teeth. "This is how it goes down, par. We keep the product outta our hands unless there's a sale. Over here, we moving dimes and twenties of that white rock. The stash is over there." Gravy pointed to the pole on the jungle gym they were standing near.

Numbers looked but didn't see anything.

"Exactly." Gravy shook his head, confusing Numbers like he planned to do. "The product is in a paper bag right there by the pole; just in case Jake rolls on us, we can walk away and they can't pin it on us. That shit could be anybody's. The main thing is to keep your eyes open. I'll school you to the fiends and who our regular customers are. After a while you'll know who's who. No credit! We don't do that over here. If they ain't got the cash, they can't get a blast!"

Numbers absorbed the ins and outs of the entry level of the drug game, at least all that Gravy had to offer. The shit wasn't difficult and the money was good; he just hoped his new grind didn't lead to jail time.

At first it was slow, but as the sun went down, more and more fiends came to get their fix. The pharmaceutical business was truly a grand old hustle.

Jarvis was also a momma's boy. He loved his mother dearly, and his mother loved him with all her heart—except when she got drunk. Over the last few years she'd succumbed more and more to the call of the bottle. Sober, she was a doting mom, but drunk she was Mrs. Hyde. When she was on the sauce she couldn't stand the sight of Jarvis, since he reminded her of his good-for-nothing daddy.

Numbers hated to go to Jarvis's apartment to get him. When he did he prayed Ms. Barbara would be sober. Today he needed his friend. Numbers had static brewing with Crush from the third side. Ever since Coney gave Numbers his own area to work, Crush had been trying to move in on his clientele. Jarvis had gone to high school with Crush, so Numbers hoped he could squash it. Even if he couldn't, Numbers knew Jarvis would have no problem watching his back. Numbers wasn't scared of Crush, but he knew if he faced him alone, he wouldn't get a fair fight.

Numbers let the metal door knocker hit the worn bronze plate three times and waited for a response. He could hear a raised voice coming from inside. Numbers thought to turn and walk away, but he needed Jarvis.

Jarvis's oldest sister, Cathy, wearily came to the door. She didn't bother to greet him or invite him in, just left the door open and headed back to her position on the old sofa in front of an even older TV. She was pregnant again and barely eighteen. Her phat ass kept men swooning. Numbers entered and it was clear the raised voice had been Ms. Barbara's.

Ms. Barbara sat at the dining table in a blue cotton wash-deprived nightgown in the middle of the day looking like she had nowhere to go fast. Her hair was matted and her right hand was clamped around a glass holding a little bit of ice and brown liquid. Rum, no doubt, her choice beverage. She took a long drink from her glass. "You ain't shit!" she yelled. "You ain't never gonna be shit! I can't stand the sight of your big-head ass! You're just like your father. Shit!" She ranted, slurring her words at Jarvis, who was in the kitchen.

"Momma, leave Jarvis alone," Cathy pleaded.

"Shut your little tramp pie-hole 'fo' I kick your ass out on the street with him!"

"Whatever, Momma. I ain't going nowhere. You need my welfare check to get your liquor," she muttered under her breath.

"Big Head, get over here. Ya friend here!" Ms. Barbara ordered.

Jarvis emerged from the kitchen with a full garbage bag in hand, looking defeated.

"Dupree, take your friend somewhere and get his worthless ass a job. He ain't gonna be shit just like his daddy! He needs to be more like you. You're a good boy. I knew I shoulda had an abortion!" She gulped down her drink, then reached for the bottle.

Numbers could feel the hurt for his friend deep down in his soul. He wanted to say something to Ms. Barbara but held his tongue.

"Momma, that ain't right," Cathy called out. "She don't mean that, Jarvis."

"That boy know I love him," Ms. Barbara said, changing her tune in a sudden moment of clarity. "Come here and kiss your momma, boy."

Jarvis reluctantly went to her and gave a swift peck to her forehead, fighting back his tears.

"Hey, Jar." Numbers greeted him.

Jar motioned a greeting, not really able to speak, his vocal cords tied up with hurt. "Momma, I'm going out," he managed to say in a shaky voice.

"Don't come back if you ain't got no got-damn money, shit! You lazy fucker!" That quickly she turned on him again.

Jarvis couldn't understand why his mother was so hard on him. His brother Marcus had been in and out of juvie and had now landed himself in the big house. His oldest sister was pregnant for the second time, and his other sister seemed as though she would follow that path. Jarvis's oldest sibling joined the service when he was old enough and rarely kept in touch. Jarvis, on the other hand, did as he was told and never got into trouble other than his frequent fights.

Even though Numbers was his best friend and had seen his mother go off on these tirades before, it still embarrassed Jarvis.

Everyone—the girls he liked, his mother, everyone else—seemed to prefer Numbers over him and made him feel less than Numbers's equal. Numbers never treated him that way, but it didn't matter; Jarvis was envious of him. Little did Numbers know Jarvis was still smarting over not getting Waketta. His mother's barbs fueled Jarvis's resentment.

Numbers, at the pay phone on the corner of North Portland, dropped the receiver back in its cradle. He crossed Myrtle Avenue against the light, scooting past a B54 bus headed east. He was on his way back to the park wall, where Jarvis and Waketta were posted up making bang-bangs, when his pager went off again. He was less than twenty feet from the wall when he read the screen: 101-911. That was Rosa's code. The 101 was her building's number, and the 911 meant there was an emergency.

Jarvis was watching from the wall when Numbers made a U-turn, heading back toward the pay phone. *Nothing un-usual,* Jarvis thought. He was used to Numbers riding the horn.

There was a girl on the jack as Numbers approached. He hoped that he wouldn't have to go through too much trouble convincing her to give it up, but she hung up before he reached her. He fished some change from the pocket of his 501 Levi's jeans, fed a quarter into the slot, and dialed Rosa-Marie's number. The phone barely rang once before Rosa-Marie picked up.

"Rosa, what's going on, Mami?" Numbers spoke in his usual calm voice—not much rattled him.

"Papi, I need you to come . . ." was the only part he understood. She was speaking in machine-gun-fast Spanish. Numbers was far from fluent in Spanish, but he understood her when she spoke at a normal pace. Things definitely weren't normal.

Instead of asking her to repeat herself he said, "I'm on my way." Then he quickly hung up and walked up North Portland toward her building—she lived two-thirds of the way up the block.

Rosa was a good girl who spoke her mind when she had to, but for the most part she never argued just for argument's sake. Genuinely sweet, she rarely complained, and it didn't hurt any that she was beautiful.

To be honest, he was surprised they had lasted this long with all the interference and static from Rosa's mother. Ms. Vasquez had done everything in her power to keep the two apart, including setting her daughter up to go out on dates with Puerto Rican suitors to make sure she wouldn't get mixed up with a good-for-nothing black boy. At this point in Numbers's life, he couldn't blame Rosa's mother. He was exactly the type of man she didn't want her daughter to end up with: a drug-dealing street thug.

It was midway through September, and Numbers could feel the season changing in the air. He was wearing a blue cardigan sweater over a white mock neck and a pair of crisp white-on-white shell-toe Adidas. After greeting a few people who were sitting on the benches outside of Rosa-Marie's building, he sprinted up the three flights of stairs to her apartment.

Rosa answered the door looking like she'd been crying for half her life and mourning for the other. Her eyes were bloodshot when she fell into Numbers's arms, sobbing heavily. Her body heaved with every labored breath. Numbers held her until he felt like she'd gotten it all out. Unsure what was going on, he looked around the apartment to see if her mother was home. If she was, she'd be right up in their business. He didn't see her. She was probably at church. Ms. Vasquez was a devout Catholic. She kept a small army of Virgin Mary statues, a handful of Jesus pictures, and candles and holy shrines exhibited around the apartment.

"Baby, tell me what's wrong." Numbers said, stroking her silky long black hair. He hated to see his lady crying.

"Where do I start?" she said in between tears. "I don't know what to do. My mother's gonna disown me, then kick me out."

"What are you talking about?" Numbers lifted her chin with his index finger so that he could kiss her softly on the mouth. "Start from the beginning."

There was a long pause. "I'm pregnant."

Everything went quiet all at once. The noise outside ceased; the kids stopped playing; the cars were no longer whizzing up and down the street honking horns, and their brakes were no longer screeching. Numbers felt like he was dreaming and the world had come to a stop.

"Baby, you say you're pregnant?" The world started to come back to life. A smile invaded his face.

Rosa was surprised by Numbers's reaction. She'd thought for sure he would be upset. But he took the news well, and that relieved her somewhat, but not much. Her mother would be another story.

"What are we gonna do, Dupree? My mother is gonna go loco when she finds out." He knew Rosa wasn't exaggerating. Ms. Vasquez only tolerated him because she knew her daughter really loved him. But a baby without a proposal, ring, and wedding would be more than she could handle.

"Listen, you're my girl and everything's gonna be all right, okay? I'm gonna take care of you and the baby. Do you trust me, Rose?"

Rosa nodded, smiling slightly, letting him know she trusted him with her everything. This was the man she wanted, the only man she wanted.

"Mami, how far along are you?" He spoke to her soft and lovingly. She loved when he called her Mami.

"Nine weeks. I'm due at the end of April." She wiped the tears from her face.

"Okay." Numbers calculated how much time she had. "I'll figure this out. Just don't tell your mother yet. Now go clean yourself up before she gets home and sees you like this. She'll know something's up." He patted her on her butt and sent her on her way. Rosa went to the bathroom to get herself together, and Numbers exited the crib.

"Jar, let me kick it with you," Numbers hollered over to Jarvis, who was sitting on the park wall watching out for Waketta pumping the product. Jarvis slid off the wall and walked toward Numbers, who was near the entrance of the park. Waketta looked over to Numbers and winked. He smiled back. Jarvis saw the interaction and gave a disapproving stare.

Jarvis and Numbers sat on the benches near the b-ball court, facing the street. Evening was approaching quickly.

"What the deal, Numbs? What's happening?" He could tell by his friend's face that something was up. "What's the dumb look for, dunny?"

"You about to be a godfather," Numbers said, showing two rows of almost perfect teeth courtesy of New York City dental benefits for employees and their families.

"Who you got pregnant, son?"

"Stop bugging. You know it's Rosa." Numbers nudged Jarvis in the side with his forearm.

"Word?" Jarvis was excited for him. "Congratulations, bruh. So what it is, a girl or a boy?"

"Don't know yet. Just found out, man. I'm amped about it, though. But listen, don't tell Waketta. I need to break this to her gently or she'll freaking spaz out." He was looking in the direction where Waketta was posted up. She was serving a crackhead. Numbers changed the subject. "What the money looking like today?"

"It's all gravy, as Gravy would say." Jarvis laughed. "Something I gotta run by you though." Jarvis was looking off toward Myrtle Avenue. "I think something's going on with Ketta."

"Something like what?"

"Man, I don't know how to tell you this other than coming right out and saying it. I think she's getting banged by Crush. I ain't seen her with him, but that's what I heard. If it's true, that's some real bullshit." Numbers kept his composure, but Jarvis knew that the news affected him. "So what you gonna do?"

"Should I ask her 'bout it? It ain't none of my business. Though that shit would be foul. She knows there's bad blood between us and that nigger be trying to disrespect my hustle. What you think?"

"Nah, don't ask her. Let's just wait and see what happens. You don't want her to think you sweating her." Jar looked his friend in the eyes. "You ain't sweating that, right?"

"Absolutely not," he lied, not wanting to let Jarvis know how much he cared about Waketta. He'd decided after Jarvis had blurted out what went down between him and Waketta that he'd keep him out of their affairs.

When Numbers had gotten into the game over three years ago, he promised himself he would only be in it six months, until he stacked enough money to take care of his family through Ta-Ta's ordeal. They ultimately operated on Ta-Ta to remove the tumor, and the radiation treatment she received over a year's time proved successful. The cancer went into remission. The day the doctor told them that, a great burden was lifted from the family's shoulders, mentally and financially. After that Numbers tried to get out of the game on several occasions, but something always kept him stuck in it like cement shoes. Now, with Rosa pregnant, once again getting out of the game wasn't an option. How could he support his family, his baby, and its mother without this income?

Besides, he was twenty-three; it was past time for him to leave the nest. His mother knew what he was into, but she turned a blind eye. She understood why he started down this path, but hoped he wouldn't get caught up in it. Now he was. Almost four years had elapsed since he first started slinging for Coney, and money was rolling in regular like the waves at Jones Beach. He was now one of Coney's top earners. Coney let Numbers set up his own shop at the park with his own crew, the Park Wall Hustlers. He, Jarvis, Broz, and Waketta were PWH. They were balling out of control, getting money and spending it as fast as it was coming in. Numbers had always been fly, but now they all sported fresh gear and jewels. They all purchased cars except for Broz; he just drove everyone else's shit. Even though money was coming in fast, it wasn't easy. Between the rival dealers trying to move in on their territory and the same two corrupt cops, O'Doul and Lockhart (who were now detectives), always trying to lock them down or take their cash, they had to stay on their toes.

Waketta never forgot how Lockhart violated her on the roof all those years ago and how his partner, O'Doul, stood there and watched. If she as much as heard someone call out one of their names, she got heated. She wanted payback, and Numbers shared her pain. Those swine needed to be taught a lesson, and Numbers came up with a plan for reprisal. Never mind that Crispy Carl had advised him years back to let karma take care of it.

Although Broz hadn't been victimized by the rogue cops, he was down with the scheme. Jarvis chose not to be involved. He said he had other business to attend to. Numbers was cool with it. He didn't need that many hands in the pot anyway. The plan was to call for the detectives on their night shift to come to Crispy Carl's building. Lockhart was sexing some cop lover named Tanya who lived there on the eighth floor with her sixteen-year-old son. Tanya wasn't a good looker by any means, but to think of her having sex with Lockhart's foulness was revolting.

Crispy Carl lived on the third floor. His window faced the entrance of the building, perfect for the setup.

A couple of weeks after they'd formulated the plan, it all fell into place. Tanya and her son left the apartment together to go to the movies. From a pay phone, Broz placed a call to Detective Lockhart at the Eighty-eighth Precinct, saying he was Tanya's son and it was very important for him to stop by. Numbers and the crew had obtained his direct number previously after a shooting in the hood. Lockhart had gone door to door giving out his card in hopes of getting some information that would help solve the case. Crispy Carl was given one of those cards. All Numbers and Waketta had to do was wait.

It was a brisk winter night, and not many people were outside. Dressed in all black, Numbers and Waketta sat in Crispy Carl's bedroom looking out the window. With all the lights out, the apartment was completely dark. Numbers opened the newly installed storm windows, courtesy of the New York City Housing Authority, about three inches. It was a nice little stakeout. They fooled around, drank, and smoked to kill time.

Besides them, the apartment was empty. Crispy Carl had been admitted to the hospital two days prior for a condition he declined to discuss with Numbers. Numbers was concerned about his old friend, but Carl assured him he was okay. He'd given Numbers a key to his crib a while back so he could come and go as he pleased.

After they'd waited more than an hour, Lockhart and O'Doul's car finally pulled up. They took their sweet time getting out, as usual. A motherfucker could get murked and buried waiting for these assholes. First, Lockhart managed to hoist his overweight and underexercised body out of the car. Then O'Doul slid his equally fat ass out the passenger side. They both looked like they were living high on the hog.

Numbers and Waketta positioned themselves in the window, taking aim at the two bully porkers.

"You ready?" Numbers whispered to Waketta.

"You damn skippy I'm ready," she whispered back.

They slid the barrels of their rifles out the three-inch opening of the window.

Numbers counted them off with a whisper: "One . . . two . . . three . . . fire."

They let off twenty to thirty rounds each from their rifles.

The first shot hit Lockhart in the face, near his right eye. He screamed like a bitch, not knowing what had happened.

O'Doul yelled, "I'm hit!" He'd taken one in the neck, one in the ear, and several in his upper body. The two policemen almost ran into each other attempting to make it to cover. Shots seemed to be raining from the sky, and they couldn't escape. Lockhart drew his gun as he made it to cover behind the front wheel of the squad car. O'Doul's fat ass dove over the front end of the car and nearly landed on Lockhart's head as he slid to what he hoped was safety. Then it was all over. They stayed hidden behind their unmarked car attempting to peek up at the building, frantically looking for signs of where the shots had come from. "Lockhart, what the fuck, oh shit, you okay?" O'Doul's hands and body were covered with red.

"O'Doul, I think it's paint. It's fucking paint! These fucking porch monkeys shot us up with paintballs." Lockhart was panting and sweating, both scared and happy to be alive.

Numbers and Waketta were in the window fighting back their laughter. It was hilarious to see the fat white cops scatter for cover thinking they were dead. Waketta felt relief wash over her body. She was vindicated. She had made the cops feel the humiliation she felt. It was *grand*!

Numbers had exacted his revenge, but to see Waketta's reaction was more than he had bargained for. It really made it all worthwhile. They sat, waiting to see what would happen next. They'd gambled that the pigs would be too embarrassed to call for backup, but if they did, it would be okay, too. Numbers and Waketta could wait it out making love to each other. It was a good night.

Waketta

"Room service," a voice chimed from outside room 3208 of the Marriott Marquis Hotel in Times Square. Waketta got up off the king-sized bed in her bra and thong, her ass bouncing all the way to the door. She opened it and a middle-aged white room-service attendant stood there with their order. He looked like he had been doing this job way too long. At the sight of Waketta's five-foot-nine chocolate, voluptuous body standing there half-naked, he damn near went into heart palpitations.

"You just gonna stand there or you gonna bring it in?" She turned around, letting the door go and showing him her pretty phat round ass. He tried to avert his eyes, but they weren't following instructions.

Numbers was in the bathroom taking a shower. "Baby, the champagne and food here," Waketta called to him.

"Where would you like this, miss?" The old man's face was red, and he almost tripped over the carpet.

"Anywhere is good." Waketta jumped onto the bed, covering her lower body with the sheet and leaving her upper body exposed.

The attendant rolled the tray near the foot of the bed and set everything out.

"Would you like me to pop the champagne?"

"Nah, that's cool," Waketta answered, holding out two $100 bills. She was more concerned with the movie she was watching on the tube.

He walked over and collected the payment from Waketta, transfixed by her breasts. He could only dream of touching this young beauty with vibrant eyes and juicy, full lips. But for all her beauty, she was still ghetto.

"Aiight, duke, keep the change and beat it."

"Anything else, miss?" he asked, hoping he could find a reason to stay or at least come back.

"We good," she replied without looking up from the TV.

The attendant exited and closed the door behind him, peeking one last time before it completely shut.

Numbers came out of the bathroom wearing paisley boxer shorts. He locked the dead bolt and privacy latch, not wanting to be interrupted by housekeeping. Then he placed his damp towel near the bottom of the door to stop any smoke from seeping out.

"Light up, Ketta."

Waketta slowly took her eyes off the TV to reach into her purse and pull out a ready-rolled blunt. Numbers walked over to the dinner cart and unwrapped and popped the Moët. He poured two flutes, handing one to Waketta. "A toss to my ride-or-die chick," he said, and smiled at his sexy honey dip. She was at the edge of the bed on her knees, smiling back at her man as she took a sip.

"Till the wheels fall off!" she said, reaching out to Numbers, signaling for him to come closer. He could tell she meant every word. She extended the blunt to his lips. He inhaled and exhaled several times, looking in her pretty marble-brown eyes, knowing he was going to serve her his hardness all night long. She placed her flute on the nightstand, rested the blunt next to it in a makeshift ashtray, and moved closer, kissing Numbers on his neck. She slowly began to move her luscious lips down his torso. Waketta knew what Numbers liked. He'd been training her for six or so years. She could have had just about any man she chose in and out the hood, but she wanted Numbers. She knew she was the side piece, and she accepted that it was what it was.

Waketta sat on the edge of the bed with Numbers in between her legs. She kissed his tight stomach, making herself wet as she anticipated his manhood in her mouth. Unable to wait any longer, she placed two fingers inside the elastic of his boxers and pulled them down.

Before she could go down, Numbers grabbed her around her neck. She gasped in excitement as he placed his lips on hers, kissing her passionately. Her nipples hardened. When he released her neck, her head drifted back down past his abdomen. She wrapped her mouth around his throbbing penis and began rotating her tongue around the tip of it. He breathed deeply, enjoying her initial touch, knowing it was going to get better. She moaned as she slurped his dick vigorously, massaging his balls with one hand.

"Come in my mouth, baby, please." She spoke with her mouth full. "I want to suck your dick forever. Let me taste it."

Numbers's legs trembled with bliss. He wanted to satisfy her desire. "Yes, Ketta, you know you mines forever. Make it cum, baby. Ooh, you got it. Make it cum," he said, panting. She stroked, massaged, and slurped him, making his dick hard as a rubber dumbbell. She could feel the babies pulsating and pounding, trying to break out. She deep-throated his cock, making herself gag on it. She knew Numbers loved when she tried to swallow his large muscle even though she couldn't. This was it. He could no longer contain himself. She knew it was coming. She spoke almost like a ventriloquist, still slobbering on it, "Yes, baby, cum."

Numbers complied.

Waketta let the semen shoot off the back of her throat, savoring every trickle. Numbers yelled with fulfillment.

"Ssshhh. Security gonna think I'm killing your ass up in here," she said, giggling, kissing the tip of it until she was sure she'd swallowed every bit of him.

Numbers climbed into the bed with Waketta and gave her what she deserved for the next hour and a half. She came until she almost passed out. After she had taken all she could handle, she lay in Numbers's arms caressing his chest. They both looked up at the ceiling, in their own separate worlds.

"Baby, can we talk?" Waketta said, not sounding like her usual loud self. Numbers had a way of making her feel like a woman, soft and feminine. That's why she loved him so much. She didn't have to be strong around him—she could be a girl. Numbers sat up and took a long swallow of his room-temperature champagne, then puffed the blunt.

"Yeah, Ketta. I want to talk to you, too." Waketta sat up against the headboard. Curled up under the plush hotel bedding, she looked around trying to find a way to start her conversation. He saw that she was having a hard time finding the words, so he started. "Ketta, you know I love you . . . and care about you . . . and I would do anything for you." He looked at her to make sure she understood he was sincere.

Waketta knew these things without him saying them, but it

sounded good coming from his mouth. He was her rock, her friend, and her lover.

"Well, me and Ro—"

"I know about the baby," she said, cutting him off.

Numbers searched his brain trying to figure out how she knew. Who'd told her? Was it Rosa? Mad questions ran through his mind. "I apologize, Ketta. I was gonna tell you sooner. I just didn't know when the right time was to do it."

"It's okay . . . I mean . . . I knew what I was getting into when we started this. I wish it could be different, but . . ." She began to tear up and the words got lost in her throat.

Numbers couldn't help but feel like a fuck-up. Like he was leading her on. He should just break it off with her, but that was really not an option, truth be told. He loved her as much as he loved Rosa. He wanted them both in his life and would do whatever it took to keep them. "If you don't want to fuck with me anymore, I understand," he said to her, lying to himself.

"Numbers, I could never stop being with you, I love you too much," she confessed, straining to get her words out. "Why would you say something like that? It's not like that."

"Then what is it that you wanted to talk to me about?"

She hesitated, then asked, "What's going on with you and Jar?" She looked at her man to see how he took her question.

"What you mean, what's going on?" He looked at her curiously.

"I'm saying, I know that's your boy and he's been your boy way before we became friends, but I was wondering if everything's all right between you two."

"Yeah, we cool. Why?" Numbers didn't say it, but he felt like Jarvis had been acting a little distant too.

"'Cuz I think something's going on with him. I seen him fucking with dude from the third side, that nigger Crush. I'm like *Why he fucking with that dude, knowing you and him got beef?*" Waketta paused, letting Numbers take it all in.

He took a few more hits from the blunt, thinking about what she said. Some funny shit was going on. Jarvis had just told him something similar about Waketta. *What the fuck?*

"Word? Don't worry, baby. I got it." Whatever it was, he intended to get to the bottom of it.

Crispy Carl had warned him about getting money. *Remember this, young hustler: mo' dollars, mo' deceit, and the deceit will usually come from the people closest to you.*

Numbers's beeper went off. It was two-thirty in the morning. Who could it be? Looking at the screen, he saw Crispy Carl's code. *Must have thought him up,* Numbers believed. But Crispy Carl would have to wait until he woke up in the morning. There was more head to get tonight.

"Enough talk for now, Ketta. It's time for round two."

She obliged.

After being released from the hospital a week earlier, Crispy Carl heard about the two dicks being shot up with paintballs in front of his building but had no idea Numbers was responsible and his pad was ground zero. His health was declining rapidly, but it tickled his fancy to hear the story of the coppers running scared for their lives.

After parking his car on Carlton Avenue, Numbers sent Waketta on a run. His mind was still reeling from the conversation they'd had earlier that morning. He needed to talk with Crispy Carl. He knew Carl could help him figure it out or least give him some advice on how to move forward. It was cold outside. Numbers zipped his Woolrich snow coat all the way up but left the hood down. He didn't trust not being able to see his peripheral. After all, this was still the Fort Greene projects and niggers were grimy.

He entered the building and collected his mail. He pressed the elevator button, then decided not to wait and climbed the stairs to the third floor. He knocked on the door of apartment 3D as a courtesy, unlocking the door with his key at the same time. As soon as the door opened, he was assaulted by the smell of urine and shit. The place was in complete disarray.

Numbers called out, "Carl, where you at?" No answer. "Carl, you okay?" *Something isn't right. I shoulda answered Crispy Carl's page when I got it this morning.* He blamed himself.

He heard a soft moan coming from the bathroom. Rushing toward the sound, Numbers found Crispy Carl sprawled out on the cold tile, lying in his own feces. He was alive but barely. He looked weak and fragile. Numbers ran to the phone and called 911, opened all the windows, then hurried back to Crispy Carl's side. Every day of Crispy Carl's sixty-odd years of hard living showed on his face.

If someone would have told Numbers he would be washing excrement from a grown man, he'd have bet his life to the contrary. But he couldn't let his mentor and friend be seen like this. Crispy Carl prided himself on being sharp—shit, he was Crispy Motherfucking Carl. So Numbers set aside his ego and did what he had to do. It was a filthy, nasty task, but Crispy Carl was like a father to him. Nothing could change that, so the least he could do was keep the man's dignity intact.

Crispy went in and out of consciousness as Numbers cleaned him up, then the apartment. The ambulance took so long to arrive, he could have cleaned the whole apartment twice. He moved Crispy Carl to the couch while they waited. He noticed that his mentor's breathing was even more labored now.

"Mr. Carl, can you hear me? It's me, Numbers." Numbers's eyes welled up. "Sip on this," he said, raising Crispy Carl's head in order to give him a sip of water. He kneeled in front of him on the couch so Carl could see him.

"Numbers," Crispy Carl said. His voice was barely a whisper. "I been waiting for you. You better not be out there fucking with my hoes." There was a trace of a smile on his face. It probably took all the energy he had to do it, but he was smiling.

"Easy, Mr. Carl, the ambulance is on its way." At least Numbers hoped it was. Everyone knew that 911 was a joke in the hood. He had called the emergency line more than forty minutes ago.

Crispy Carl wheezed and gasped for air and continued to speak weakly. Numbers leaned as close to his mouth as he could in order to hear him. "You're like a son to me," he said. "Thank you for your friendship."

Does Mr. Carl know how much he's done for me over the years? What he's been to me? Numbers wondered. "I know, Mr. Carl," he answered, trying to hold back tears, finally hearing the ambulance sirens in the background nearing the projects. "The ambulance is here." Numbers was overwhelmed. Tears streamed down his caramel cheeks.

"Remember everything I taught you . . . be better than me . . . be better than you think you can be. Full circle." Crispy Carl faded.

The paramedics did all they could do to revive Crispy Carl, but his spirit had already moved on to a better place.

The wake and funeral were short and sweet. It was said that he had a daughter and son, but no one knew who they were or where they lived. Most of the people who attended the funeral were Crispy Carl's old acquaintances and card-game comrades. The others were Numbers's friends who knew how close the two had been. Since Numbers was his only real family, he wrote the eulogy.

A player is as a player does. Crispy Carl was the ultimate player because he played the game with no regrets. He believed in being real to himself first, so it made it easy to be real to everyone else. He may not have walked the straight and narrow, but he walked with his head held high, with integrity and dignity. He wasn't the type to tell you what to do, but he was sure to tell you what it was.

"Crispy" Carl Stevenson once told me when one door closes, another one opens. Though the chapters to his life have closed, his guidance has opened up endless possibilities for me. I was blessed to be touched by this angel in the pimp suit. He was a father figure, a man of honor. He was my friend. As he would always say to me, I say to him now: I'll catch you on the full circle. May God be your shepherd. Amen.

"Rosa, come on, I want to show you something," Numbers beckoned to Rosa-Marie to get dressed and come with him.

"I'm moving as fast I can with this belly, and I don't want to go out—it's cold outside," she complained. She was doing a lot of that these days; she was five months pregnant.

"You won't regret it, I promise."

"*¿Dónde usted que toma a mi hija?*" Ms. Vasquez interrogated Numbers about where they were going. She was still infuriated that Numbers had impregnated her only daughter. And they hadn't even had the decency to tell her. She'd only found out once Rosa-Marie could no longer hide her growing stomach under her clothing. Of course she blew her top and told her daughter she would have to get out, she disgusted her and disgraced the family. Rosa moved in with Numbers for a few weeks, but it was already too crowded in the two-bedroom with his mother, two sisters, and himself. After pleading with her mother, who did miss her, she was allowed to move back in. Though Numbers had the means to get them an apartment outside of the projects, he thought it best for Rosa to stay with her mother while she was pregnant. He was running the streets all the time, and Ms. Vasquez could watch out for Rosa. As much as Ms. Vasquez wanted to dislike Numbers, she had to admit he treated her baby well and made her happy.

"Jupree"—Ms. Vasquez said his name incorrectly every time—"you hurry and bring Rosa back, okay?" she grumbled.

Before Numbers could answer, Rosa waddled out of the bedroom with her long black hair in a ponytail. She hated doing her own hair these days. Dressed for comfort, not fashion, she wore a pair of white Reeboks, loose-fitting jeans, and an oversized yellow blouse. She went to the closet and grabbed the navy-blue three-quarter shearling coat Numbers had bought for her and put that on. She hated the cold weather. After wrapping her neck with a scarf, she scooped gloves and earmuffs of the same color as the coat out of its pockets and put them on. "I'm ready," she said, exhausted.

Numbers was exhausted just watching her put on all the garments. He looked at his beautiful future baby mother and held out his arm, bent at the elbow. She smiled at him and put her hand through the opening, allowing Numbers to escort her out the door.

"Este detrás en un poco mientra que la madre," Rosa told her mother—she would be back shortly.

"See you later, Ms. Vasquez," Numbers said.

Ms. Vasquez just huffed at them both.

Numbers and Rosa-Marie walked around building 101, past the basketball court toward Carlton Avenue, arm in arm.

"Where are we going, Dupree?" Rosa queried.

"Right here!"

They were standing in front of building 60. A rough, dirty-looking thirty-something-year-old man came up the pathway from the connecting building, 75, with his coat open, oblivious to the wind.

"Yo, Numbers, can I get a two-oh?" the fiend asked, as if they were old friends. Rosa looked at Numbers. She was aware of his illegal activities, but this was the first time she witnessed it. Numbers gave her that much respect. The deadly sneer he flashed the fiend, though, told the man he had made a mistake. First off, Numbers hadn't dealt drugs hand to hand since he formed PWH. Second, his crew only did business by the park.

"You playing yourself," Numbers said in an even tone.

"I'll go to the park and see what's jumping off up there. Sorry, Numbers. Excuse me, miss." He apologized repeatedly, knowing he fucked up. He picked up his pace as he limped away.

If Numbers hadn't been with his lady, he might have shown some compassion for the man—after all, he knew Archie from way back. But he was nothing more than another customer now, and it was hard to believe his promising basketball future was all but an illusion.

"Excuse me, baby," Numbers apologized.

She said nothing about it and continued walking with Numbers into building 60.

"Isn't this where your friend used to live? Why are we coming here?" She was speaking about Crispy Carl. Three weeks and four days had passed since he was laid to rest.

Numbers smiled at her as the door to the elevator slid open; he ushered her in and pressed the button for floor 3.

When the elevator stopped, Numbers led Rosa to the door directly across from them; he was dangling a key in front of her.

"Take it. Open the door," he urged.

Looking at Numbers curiously, she took the key and unlocked the door. She stepped inside and was speechless. The apartment was spotless, and other than beige venetian blinds in the windows, it was empty. The walls were painted a matte cream, and beige carpet was installed throughout the one-bedroom apartment. There were no signs that the dwelling was once an old pimp's palace. Numbers had given all of Crispy Carl's belongings and furniture to his few friends who were still alive or to the Salvation Army. The housing authority didn't know Crispy Carl was dead, and Numbers wasn't about to tell them. He would continue to pay the $235.32 a month for rent. He spent that much on any given night bullshitting.

"So what do you think, baby? This is our new apartment; we have to dress it up of course, but it's ours," he said, and spun around with his arms extended as if presenting the world to her.

She ran into his embrace. "I love it." She kissed him hard, sticking her tongue in his mouth. Her succulent kiss aroused him enough to peel off their clothing and ravish her childbearing body on the plush new carpet.

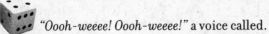 *"Oooh-weeee! Oooh-weeee!"* a voice called.

"Baby, baby, wake up, somebody's calling you."

"Huh . . . what . . ." Numbers responded, groggy and disoriented. There was no sun shining through the blinds. The overcast skies gave the early morning the semblance of dusk, and precipitation seemed imminent on this second Monday in January.

"Oooh-weeee! Oooh-weeee!"

Numbers finally heard the call, and he knew by the tone who it was. He looked over at the clock: 7:15 A.M. *Why is Jar waking me this early? It better be important.* He rolled out of the queen-sized bed and made it over to the window.

"Yo!" he called down to Jarvis. "What up?"

Jarvis pointed up, gesturing to Numbers that he was coming upstairs. Numbers nodded. By the time Numbers had stepped into his jeans, Jarvis was knocking on his door.

"What's popping, Jar?" Numbers said as he opened the door, still not quite fully awake.

"Coney got bagged last night," Jarvis announced.

"What?" He wasn't sure if he'd heard Jarvis correctly.

"Coney's locked up! They said he got caught with weight on 'im, too."

How could that be? Numbers wondered. Coney never held any weight—unless he was picking up from his connect. Even then he was extra cautious. He'd have one of his mules float it back to his safe house under his watchful eye. How could he possibly have gotten jammed up?

"Nothing we can do but wait it out. This could be a problem. Gravy already knocked, if Coney under too . . ." Numbers stopped mid-sentence. Jarvis knew the look on his boy's face. He was either calculating numbers or coming up with a fresh strategy.

Numbers estimated that if they kept selling at the clip they were going, they'd sell out by Friday. They'd have a little over thirty thousand dollars; 25 percent of that was his and the crew's take. Hopefully, Coney would be back on the street by then and he could re-up. But what if Coney didn't get cut loose? Numbers had no idea how or where to get the type of quality product they would need to continue their hustle. Coney never let anyone meet his supplier, nor did he ever mention where he got his drugs from—that was one of the ways he stayed in control. Numbers hoped they didn't have bigger problems. *What if 5-O was watching Coney's whole operation?*

Numbers sat on his brown Italian-leather sofa and put his feet on the corresponding ottoman. Directly in front of him, next to the door, was a big-screen Sony Trinitron TV.

The apartment was looking like the hood version of *Better*

Homes and Gardens. The living room, dining room, and kitchen were one big space and not that large of an area, but Rosa displayed an interior designer's touch.

"Who's working the park wall today, Jar?"

"Broz and Shorty."

"Okay, tell 'em to be extra cautious. They might be watching us, you never know. Better yet, tell 'em to take a day off. Nobody in our camp pumps anything today," Numbers decided.

"I don't think that's a good idea." Jarvis wasn't feeling Numbers on this call. Getting money had changed Jarvis considerably, and he wanted it no matter what. He'd become arrogant, touchy, selfish, and greedy.

"We straight, Jar. A day off won't kill us." Numbers was smiling at his childhood friend but making sure Jarvis understood what he wanted done.

"I think that's a mistake," Jarvis said condescendingly.

"What up with you, Jar? You been acting funny lately. You got a problem with me or something?"

Jarvis avoided Numbers's eyes. "Nah, we cool. Just got a lot on my mind with my family and stuff," Jarvis said.

"You know if you need me, I'm here for you." Numbers put his feet down on the carpet and sat up.

"No doubt," Jarvis reluctantly conceded.

Numbers knew Jarvis was dealing with his mother's alcoholism. His oldest sister had just up and disappeared, leaving her two children behind, and his other sister had one on the way, and the brother that was around was a jailbird. Jarvis inherited the burden of taking care of all of them and everything that came with it. Numbers understood the plight of being the man of the house oh so well, although his situation had never been anywhere near as crucial.

"Jar, trust me on this one. Just give the word for everyone to lay low for today." He got up and gave his boy a pound and hug. When Jarvis left, Numbers locked the door and went back to bed.

It was 5:15 P.M. when Numbers's Sky Pager sounded off. He picked the device up off the nightstand, looked at the numbers, then grabbed the jack immediately, dialing out.

"Yeah, what up? . . . Who? . . . Get the fuck outta here!" he said into the phone.

Rosa sat up in the bed looking at her man, hearing the alarm in his voice. She knew Numbers wouldn't tell her what was happening, but that didn't curb her curiosity.

"Get at Ketta and Jar. I'll meet you at my mom's building," he commanded before hanging up the phone.

"What's wrong, baby?" Rosa asked, not expecting an answer.

"Nothing, Rose. Do me a favor and make me some tea."

She rolled out of bed and waddled to the kitchen to boil water.

Once she left the room, Numbers got up quietly, wasting no time going into the closet to his safe. He moved quickly, opening the safe before Rosa caught wind of what he was doing. He looked over his shoulder to make sure she was occupied before taking out a black .380, which he stuffed in his pants pocket. He locked the safe, then sat back on the bed and began putting on his boots.

When Numbers exited the building it was close to five-fifty and darkness was creeping in fast. A stiff wind was swirling and whooshing at his back as he walked into the rear of his mother's building. The first thing he heard was Waketta's mouth. When he opened the creaky door leading to the first-floor hallway, everyone went quiet for a moment until Waketta, Broz, and Jarvis saw it was him.

Waketta picked up where she'd left off. "Let's go whip them bitches' asses. How the fuck they gonna pump in our park?" she said, talking to Numbers now. "Crush's flunkies pumping product in our spot. What we gonna do?"

"I told you we shouldn't take a day off," Jarvis chimed in with an I-told-you-so attitude.

That was fast. Numbers wondered how they knew PWH was lying low today. Later for the guessing game. Numbers would go to the source, run up on whoever was in the park, and get answers.

"Is everybody packing?" Numbers checked his clique.

"And you know it," said Waketta, always the first one to speak up.

Broz and Jarvis nodded in affirmation.

"Aiight, let's roll on 'em." Numbers led his crew out of the building, glancing at his mother's first-floor window to see if any of his family members were aware of his presence. The shades were down. PWH walked across the courtyard past the front of building 81 onto North Portland Avenue.

They hurried up the block with Broz trailing. For a big boy, he could move fast, but he always chose to dally. When they reached the avenue it was just as Broz informed Jarvis: Crush's boys were slinging in their park. Coney had schooled him early on that shit like this was unacceptable.

A medium flow of traffic cruised east and west on Myrtle Avenue, but there were not many pedestrians. The windchill must have kept many people inside. PWH, all dressed in dark garments, marched against the DON'T WALK sign looking like the GoodFellas. Two dudes kicked it with their backs to the street, not seeing the crew walk up on them. If they'd known what was about to take place, they might have been paying more attention. They would learn to stay on point after this.

"My man, can I speak with you a moment?" Numbers asked in a calm, civil manner. The crew fanned out into a loose circle around the men.

"What up, par?" The taller of the two guys said thuggishly, unaware he was speaking to the shopkeeper of the area they were peddling on.

"I wanted to know who gave you guys permission to push your product over here." He was boiling inside, but his demeanor didn't convey it. He'd built up this location from nothing, and he wasn't about to let two Johnny-come-latelys move in on his territory.

The tall dude answered indignantly, "Permission? Duke, we sling where the fu—" Before the last word came all the way out, Waketta came down on his skull with the butt of the .380 she had palmed. It was identical to the pistol Numbers was carrying, still concealed in his pocket. Dude folded over, grabbing his dome piece, blood seeping through his clutching fingers.

His partner wanted no part of the business. He jumped up and tried to flee from the loose entrapment, but Broz stuck out his fat foot, tripping him; he fell hard, scraping his face on the sidewalk. He bounced right back up in fear for his life and continued running down the hill toward the third side of the projects, looking back once to see if he was being chased. He wasn't.

"The man asked you a question," Waketta demanded.

Attempting to clear his head, the soldier looked up, then at Numbers, and at Jarvis. He was about to fix his mouth to say something when Jarvis rammed his size 9½ Timberland into his gut. The dude moaned in pain. Jarvis hovered over him, daring him to say the wrong thing again.

"Crush . . . it was Crush," he whimpered. "He said this was our spot now."

Numbers bent down so he would be on eye level with the young man. "Tell Crush to respect the boundaries and we won't have any unnecessary problems. Got that?"

"Let me put a cap in his ass," Waketta begged.

"Nah, baby, he got the message. Don't you?" Numbers looked at the dude in a manner that could not be misunderstood.

Dude nodded in compliance.

It was confirmed that Coney was locked up, but no one was sure of the particulars. Everyone speculated it was drug-related. But what Numbers did know for sure was that Coney had been incarcerated for the past two weeks and the PWH were out of product. Shit was dry. Other than Coney's money, the crew didn't have much reserve cash. Things were getting tighter than six fat men in a Pinto.

It was early morning; Mike's Coffee Shop was bustling, as usual. A small, quaint spot on the corner of DeKalb Avenue and Hall Street, diagonally across from Pratt Institute, Mike's held, at most, fifty people. Numbers and Jarvis used to go there often when they worked the summer youth program. The PWH sat in the last booth across from the kitchen, near the one restroom in the back, plotting their next move.

A stubby Mexican waiter with a dark mustache approached. "Are you ready to order?"

"I'm ready," Broz was quick to respond.

"Your fat ass is always ready," Jarvis ragged on him, and the others laughed.

"Why you always got something to say, Horse Skull?" Broz snapped back, and this round of giggles was with him, not against him.

"Give us a minute. For now just bring us four waters with lemon and four hot teas. Thanks," Numbers said.

"Make that three teas. I want a hot chocolate with whipped cream," Broz interjected.

"Okay, be right back." The waiter scurried off.

"So what's the plan, ol' great leader?" Jarvis started the conversation.

Numbers ignored his sarcasm. "I got word from one of Coney's boys that Coney should be back on the streets in a couple of days."

"And what if he's not?" Jarvis asked, challenging. He was pissed off at Numbers because he was remaining loyal to Coney, which meant they weren't getting paid.

"Then we wait it out," Numbers replied, weary of his best friend's contempt for his authority as leader of the crew. "How do you think we should proceed, almighty preceptor? Since it seems as though you have the remedy for what ails us." Numbers spoke, exhibiting some of the education he was afforded at his premier high school.

"What? Fuck you." Jarvis knew Numbers was fucking with him, but he didn't know what that shit Numbers said meant.

"Easy on the testosterone, guys, let's just figure this out," Waketta said, endeavoring to cool tempers down.

"Yeah, I got a plan," Jarvis continued, a bit calmer. "I think we should get weight from Crush."

"Crush?" Waketta and Broz both burst out, surprised to hear that name. After all, they had just pistol-whipped one of his workers not two weeks ago. Why would Crush be willing to supply them?

"You not serious, Jar? Crush?" Baffled, Numbers looked at Jarvis. They all did.

"Are you ready to order yet?" the waiter asked after returning with the beverages.

"Give us another minute." Numbers sent him off again.

"Listen, duke ain't sweating that ass whipping we gave his worker—he a businessman. He said he'd hit us with a brick for a good price," Jarvis explained, pouring a ton of sugar into his tea.

"Nah, Jar, we ain't fucking with dude. I don't trust that nigger. He foul. Plus Coney ain't never did us dirty," Numbers replied.

"You sure 'bout that?" Jarvis raised an eyebrow.

"What you trying to say, Jar?"

"Nothing." Jarvis took a sip from his tea.

"Fuck you mean, Jar? You started this shit. If you know something, just spit it out."

"Nothing, man. It's whatever you say."

The waiter was back for the third time, the irritation obvious in his tone. "Are you ready to order now?"

"Yeah." Numbers looked over to Waketta, who was sitting next to him on the inside of the booth. It was clear she was thinking the same thing Numbers was: *What is Jar talking about?*

Broz ordered first. "Let me get a cheese omelet with mushrooms, green peppers, french fries, extra side of bacon, a Belgian waffle, and more hot chocolate."

"We not gonna order nothing; we'll just eat off his plate," Numbers joked, lightening the atmosphere a little. Before he could order, his pager started vibrating; he looked at the number and smiled. "Let me get two eggs over easy with home fries. I'll be right back." He got up and walked out of the diner to the pay phone on the adjacent corner.

When Numbers returned, the food was there and everyone was enjoying their breakfast. Things seemed back to normal. "We back," Numbers announced.

Everyone looked up from their food.

"Coney's out the can, I'ma meet with him a little later on." It was welcome news. The crew ate, laughed, and enjoyed their meal.

Numbers met Coney at his mother's place in building 117. He knocked on the door of 11G, one of the largest apartments in the development, with three bedrooms. Only the A, F, and G apartments came with three bedrooms.

"Who is it?" the male voice on the other side of the door asked.

"Numbers."

A moment later Coney opened the door, looking none the worse for wear. He poked his head out the door to make sure Numbers was alone. Coney seemed a little paranoid. Without a word he waved Numbers into the crib. Numbers had been there before. The shades and curtains were closed; the only light came from the project light fixture on the wall. Numbers followed Coney past the dining room set that was too big for the area into the living room on the right. A sexy female sat on the couch wearing nothing but a white tank top, panties, and a fresh hairdo; she looked familiar.

"Shorty, go in the back," Coney instructed. When she stood up Numbers couldn't help but notice the body was crazy. Then he remembered where he knew her from. She was the girl from Farragut Houses who was with the pretty boy Coney duffed out that time. *I guess he was right when he said he thought she wanted him, because she got him, or vice versa,* Numbers thought. The Jayne Kennedy twin smiled at Numbers as she left. *Maybe she wanted me, too,* he thought. Coney waited for her to leave. After hearing the bedroom door close, he spoke.

"Yeah, Numbers, the law tried to jam me up. They almost had your boy." Coney was trying to gauge Numbers's reaction. It was stoic. "If it wasn't for Spitz, I'd still be down," Coney continued. "If you ever get into any shit, Joshua Spitz is one slick motherfucker to have on your payroll. He ain't cheap though. I had to shell out fifteen grand to that Jew-boy attorney, but it's worth it to be back on the streets." Coney lay back on the plush sofa and lit up a Dutch. Numbers sat in a recliner adjacent to Coney.

"It's good to have you back," Numbers said. "So what up, Coney, how we moving? I ain't got to tell you we been missing out on major loot."

"I know, that's why I called you. This is some serious shit I'm about to drop on you, and I need you to be solid on this, don't fuck me." Coney became rigid. He shot a glare at Numbers, letting him know this was life or death. Numbers felt uneasy; whatever Coney wanted from him, he hoped he could handle it. He waited as Coney inhaled and exhaled on the blunt.

"Shit is too hot for me right now. Po-po got it in for me." He seemed reluctant to say what he really wanted to say, then he just blurted it out: "I need you to get at my connect to make the re-up."

Numbers knew this was big. One of the initial rules Coney had laid down was never to give up your supplier. Now he was entrusting Numbers to make the pickup.

"You know I don't trust no-fucking-body," Coney said, as he'd done many times before. This mantra was as consistent as U.S. taxes and death. Coney didn't trust his own mother, but he felt Numbers had proven his loyalty in many situations. If he got out of line, Coney would murder him—it was as simple as that.

"So this how it's gonna go down," Coney continued, not giving Numbers a choice in the matter. "You gonna meet my connect, Sanchez, up in Washington Heights at this chicken spot near a hundred-sixty-eighth and Broadway. Take the twenty-four K you got for me and pick up what I got there. When you get back to the hood with the goods, let me know and I'll tell you what to do with it. Now listen to me, don't be holding no long drawn-out conversations with dude. He a straight shooter, but he ain't your friend and he tend to run his mouth too fucking much. So get in and get outta there. And go by yourself! Nigga don't like crowds. You got me, Numbers?" Coney spoke as if he was giving orientation to a new employee.

"Come on, Coney, you know I wouldn't shit on you," Numbers said, wanting to alleviate his concerns. It was true, Numbers was loyal to a fault.

Looking into Numbers's eyes, Coney believed him. "My nigga." He smiled, passing Numbers the smoke.

Numbers drove his silver '89 Acura Legend into Manhattan and up the West Side Highway, blasting the Nas *Illmatic* cassette. He got off on the 125th ramp in Washington Heights and drove to 168th and Broadway. The area boasted a large Latino community. It also flaunted a healthy drug trade. You could cop nearly any drug you wanted up here, from weed to boy and anything in between.

The money was stashed in his long-john pants. Before entering New Caporal, a little Spanish fast-food chicken spot, he paged the connect. He ordered some chicken wings and yellow rice while he waited. The chicken wings were ten times better than the Chinaman's, but not as good as his mom's.

He waited there half an hour after he finished eating, and still no sign of Sanchez. He was getting antsy. Numbers did take comfort in knowing he was packing his .380, just in case things got hairy. He wished he would've brought Jar or Ketta to back him up. They would have no problem busting their gats if something went wrong.

Every time the restaurant door opened, Numbers looked to see who was entering. A couple of older Latino men came in, then a lady and her young son minutes later. They got their orders and left. Not long after that, a Latina bombshell came in. Numbers would have bet the $24,000 in his long-john pants that she was the singing sensation Selena. He was content with the two ladies in his life but would have had no problem adding her to the stable.

"Good evening, sweet lady," Numbers said in Spanish. Rosa would have a fit if she knew he was using what she taught him to pick up other women.

The female was surprised to hear Numbers speak Spanish.

"*Hola,*" she replied, giving him a big inviting smile.

"What's your name?" he continued in Spanish.

"Guadalupe," she answered. "What's yours?"

"Numbers."

"Numbers." She ran her fingers across his waves and exited out the door. Numbers wondered what that was all about. She hadn't ordered anything. Though she seemed friendly enough, Numbers speculated that he may have scared her off. He was ready to follow after her but didn't want to take the chance of missing Sanchez. He was at a disadvantage being in a strange area and not knowing what duke really looked like. He just knew he was Spanish and wore a lot of jewelry.

Moments after the gorgeous Latina girl walked out of the restaurant, a short Latino guy ambled in. He was about five foot six, with dark, close-cropped hair. He wore his black bomber jacket open, showing off no fewer than eight gold chains with Jesus medallions, crosses, and other religious pieces. He wasn't wearing a hat or scarf, so Numbers deduced he was in a car or he lived close by. It was still rather cold out, and the temperature was dropping by the hour.

"Numbers, my man! I apologize for taking so long." He spoke English with a Hispanic accent. "I'm Sanchez." Numbers had a

perplexed look on his face. How did he know who he was? Maybe Coney had described him?

"Come walk with me. My building is right up here," Sanchez said. Sanchez could see the concern in Numbers's face that this could be a setup.

"No worries, my friend. I've been doing business with Coney Island for ten years—you good here."

No one called Coney by his full handle unless they knew him for a while. Numbers walked with Sanchez up Broadway and made a right onto 170th Street. They crossed over to the left side of the block. He was leery, walking pass several seedy-looking Hispanic males. As he passed, he could hear them speak Spanish with their own dialect and slang. He understood some of what they were saying; none of it was threatening toward him. Still, he didn't let his guard down. He kept his hands in his coat like he was cold, but he was really keeping a firm grip on his gat. If Fort Greene had taught him anything, it was to always be aware of his surroundings. Numbers followed Sanchez into the third apartment building on the block, a prewar structure with no visible number on the outside. They walked up four flights to apartment D3. Inside, the apartment was decorated with bright eccentric colors and large works of art. An acrylic painting of Tony Montana in the bathtub with a cigar in his mouth covered one whole wall in the living room. The dwelling was quite comfortable.

"Can I get you something to drink?" Sanchez offered.

"No, I'm good," Numbers said, just wanting to take care of his business and get back to BK to the fullest. He stood in the long foyer at the entrance to the living room.

Sanchez could sense his uneasiness; this was a deadly game, and stickups were a part of the landscape. "Amigo, I don't do business like that. You be straight with me, I be straight with you. Come in, sit." After Numbers did what he was asked to do, Sanchez called out, "Lupe, get in here."

The brown-complexioned Latina sexiness that Numbers had been cracking on just moments ago in New Caporal came strutting out from one of the rooms carrying a cigar box. Numbers kept his hand jammed in the pocket with the gun, ready for anything. Upon seeing her the second time, it was confirmed: she was fire, no dispute. Numbers couldn't help but to get a semi-rise imagining serving her.

"You smoke?" Sanchez inquired. "I got some exotic shit from my country. This marijuana will blow your mind." He pronounced the word *marijuana* like he was saying the name of two girls: Marie and Juana.

Numbers knew that Coney said not to trust him, to get in and out, but his instincts told him Sanchez was all right. His instincts rarely let him down.

"Sanchez, no disrespect, but I'm gonna have to take a rain check; maybe the next time. I need to take care of this and get back. Next time, if that's okay with you," Numbers said, not wanting to offend him.

"*Comprendo.* Lupe." He gave her a nod, and she placed the cigar box on the coffee table and went into a back room. Sanchez's instincts were equally sharp. He got a good feeling about Numbers.

"Can I use the bathroom?" Numbers asked. He didn't want Sanchez to see where he had the money stashed.

"Yes, right through there." He pointed to a small corridor.

Numbers went into the bathroom, removed the money from his hiding spot, and came back to the living room in no time. Sanchez was waiting with two bricks of pure white on the table. Numbers laid the money on the table next to the weight. He picked up the kilos and placed one in the back of his waistband and the other in the front, tightening his belt to secure them. After zipping his blue Woolrich coat, he was ready to bounce.

"Hey, Numbre, tell C.I. to come see me sometime. I'll see you again, no?"

"Most likely."

"Okay, take this, take it, it's on me." He held out a Ziploc bag containing exotic green smoke with bright amber hairs, urging Numbers to accept it.

Numbers took the bag and smiled slightly. "Good-looking."

"Okay, my friend." Sanchez walked Numbers to the door and let him out. Numbers kept his hand on his piece until he was safely in his ride.

Numbers met with Sanchez three times in a two-week period. He would get the product and take it to Suki's place. She lived in a one-bedroom apartment on Lefferts Place. Suki was Coney's bottom bitch. Whatever he wanted or needed, she'd do it or get it for him. She wasn't looking as fly as when Numbers had first seen her some years ago, but she wasn't far off her mark. She looked as though she may have been enjoying the cocaine being stashed at her crib a little too much. Coney was careful not to be seen coming and going from the spot. He believed someone was watching him, he just didn't know who.

Numbers moved Broz up to product distributor. His new job was to go around the borough supplying Coney's soldiers once Numbers got word they needed re-up. Coney would still go around and pick up his trap. He didn't trust anybody handling his money. Even though the crew was getting money, it wasn't enough for the risk they were taking. Jarvis complained about the money every chance he got.

Today he called for Numbers from the courtyard outside his building. Numbers came down to the first-floor lobby of 60 Carlton. Jarvis was waiting there for him. The door to the lobby was closed, but you could hear the wind outside whistling like a banshee. "Jarski, what up, son?" Numbers came out the stairwell door in a jovial mood.

"How's Rosa?" Jarvis inquired.

"Man, complaining 'bout everything. I wish the baby would hurry up and drop already. It's due in April."

"You still don't know what you're having?"

"Nope, but what up? What you wanted to talk to me about?" Jarvis had left word that he really needed to speak with him.

"Coney is shorting us. He's giving us a seventy-five/twenty-five when we should be getting a sixty/forty cut," Jarvis said, getting straight to the point.

Numbers didn't say anything; he just listened to what his boy was telling him.

"Who told you that?" Numbers wanted to know where he got the 411 from.

"You can ask anybody hustling, they'll tell you the same shit."

Numbers thought better than to blow his friend off this time. "Aiight, Jar, I'ma definitely checking that shit out." As he thought about it more, Numbers began to believe there had to be some truth to what his man was saying. Jarvis had been harping on it for several months now. "But right now let's go to Lorro's Deli for a sandwich or to Louie's to get a slice of pizza. I'm starving."

"Bet," Jarvis agreed, happy to have finally gotten through to Numbers.

The whistling wind made it seem much colder than the temperature, but the weather was actually quite bearable for this time of the year. The two friends strolled up Carlton Avenue. Numbers didn't drive his vehicle when it wasn't necessary. Walking was cool with him. As they headed to the avenue, Numbers couldn't help but calculate the difference in what they were getting and what they should be making. It was significant. He would have to address this immediately.

Numbers met up with Coney later on that day. Coney was in a navy blue '93 Mercedes-Benz SEL.

"What the deal, Numbers? Everything good?" Coney smiled, sporting some new jewels and a new Rolex President. Numbers now understood how Coney was able to afford shit like that—by underpaying him and his team.

"Coney, I wanted to talk to you about my cut." He gauged Coney for a reaction.

Coney twisted his face. "What about your cut?" he shot back coldly.

"Man, I've been doing this for you for the last four years and change. I've only been getting hit off with twenty-five percent. I ain't said nothing before, but with all my new responsibilities it should be a sixty/forty cut instead of seventy-five/twenty-five."

Coney rubbed his left hand over his face, pulling down his gorilla jaw. He was laughing but not amused at all.

"Son, you bugging! I ain't splitting my shit with you sixty/forty. You can forget that shit," Coney said flat out. The tone of his voice and his refusal to give a little vexed Numbers. He was ready to wild out on Coney's ass. He'd always respected Coney, but now it looked like Coney may have misconstrued that respect for fear. He may have other young niggers petro, but Numbers had vowed to himself long ago he'd never fear no man, ever! Coney had eight years and a few pounds on him, but Numbers was taller. Growing up with Jarvis, getting in fight after fight, he'd developed above-average skills with his hands. He could handle his own with the best of them.

"Word, Coney, that how you gonna do me?" Numbers didn't try to conceal his contempt. "That shit's grimy."

"Son, I put you on to this game. Now you trying to be greedy, what the fuck," Coney rationalized, trying to turn the tables and make himself the victim. "Listen, this is what I'll do: I'll bump you up to thirty percent, aiight?" He continued as if he was doing Numbers a favor. "You good with that?" Then the nigger had the nerve to change the subject, further pushing Numbers's ire. "Yo, I been meaning to ask you what's up with ya bitty Ketta? You should let me get at that."

Numbers sat there silent, trying to calm himself down, so as not to react before he thought things through. It was almost laughable that Coney was pissed off because he was asking for his just due. But to disrespect him by asking about Ketta—knowing that she was his piece—was too much. *What's that comment all about? Is he trying to test me to see if I'll flip on his ass?* Numbers was finally able to see Coney's true colors, exactly what Jarvis was trying to tell him all along.

"Aiight, Coney you got it." Numbers got out of the car calm and collected.

Things were tense between Coney and Numbers after their discussion. Numbers's first thought was to get out of the game, but he knew he couldn't go back to nickel-and-dime hustling cards and dice. He accepted the 30 percent, but he wasn't satisfied. Numbers believed he was more calculating than Jarvis. Jarvis wanted to jump ship and roll with Crush. Crush wasn't an option for Numbers—too much bad history. *But why is Jarvis so keen to deal with him?* That was one thing Numbers couldn't figure out. He'd have to devise a better plan. He needed his own connect. Although he'd built a respectable rapport with Sanchez, Sanchez was still Coney's supplier. It was time to rethink his arrangement with Coney and play it smart until he could get out from under his thumb.

Coney believed he had made off like a bandit, but he wasn't taking any chances. He was going to keep Numbers on a short leash. He threw him a bone just to keep him content until he could get someone else to make his runs uptown or the heat was off him. When the time was right, he'd eliminate Numbers from the equation. It would be better for Coney to get rid of him than to cut him off.

Numbers and Waketta walked up to the Lexus lounge. Whenever they couldn't find Jarvis on a Thursday night, he was most likely here. They could hear the music vibrating through the walls as Waketta approached the door first, trailed by Numbers. Numbers had pull at the joint because he hooked the bouncers up with drugs or hit them up with cash when he breezed through. Waketta's pull was totally different. Her juice was from a couple of the bouncers trying to get up in her. She flirted with them, but that's all it was because she was only interested in Numbers.

"Hey, Waketta, what the deal, sugar? When we gonna hook up?" Big Mike the bouncer asked, seeing Waketta walking up looking scrumptious. She wore a pair of form-fitting Sergio Valente jeans and a leather jacket with fur around the collar and cuffs. The boots were leather with fur trim. Waketta knew how to accentuate her God-given gifts. Numbers never got jealous of men trying to get at Waketta; it was expected. She was fine like Naomi Campbell.

"Maybe one day, Big Mike," she lied. "Right now I'm on that paper chase." They traipsed past Big Mike into the lounge.

Chubb Rock's "Treat 'Em Right" was being spun by deejay Quick Rock. On Thursday night, most of the hood hung out at the Lexus on Fulton Street near Ashland Place. The Lexus was by no means upscale, it was just a place where the local hustlers, thugs, and whatnot could hang out, drink, and snatch up something to stroke for that night. The spot didn't have a sign on the exterior of the building. Most people knew its location from frequenting it or by its address—667 Fulton Street. The Lexus was about seven hundred square feet back to front. The front was the largest part. When you walked into the smoky nook, the bar was located on the left-hand side. Tables were lined up on the right, with a four-foot walkway straight up the middle. In the back was an open area where people danced. The first door on the right led to the deejay's booth. A few feet farther down, two bathrooms faced each other, with an emergency exit door in between. The Lexus was the straight hood joint. The bouncers were ex-cons or big burly dudes who were known for breaking niggers' faces. The Lexus had drama nearly every night, but still people persisted in frequenting the establishment.

This Thursday night, the Lexus had its usual thick crowd. Numbers knew most of the people, or they knew him. A lot of them were from the PJs. As they made their way through the crowd, Waketta used the opportunity to hold Numbers's hand and caress it. They found a spot near the far end of the bar. That's where they posted up, ordering a bottle of Moët White Star champagne, which Waketta paid for. Numbers wasn't tricking off cash anymore—he was trying to save as much loot as possible. That was part of his plan to get out of the game.

"You see Jar in here, Ketta?" Numbers asked, pouring two flutes.

Waketta surveyed the crowd. She caught sight of Jarvis in the far corner, talking to Crush. Under further scrutiny they seemed to be arguing. Waketta wasn't sure if Jarvis had seen them come in, but he looked mad as hell when he turned and walked up to Numbers and Waketta at the bar.

"What up with that?" Waketta asked, not giving Jarvis time to dap them up.

"It ain't nothing. I told that nigger not to have them busters selling his shit on our territory," Jarvis said.

"Yeah, okay," Waketta replied, not believing him.

"Mind your business."

Numbers noticed more and more that Waketta and Jarvis were at odds with each other. "What y'all arguing about now?" he said, giving Jarvis a pound, then pouring him a glass of bubbles. As Numbers handed Jarvis the glass, the deejay threw on some Mary J. Blige.

Waketta reacted immediately. "That's my jam!" she exclaimed. She began dancing in front of Numbers, sexy and seductive. She rubbed her ass up against him. His nature rose. Numbers bobbed to the music a little, pressing his firmness up on Waketta as she backed it up on him. She always knew how to turn him on. They had intentions of serving each other later on. The deejay followed Mary Jo with the new joint.

"Hold up, Ketta, I'll be right back. Gotta take a leak." Numbers put his flute down and turned to walk to the back of the lounge.

Jarvis decided he had to relieve himself too, so he caught up with Numbers.

"What up with Crush? What he talking 'bout?" Numbers asked Jarvis, scoping some of the phat butts dancing by.

"That nigger a clown. He ain't saying nothing, but he keep asking 'bout Ketta. You need to check Ketta. I think she sweet on dude."

"How you figure?" Numbers asked.

"I saw them getting at each other, and they looked rather friendly. Something was up."

Numbers was next on line to use the restroom. The door opened and Crystal came out. Crystal wasn't a looker, but what she lacked in beauty she made up with booty. Her waist was a petite twenty-four, but her ass was one of the roundest, shapeliest, plumpest rumps God ever created, and she knew it.

"Damn, girl, don't hurt nobody with all that ass," Numbers flirted.

She smiled.

"I'd love to put this dick up in you," Jarvis got at her.

She frowned at him and went on her way, not feeling his pick-up line.

"Fuck you, whack ho," he shot at her over the music.

Numbers tried to reel him in. "Easy, Jar, you too hard on the chicks." Jarvis was far from a ladies' man; he was too abrasive most of the time.

When Numbers exited the bathroom, Jarvis was still waiting to use it. The other room must've been occupied by females. They always made using the restroom an adventure.

"I'll see you back by the bar, Jar."

Jarvis waved him off. He was kicking it to some short ugly chick.

Numbers made his way to the bar. The little spot had gotten crowded that quick, and it was difficult to navigate through. He attempted to slide by Crystal, and she bounced her sexy ass up on him to the beat. He stayed there for a minute, letting her softness make him hard. He looked to where Waketta was and saw Crush all up in her face. His blood boiled. Every time he and Crush crossed paths, whether it was at the dice games or the corner store, Crush always shot some slick shit out of his mouth.

Crush was a light, bright nigger, average height, average weight. He kept his Afro trimmed and neat like he was an Afro Sheen model. With his strong, etched facial features, it was easy to see why women would be attracted to him until he opened his mouth. His overbite protruded so much it made him look somewhat dorky. It looked like the product of years of sucking his thumb.

Numbers walked toward them. Crush was trying to manhandle Waketta, grabbing her around the waist. Numbers really couldn't tell if she was fighting him off or not, but he didn't care. He wanted him to back off her.

"Ketta, why you got this dude all up in your face?" Numbers grilled her like he was her father. Waketta wanted to tell him that wasn't the case as she continued trying to pry herself loose from Crush. "Crush, my man, you playing the lady too close," Numbers said to Crush in his calm, cool manner.

"Look at this nigger . . . Captain Save a Ho . . . This your bitch or something?" Crush smiled, showing his horse dentures.

"Your mother's a bitch and ho," Waketta snapped at him, finally getting loose from his grasp.

"Crush, you know we don't fuck with you. Why you always running your trap, duke? Beat the road up." Numbers nudged him on his way with his left forearm.

Crush took exception to Numbers touching him. He swiped his arm away like the Karate Kid's wax-off move. Numbers reacted by coming across the top with an overhand right that clocked Crush on the jaw. All hell broke loose. Numbers didn't give Crush an opportunity to get a punch off. He rained lefts and rights to his head region. One of Crush's boys tried to get a sucker punch in on Numbers, and it grazed his dome. Waketta didn't give him another chance. She crowned the sucker puncher with the Moët bottle, laying him out.

Numbers and Crush wrestled into the back of the lounge near the bathroom and exit. The crowd scattered. Jarvis came out of the bathroom to find his boy beating Crush's ass something lovely. Seeing that Numbers didn't need any help with Crush, he made sure no else jumped in. Crush's face was bloody; he was fighting a losing battle. Waketta was over Numbers's shoulder screaming for him to stop before he killed him. By now the lights were on. The security rushed over, ready to hem up whoever was brawling in their spot. They saw Jarvis watching over the scuffle. The bouncers knew all too well who these guys were. They did not want it with them, but they had a job to do. They yelled at Jarvis to get Numbers and Crush out of the spot. They weren't about to violate the two rival gangsters and risk the chance of having beef with these crazy-ass Fort Greene niggers. Jarvis grabbed Numbers up and led him out the back exit, followed by Waketta. Crush lay on the floor, beaten and trying to recover from the thrashing.

"What up with that shit, Ketta? You fucking with that duck?" Numbers screamed at her as they walked back to his ride. Waketta was hurt that Numbers would think she was dealing with dude. Her eyes welled up, but she said nothing.

"You beat that nigger ass, Numbs. What he do to you?" Jarvis said with a chuckle as he walked behind them down Ashland and across Fulton Street, where their cars were parked. Numbers didn't answer.

"You know it's on now! We gotta watch our backs. Crush gonna want payback," Jarvis said, becoming more serious.

Numbers was unconcerned; he'd tired of dude. If it called for it he would whip Crush's ass again and again. "Fucker don't want it!"

"Jar, you gonna be able to pick Rosa up at eight or not?" Numbers spoke into his Motorola brick cell phone. He would have gone to pick up Rosa himself, but didn't want to be riding around with her dirty.

"Nah, Numbers, I can't make it over there in time. It's crazy out here, baby boy. You know Crush is gunning for you? Where the baby at?" Jarvis spoke into his cell phone.

"L'il man's home with Ms. Vasquez. He's all right. Okay, Jar, I got it." Numbers was a little bit upset that he couldn't count on his friend lately when he needed him.

"You sure you can make it back?" Jarvis asked.

"It's cool, I got her." He quickly dialed out to Coney to let him know he had to pick up and drop off his lady. Coney's only concern was his product.

Numbers was uptown with Sanchez making a pickup for Coney. Rosa-Marie needed to be driven home from Crown Heights. She was taking evening courses at Medgar Evers College. Numbers hung up and paged Waketta. She called him back in moments.

"Hey, Ketta, I need you to go pick up Rosa from class for me. Can you do that?"

"Yeah, baby, I got you and I got something to tell you. Well, I got two things to tell you. I hope you don't get mad at me. Can I see you later?"

"Okay, let's hook up. What you got to tell me?"

"No, baby, I want to tell you in person, okay?" she spoke softly.

"Oh, and I got your car. Take my Acura. Pick her up at eight P.M. You know where, right?"

"Yes, I got it. See you later, sexy."

"Okay."

Numbers hung up the phone. It was seven-fifteen in the evening. He was completing his transaction with Sanchez and would be headed back down to Brooklyn in a few minutes.

At 7:55, Waketta pulled the silver Acura coup up in front of Medgar Evers College on Bedford and waited for Rosa to come out. Unable to see who was in the car because of the dark limousine tint on the windows, Rosa took it for granted it was Numbers as she opened the door to get in. She was taken aback to see Waketta in the driver's seat. She scoffed slightly and rested into the passenger seat.

"Hey, Rose," Waketta greeted her with a smile. Rosa-Marie looked teed off.

"Where's Numbers?" she asked coldly.

"On his way back from uptown."

Waketta didn't understand why Rosa was acting like this. They were on good terms. They'd never had a problem between the two of them. After all, Waketta was the godmother to her son. Waketta didn't pry, just chalked it up to Rosa probably having had a long, hard day. She pulled off and headed north back to downtown Brooklyn. They rode home in an uneasy silence.

Crush picked up his home phone. "Yeah, what up, my dude?" He listened to the voice on the phone. "Nah, we not gonna kill duke, just gonna put the fear of God in his ass. Yeah, I told you, we gonna shoot up his tires or something. Word is bond!" Crush assured the caller, meaning his word meant jack shit due to the fact he wasn't a 5 percenter. "After we done tonight, that nigger Numbers ain't gonna want no part of this game. That's my word!"

Crush pressed the button to end the call, then listened for the dial tone and punched in an eleven-digit number. He listened for the beep, then put his code in. In moments, his phone was ringing again. "Yeah, it's on. Yep, that's what he's driving. Do what I told you to do," he said into the phone. "He should be pulling up on the block in the next fifteen minutes or so, so get over there and get his bitch ass." With that command, he hung up.

Numbers drove across the Brooklyn Bridge and made a left onto Tillary Street, then a right on Flatbush Avenue Extension, and a left onto Fulton. The dashboard clock, which was five minutes fast, read 8:15. He was making his way to Suki's to drop off the goods, then he'd do a quick turnaround and head back to the hood. Rosa called him a couple of times, but he couldn't pick up. He was curious about why she was blowing up his phone and pager.

Waketta was on Myrtle Avenue approaching Adelphi Street when Rosa-Marie finally broke her silence; she was clearly beside herself with anger.

"What's up with you and Dupree?" Rosa asked, using Numbers's government name.

The question took Waketta by surprise. She mustered up a smile. "What are you talking about?" she asked, trying to make light of the question.

"Don't play stupid, Ketta. What's going on with you and my man?" she asked sternly and unwavering.

"I don't know what you're getting at," Waketta fibbed. *What's this all about? Why is Rosa getting at me like this? Where's all this coming from?*

"Right before I got out of class I got a voice message that said, '*I bet you don't know Numbers and Ketta are fucking each other, you dumb cunt.*' So I'm asking you again: Are you fucking my man?"

"No. Hell no! You can't be serious, Rosa. Me and Numbers is cool—you know that!" Waketta started getting loud. For the first time she felt terrible for being with Numbers. She felt bad for lying to Rosa, but she couldn't tell her the truth—it would devastate her. Even worse, she'd be betraying Numbers, which is something she absolutely wouldn't do. Her loyalty was to him, so she lied. Now she wasn't sure if she could tell Numbers her news—it was all too much. Her mind was racing. *Who the fuck would do some grimy shit like this?* She had an idea.

A horn honked from behind. The light was green and Waketta hadn't noticed it. She got moving.

Rosa didn't know what to believe. Why would someone leave her a voice message saying these foul, hurtful things? They turned onto North Portland Avenue, cruising slowly up the block, approaching her mother's building. There was a lot of movement on the street on this June pre-summer night. Waketta pulled into an open space near the walkway to Rosa-Marie's mother's building.

Numbers rolled onto Lefferts Place looking for a parking spot near the building. He hated when there were too many people hanging out in front of Suki's complex, like there were tonight. He wanted to run in, drop the keys off with Coney, and break out.

He put his pistol in his belt; the dark-tinted windows shielded him from prying eyes.

A dark-colored Chevy rolled down the block, two men inside. They spotted their target stopped on the right side of the road. The driver was Spank, the dude that PWH put it on by the park last winter for selling product on their turf. He was still smarting from that ass whipping, and he wanted payback. The guy in the passenger seat was Holiday, Crush's little brother. He was always up for a murderous deed.

"You ready to do this, slouch?" Spank asked his partner.

"Born ready, nicca. Let's scorch his ass with this heat." Holiday laughed deviously.

They crept up slowly next to the parked ride, bumping Biggie's "Somebody's Gotta Die." Holiday extended his Glock out the window and let off multiple rounds, shattering the back window, then the driver's-side window. Screams echoed in the night and people ran for cover. The two assassins sped off down the street, not waiting to see if they'd hit their target. A police cruiser was just turning onto the block and it rammed the escaping Chevy. A gun battled ensued and when it was over Spank and Holiday lay fatally wounded in the crumpled vehicle.

Numbers's pager was blowing up 911, 911, 911. He dropped the product off with Coney and went back to his ride. He just missed a call on his phone. He dialed that last 911 one call from his beeper. It was Broz.

"Numbers, you need to get to the PJs quick—they shot up your ride. Hurry!" Broz yelled frantically.

"Is Rosa all right? Is Waketta okay?" Numbers asked, his heartbeat becoming rapid.

"Hurry, Numbers. It's bad. We by Rosa's mom's building." Numbers heard cracking and pain in Broz's voice. He threw down the phone and sped to the projects, running lights when he had to.

When he reached North Portland, the street was blocked, so he parked the silver Honda and sprinted down the block. The closer he got, the faster his heart raced. He didn't know what to expect. He thought he was losing his mind. As he neared the crime scene, he saw his car taped off by police and his mother standing next to an ambulance crying. Then he saw Rosa sitting in the ambulance being looked at. *She's okay.* He felt the pressure ease off his heart. He kept looking, searching—*Where is Waketta?* He got to his mother and hugged her tightly. She cried in his arms, and whispered, "I'm so sorry, baby."

Why is she sorry? "Where's Ketta, Mommy?" She held him tightly, not wanting to let him go. He looked toward the driver's seat of his car and saw her. Waketta was dead. They had snatched her from his life. He screamed in unimaginable agony, then collapsed.

Waketta's body was laid to rest on June 21, 1998, the first day of summer. The day started out with overcast skies but cleared up when the family tossed the first handful of soil onto the casket. It was a beautiful ceremony.

Right afterward, Waketta's mother, Ms. Dixie, pulled Numbers aside. "Numbers, can I speak with you a minute?" Grief was engraved on her face. She looked like she would never smile again.

"Yes, Ms. Dixie." Numbers couldn't look in her eyes.

"Baby, I know how much you cared about my daughter. She told me how you always looked out for her." She paused, wiping a tear from her eye. "You know Ketta had a great sense of humor." She was able to form a smile. "And she was also very secretive. I want to ask you if you knew who she was dating."

"Dating, Ms. Dixie? No I don't," he lied, surprised the conversation was going in this direction. "May I ask why you're asking?"

"Well, according to the medical examiner, she was ten weeks pregnant." Ms. Dixie's head dropped and tears poured out of her eyes.

Numbers was floored. He knew it was his baby. He became light-headed and dizzy with guilt. It was his fault Waketta and their unborn child were dead, but he couldn't tell that to Ms. Dixie. This was the darkest day of his life.

Numbers became so depressed that he could barely eat or focus. He stopped hustling. He stayed in the house and spent most of his time with his son. He didn't answer his pager or his phone. Almost a month had passed since Waketta died, and he hadn't spoken to Jarvis, Broz, or Coney since the funeral. Rosa thought she was losing him. She didn't know how to get through to him.

One morning Numbers was at his mother's apartment attempting to eat breakfast. Jenny looked at her son with a mother's concern. She could tell his heart was heavy and he was still laboring over the loss of his childhood friend.

"I spoke to your Aunt Camille. She asked how you were doing. She suggested you come down and spend some time with her and the boys."

Numbers looked up from his plate, calculating. "I ain't been down there in as much as fifteen years or so." Jenny's next-to-oldest sister lived in Norfolk, Virginia, on a navy base with her two sons, who were around Numbers's age. Numbers thought the visit might be just what he needed. He decided it was time to take a road trip, get his family out of the city for a while.

He entered his apartment. Rosa was on the sofa watching TV. R.C. was in his playpen. His name was Reginald Carlton, after

Numbers and Crispy Carl. Numbers picked him up and kissed him on his round plump cheeks. "Rosa, I think we should go away for a little while."

"Where?"

"My mom's sister lives in Norfolk, Virginia. We should go down there and kick back. What you think?"

"What about school?"

"Oh, yeah, forgot about school," he said, his face becoming solemn. "Rosa, I hope you understand, but I need to get out of here or I'ma murder somebody." This was the first time Numbers said what he was feeling out loud. He knew who was responsible for Waketta's murder, and he swore to himself that person would pay.

Rosa looked at her man's face and saw the desperation. She knew he wasn't lying. She loved him. She would follow him to the ends of the earth.

"Okay, Papi. When we leaving?"

Numbers held his baby boy above his head. "What up, R.C.? Are you ready for a road trip?" Speaking to his son, he sounded more upbeat than he'd been in a month. His son smiled, laughed, and cooed down at him as if giving affirmation to his daddy.

Numbers had saved up a good little nest egg, accumulating more than $39,000 in the last five months. He'd wanted to get out of the game when he reached $100,000 but the loss of one of his best friends and his lover hastened his desire to retire. The city was closing in on him, making him feel like a claustrophobic locked in a broom closet. He needed to get away.

Numbers and his family left in the middle of the night. He didn't want anyone to know he was going out of town. Leaving the projects without someone seeing was a task in itself. He told his mother not to tell anyone, including Jarvis, where he was going.

It was 1:40 A.M. when he got through the Holland Tunnel and

gassed up. The baby was already asleep in his car seat in the back. Rosa sat in the passenger seat looking as beautiful as ever, but she was troubled.

"Numbers, baby, can we talk?" She initiated the conversation reluctantly.

"Yeah, what's going on?" He reached over to the dashboard to turn the volume down on the Kenwood system.

"It's about Ketta and the day she died." She looked at Numbers, and his face grew tense. "Well, the day she came to pick me up, I received a voice mail from a guy."

"What guy? Who?" Numbers responded jealously.

"That's just it. I don't know who it was, but, well . . ."

"I'm listening," he said, wishing she would get to the point.

"Well, the message said that you and Ketta were sleeping together." She was finally able to get it out. "I asked Ketta about it that day."

Numbers was caught totally off guard. "Me and Ketta? That shit's crazy. We were like brother and sister," he lied, hoping his facial expression didn't betray him.

"That's kinda what she said, but why would somebody leave me a message like that?" Rosa wanted to believe her man.

"I don't know, all this shit is crazy. I don't know why this shit went down the way it went down." He wasn't being entirely honest with her—after all, this was a cutthroat business he was in.

"Baby, it was bothering me. I had to ask and get it off my chest. I hope you understand." She leaned across the seat and kissed him on the cheek. Then she leaned back and rested her eyes, seeming content.

She drifted off to sleep, and Numbers had hours to think. He couldn't remember the last time he could relax and think. It was three-thirty in the morning by the time they got to exit 1 on the New Jersey Turnpike. It was drizzling as they rode over the bridge into Delaware, and it turned into rain as he drove down 95 South.

Numbers's mind began to work as rapidly as the raindrops hitting the '91 Nissan Maxima's burgundy paint job. He thought about all that had transpired over the last year or so. He thought about what Rosa had just told him. Only a few people knew he was messing with Waketta on that level. Beyond Jarvis, Broz, and maybe Coney, everyone else could only speculate. *Was there any truth to what Jarvis was saying about Waketta messing with Crush, and if so, was it his baby she was carrying? And what about Waketta asking if he and Jarvis were still the best of friends and questioning his loyalty? Was her pregnancy the news Ketta wanted to tell me?* He wondered how Crush knew they wouldn't be working their track the day they had to go to the park and check his soldiers. *Somebody had to give me up to Crush the day Ketta was killed. How did they know what time I'd be there? Was it Coney? I did tell Coney I was going to be late getting to him because I had to pick up Rosa. Plus, Coney wasn't there when I arrived. If I would've been driving that night, I would be dead.* He thought about Coney's greedy, trifling ass. *Yeah, it had to be him. Who else could it be? Or maybe it was more than one person?* Then his thoughts bounced quickly to his trip. This excursion was exactly what he needed to clear his mental. He hadn't seen it before, but someone really had it in for him. *Who?*

It was close to 9 A.M. when Numbers pulled up in the driveway of 16 Garvin Street. Camille lived in a four-bedroom, one-level house. Her husband, Charles, a navy man, spent most of his time out at sea. He was stationed on the Gulf Coast.

"Numbers, honey, I'm so glad you came to visit," Aunt Camille said as she came bounding out the front door.

"Hi, Aunt Camille," Numbers said as they embraced.

"You remember Rosa-Marie?"

Aunt Camille gave Rosa a hug and kiss. "Of course! How could I forget such a beautiful girl?"

"Thank you!" Rosa said, feeling the sincere warmth from her man's aunt. It was the same way Ms. Jenny made her feel.

"Now, where's my great-nephew?" Aunt Camille was bursting with excitement over seeing R.C.

Rosa reached in the backseat, unfastened her son, and presented him to his great-aunt. At first he began to cry, but Camille was able to make him feel right at home against her big bosoms.

Numbers left all the bags except for the baby's in the ride until later. Camille had prepared them a big down-south breakfast.

Matthew and Melvin were the youngest of Camille's four children and, at the ages of twenty-three and twenty-two, the only two who still lived at home. They were sizable young men; although they were about the same height as Numbers, they were built like running backs. They rarely got up this early. Melvin dragged himself out of his bedroom, and Matt emerged from the bathroom to greet his cousin and family.

"What up, cuz?" Matt bellowed with his strong southern twang. Mel was still a little groggy. He gave his cousin a pound and a hug. They hadn't seen each other for close to fifteen years. Their eyes couldn't help but open wider at the sight of Rosa looking like a Latina movie star.

"How long y'all staying?" Matt asked.

"Not sure," Numbers replied.

"Well, you know you're welcome to stay as long as you want," Aunt Camille said.

They sat down at the table, and Numbers filled his belly to the max, enjoying getting reacquainted with his family.

It was good to finally breathe—do nothing else but breathe.

Numbers cut off all ties with everyone after the funeral. He could not bear to speak to any of his crew, let alone look in their faces. He was sure they blamed him for Ketta's death. Shit, he blamed himself.

When he last spoke to his mother, she'd said Broz and Jarvis came by regularly asking for him. He hoped they understood that his leaving wasn't about them, it was something he needed to do for himself. Numbers and Rosa enjoyed the climate and the change of pace of living outside of the city. They decided to relocate to Virginia. Staying with his aunt and cousins was cool for the first three weeks, but then he realized that his family needed their own place. A week later, they found a two-bedroom with washer and dryer, wall-to-wall carpeting, and other amenities in Virginia Beach. They would never have found anything this proper for the price in New York City. The apartment was about twenty minutes away from his Aunt Camille's place.

Over the next several months Numbers spent most of his time in their apartment. Rosa enrolled in classes at Norfolk State University. Her sights were set on a degree in business management, and despite her previous attempts, she vowed to graduate this time. Rosa knew how to handle cash and stashed most of the money Numbers gave her for a rainy day.

Numbers didn't hang out with his cousins much. He didn't feel up to it. Other than taking Rosa out to dinner and to an occasional nightclub, he wasn't doing much with his days at all. His mind was unable to rest easy. Waketta's murder was constantly digging at him. He couldn't smoke enough blunts or play enough video games to dampen his hurt. He knew what he had to do. Finally he put a call in to New York and set his plan in motion.

"Hello, where are my two favorite men?" Rosa beckoned, coming through the front door and resting her book bag in the foyer. R.C. came crawling toward the sound of his mother's voice. He was nine months old now. His hair was dark and wavy, and his complexion was light brown like his mother's.

"There's my little boobie. There he go," Rosa said in a small playful voice that made R.C. giggle and laugh. She picked him up and kissed his baby cheeks. "Where's your daddy?" she continued. "Show me where Daddy's at. Are you hungry? Did Daddy feed you?" She blew into his belly, making a funny noise. R.C. flailed his little body, laughing and giggling. She walked to the master bedroom.

"Hey, baby, what you up to?" The joy on her face turned to confusion. Seeing Numbers packing, she asked, "You going somewhere?" Numbers was slow to answer, so she continued to press. "Where are you going?"

"I need to get away," he said, not looking up and continuing to pack.

"You're leaving us here? Where you going that you can't take us?" Rosa was getting upset.

"I just want to get away, go to Atlantic City for a day or two or something."

"How can you just up and leave us?" she said. "That's some bullshit" was a close translation for what she said to him in Spanish. She turned and stormed out of the room with her son playing with her hair.

Numbers knew she would react unfavorably but hadn't thought she'd be this upset.

"Rosa, Rosa, you're right!" he exclaimed following her into the front. "Let's all go. We'll leave tomorrow morning. Okay?" He hoped this would appease her. "But you know I'm going to gamble, so I'll be down in the casino awhile. I don't want to hear no whining."

She smiled, kissing R.C., pleased that she'd gotten her way. "R.C., we're going on a road trip. You hear that? We're going shopping in Atlantic City," she said in a playful baby voice.

Saturday morning, Numbers went out and loaded up the rental car. Rosa followed shortly after. It was 10:37 when they headed out. It was 3:29 in the afternoon when they pulled into the Trump Plaza parking lot. After setting their luggage down in their two-room suite and freshening up, Numbers took his family out to eat. They were back in the room taking a nap by 7 P.M.

Numbers awoke a little before ten. He threw on his jeans, long-sleeved crewneck, black hoodie, and black Nikes, then put a black cap in his right pocket. Rosa woke up, hearing movement in the adjoining room. Only a sliver of light from the Atlantic City nightlife snuck through the break in the curtains. She covered up the baby, who was sleeping next to her. She saw light coming from the other room and heard the TV.

"Who you going to kill?" Rosa asked jokingly, coming out of the bedroom seeing Numbers dressed in all black.

"I'ma murder the blackjack table," he answered with a controlled smile. He thought it was ironic she would make that quip.

"When you coming back?"

"Don't know. When I win enough or get tired."

"Okay, baby, then win us a lotta money and hurry up back so I can give you some of this good stuff," she said as she wiggled her sweet ass at him.

If Numbers didn't have business to take care of, he probably would have stayed there and gotten some of her good stuff. Numbers went into the bedroom, kissed his son on the cheek, and looked at him for a moment. He looked like Rosa, sleeping so peacefully. He came back to the living room and kissed his lady passionately, as if it was the last time he'd see her. Rosa felt something different in his kiss, but couldn't place it. He left.

In the casino, clouds of smoke hovered above the huge space like an overcast sky. The sounds of bells from the one-armed bandits and coins descending to their temporary resting place in the machines until the casino workers came to retrieve them were never-ending. Scantily clad hostesses bounced to and fro, taking drink orders, putting extra-big smiles on their faces to obtain higher tips. It was Numbers's second time in Atlantic City. He'd visited once before with Crispy Carl, right after his twenty-first birthday.

He felt at home in the stench of cigarettes, musk, and money. This is where he was supposed to be, and he wondered why he hadn't frequented the casinos more often. He strolled past the roulette and craps tables. He had no desire to play roulette, but he thought about trying craps later. He breezed by various blackjack tables with their varying rules and minimum bets until he came upon the right one for him—blackjack 21, with one deck of cards. He sat in the last seat, next to the dealer. Crispy Carl told him it was the best seat, because he would have the last decision to hit or let the dealer take the brick. A Middle Eastern woman, whose name tag read SEDALIA, shuffled the deck. In addition to Numbers, there were three other players at the table. The minimum bet was $50; the maximum was $10,000. None of the other players placed a bet lower then $150. Numbers tossed twenty-five $20 bills onto the green-cushioned table.

"Five hundred dollars coming in!" Sedalia called to the pit boss.

An African-American woman in her late thirties walked over, looked at Numbers and then at the table. "Five hundred. Good. Would you like a Trump player's card, sir?" she inquired politely.

"Nah, not yet," Numbers replied. Then seeing the dealer reaching for $25 and $50 chips, he instructed, "Hundred-dollar chips are good."

The dealer slid the chips in front of him. He immediately bet the entire 500 dollars. The cards were dealt.

The first player got a 7 of clubs, the second a 10 of diamonds, the third a king of spades. Numbers caught a 6 of hearts. The dealer's first card went facedown. The dealer dealt the second cards. The first player caught a 10 of clubs; he had 17. The second player's card was an 8 of spades; he was dealt an 18 hand. The third person's card was a 4 of hearts; his hand was 14. Numbers got a 7 to go with his 6; his cards showed 13. The dealer's faceup card was a 9.

Sedalia looked to the first player; he waved her off, swiping his hand over his cards from left to right; his palm downward. The second player did the same thing. The third tapped two fingers on his cards, signaling the dealer to give him a card. She turned up a 6 for him. His hand read 20; he waved her off. He was good with that number.

Numbers was watching the table; he knew what played. He had 13 and the dealer was showing a 9, which meant she most likely had 10 in the hole, if you believed the common blackjack wisdom, which said that Numbers should take a hit and attempt to beat the dealer. But Numbers believed the dealer had a 5 in the hole. Even though he hadn't called cards in a while, it was like second nature. Numbers waved her off of his 13.

"You want to stay with thirteen?" she asked. The other players grumbled at Numbers, feeling he was making a mistake. When Numbers didn't respond to the dealer, she turned up her down card. It was a 5 of spades, just like Numbers had suspected. She would have to take another card.

Numbers was confident that he was good with the cards he had. He didn't take the hit because he believed the next card was a brick. The second player was sure Numbers had made the wrong play, and he voiced his opinion. "You don't know how to play the game." Numbers paid him no attention.

The dealer took her card; it was a queen of diamonds. The house busted. Everyone at the table won.

Numbers took up his $1,000 Trump currency and cashed in at the nearest cashier. It was time to take care of his real objective.

After a two-hour ride, Numbers paid the toll at the Holland Tunnel. It was 1:03 A.M., and there was no traffic. He'd made good time from Atlantic City. Numbers made Jarvis, the only one who knew he was coming, promise not to tell anyone. It was time to take care of unfinished business. He wanted this to be a stealth visit, no hoopla—in and out.

WELCOME TO BROOKLYN, read the sign coming off the Brooklyn Bridge. Numbers drove to the waterfront, which was dilapidated and desolate. It was 1:22 A.M. He was right on time to meet Jarvis with the package. He turned the car around and faced the way he came in, then waited impatiently in the rental with the lights off and gun in hand. Ten minutes passed before there was any sign of anyone or anything. Headlights approached from the same direction Numbers had come from. He waited quietly, praying it wasn't Jake, though he knew no one came down here much. This was where he used to bring Waketta to get head undisturbed. He missed her more than the civil rights movement missed Dr. Martin Luther King. There was no bringing her back, but tonight there would be retribution.

The car drew near and flashed its headlights twice. Numbers flashed back three times. The signals locked; it was Jarvis. Numbers kept a grip on his gun as he and Jarvis exited their rides.

"What up, brother? Good to see you."

"Same here. What's good?" Jarvis asked.

"You tell me. You got that?"

"For sure, Numbs, I got the package." Jarvis moved to the trunk of the Lexus. He also wore all black with a pair of black gloves; he looked like a Black Panther or a hood ninja. He unlocked the trunk and moved back so Numbers could view the goods. Now that the moment of truth was upon him, Numbers didn't know how to feel. Initially he'd been resigned to closing this chapter no questions asked. Just end it. That was no longer an option—he wanted answers.

Dude looked as though Jarvis had worked him over good. His body seemed lifeless. His hands were duct-taped behind him, his eyes and mouth were taped shut, and his feet were taped together.

"Damn, did you kill 'im already?"

Jarvis shook his head no.

Numbers nudged the body in the rib cage with the .380 he'd never fired, other than on the roof of the project buildings. The body squirmed and mumbled.

"What up, player? Do you know who this is?"

The body reacted, confirming he recognized Numbers's voice.

"Yeah, you're fucked in the game now, you bitch-made nigger. You had to keep fucking with me, right? Who's the pussy now? I got one question for you, and if you answer me honestly, I may let you live. You got it?"

The man nodded, now sobbing. Numbers moved closer and violently ripped the duct tape off his mouth.

"Aarghh!" The captive let out a yell that would only be heard by Numbers and Jarvis. He began to beg for his life. "What the fuck, Numbers? Why it got to go down like this?"

"Shut the fuck up, Crush!" Numbers hit him with the back of his small weapon.

Crush whimpered but didn't say another word.

"Crush, I'm gonna ask you one time and one time only. Why did you kill Waketta?" Crush heard the click of the weapon and knew it might be the last thing he ever said.

"Let's just smoke this fool," Jarvis interjected impatiently, speaking in a lower tone than usual in an attempt to disguise his voice.

Crush recognized the voice. He spit blood attempting to speak, "Ja—"

Blam! Blam! Jarvis put two into Crush's medulla. He was dead.

Numbers was stunned. "What the fuck, Jar? Why you did that?"

"Numbs, fuck all that talking shit. We came down here to do a job. We ain't police. That nigger murdered Ketta! That's it! He got what he had coming to him, period." Jarvis tossed the gun in with Crush's body, slammed the trunk closed, and walked toward the passenger side of Numbers's ride.

Numbers stood there for a moment, staring at the closed trunk. He derived no satisfaction from Crush's death, though he'd thought he would. But he felt no regret either. The streets had made his heart cold, but not as cold as Jarvis's.

"Let's go, Numbs!"

Numbers and Jarvis drove out of the dark, abandoned streets of the Brooklyn waterfront in silence. Numbers pulled over on the corner of North Portland and Park Avenue, the back of 56 Monument Walk. They sat there for a few minutes.

"When you coming back up top, Numbs?" Jarvis broke the silence.

"Don't know. Gonna lay low for a while and figure out what I'm gonna do," Numbers replied solemnly.

"Man, all you know is hustling. What you mean, you got to figure it out? It's figured out already. You're gonna hustle on these streets, my nig, ain't nothing else."

Numbers couldn't argue with him. Hustling was all he knew other than his short stint flipping burgers. "Yeah, I guess you're right," he answered, wishing what Jarvis said wasn't true. Still, he would do whatever he could to stay away from dealing drugs again.

Numbers's younger cousins wanted to take him around Norfolk and show him the landscape. Why not? Numbers decided his schedule was wide open. Rosa wanted Numbers to get out and do something. He'd basically been cooped up in the house for the six months they'd been down there. He was starting to drive her batty. He opted to use this time to get to know his cousins and find out their angle. Crispy Carl had told Numbers everyone had an angle. They might not reveal it at first, but given enough time and opportunity, you could learn everyone's angle.

Matt and Mel looked like regular ol' country bumpkins. They didn't wear the latest fashions and weren't at all trendy. They were thick as thieves; it was hard to believe they weren't twins. They looked almost identical, to the point that it was difficult for Numbers to differentiate between them for a long time; even their mother would get them confused if she wasn't paying attention.

Matt and Mel came and scooped Numbers up in an old-school gray Oldsmobile Cutlass Supreme with cranberry interior.

"Where we off to?" Numbers asked, settling into the cloth-cushioned backseat. He always wanted to know for his own safety where he was going; it was hard for Numbers to trust anyone, even if they were his cousins.

"We going over to the hood, cuz," Matt replied with a southern drawl.

"Cuz, we been telling them you was down here from the big city and these fools think we lying," Mel added. "We got some boys who be rapping. They trying to get in that rap game. Maybe you can put 'em onto somebody in the city like Puff Daddy."

"I don't do that music shit." Numbers sat back taking in the sights. It was a cool winter day, about forty-five degrees, but it felt more like sixty. Matt drove out of the complex toward the highway. Numbers studied the route. They departed the Princess Anne section of Virginia Beach proceeding to Virginia Beach Boulevard. They rode the boulevard west. The sign read Route 58. Numbers had traveled this way a number of times to take or pick up Rosa from school.

"Yo, cuz mane, it's this hot little freak that lives 'round the way name Wynter," Matt began.

"Mane, that booty is bodacious," Mel picked up. "I told her my cousin from New York was in town and she been asking 'bout you ever since. She ain't never been to the city, so she all charged 'bout meeting you."

Numbers just listened to his cousins ramble on. His instincts cautioned him to take it slow with these family members.

"Hey, Numbers, want a puff on this swisher?" Mel held a

brown cigar over his left shoulder that looked like a blunt and smelled like pot.

"What's a swisher?"

"It's the cigar we roll our pot in," Matt explained. "I hear y'all smoke those El Productos. We got these swisher sweets."

"Nah, not as much anymore. We smoke Dutch Masters or Backwoods now," Numbers said. He fingered the blunt, surveyed it, then took a couple of quick puffs; it was subpar weed by Numbers's standards—worse than what he usually smoked and nowhere near as good as what Sanchez used to hit him off with.

"Man, I'm gonna have to get y'all some real shit next time I go back up top," Numbers complained, but he continued to smoke.

"Numbers, cuz, if you can get a mess of good smoke—" Matt said.

"—we can make a bank. That's for real," Mel finished, excitedly.

Numbers didn't have any intentions of getting any weight to sell anything. He was resigned to leaving the illegal street-substance hustle alone, although he knew he needed to come up with a new hustle to bring money in soon. His bankroll was a little under thirty thousand dollars, and the cost of living was half the amount of New York. Nevertheless, that money wouldn't last him forever.

They continued on Virginia Beach Boulevard for about half an hour, give or take, until they reached Llewellyn Avenue. They made a right on Llewellyn north until they reached West Twenty-seventh and crossed over to DeBree Avenue. They were now in the hood they called Park Place. It wasn't hard to tell they were in the ghetto. Though it wasn't the concrete jungle Numbers was accustomed to, it was the ghetto nonetheless. There were fewer trees than there were in the Virginia Beach area he now lived in. The blocks were speckled with mostly two-level houses with lawns and driveways. It looked as though the community may have once thrived. Easily half the houses needed painting and repair, if they weren't abandoned altogether. It looked as though the landscapers were barred from this part of town. Only a few residents kept their yards trimmed. But even with the run-down condition of some of the properties, Numbers thought they had it good. At least they lived in houses and not on top of each other, packed together like slaves on a ship.

Matt pulled the car up on Twenty-seventh Street and DeBree. There were only three houses on the right side of the block. The rest of the lots were empty. None of the properties were numbered. They pulled into the driveway of the middle house.

"What's over here?" Numbers inquired.

"Oh, this John-John's place. He live here with his sister, Wynter, the one I was telling you 'bout with the ass," Matt said, making a round gesture with both hands. Mel smiled a little, agreeing.

Numbers followed his cousins as they walked into the crib without knocking. They were in the living room; off to the left was the dining room and a door behind it that led to the kitchen. Straight in front of them was a hallway, which led to a bathroom and a bedroom. Next to the hallway, right behind the living room's back wall, were stairs leading to the second level. The living room was sparsely furnished, but it was neat, except for a few toys tossed here and there.

"Aye, John-John!" Mel yelled.

"He ain't here and why the hell y'all keep walking in my house like y'all live here?" a mocha-complexioned female screamed at the cousins, coming into the living room, carrying a toddler in her right arm; she seemed to be connected to her thick hip like it was her natural resting position. Numbers was pleasantly surprised to see a fine-ass chick in this battered neighborhood. Even with her hair in a scarf you could see her potential. She traipsed into the living room and sat the baby in the playpen right in front of the TV. She wore a pair of gray warm-up pants that were cut into shorts—her ass wasn't as plump as his cousins made it out to be, but he could see why they described it as such—and a tied-up T-shirt showing her belly button. Her stomach was flat and tight. *The baby couldn't be hers,* Numbers thought. Her waist-to-hip ratio made her look extra curvaceous, though her small titties didn't seem to match her body. Numbers surveyed what she had to offer the world and rated her a six and a half. He would have to see her dressed up or butt-naked to really assess her point scale. Her numbers could only go up from here. He surely wouldn't turn down a blow job from those moist, inviting lips.

"M and M, who y'all bringing in my place?" She stood by the playpen with her hand on her left hip. Everyone called them M and M because they were always together, and it was easier than trying to figure out which one was which.

"Girl, be quiet," Matt ordered, like he was used to hearing her flap her gums.

"This our cousin we been telling you 'bout," Mel added.

"Y'all wrong for that! Bringing him up in here while I'm looking like this." It was obvious from the way she attempted to adjust herself that she was a little bit embarrassed.

"You good. I'm Numbers." Numbers gave her an easy smile.

"Wynter." Her full lips formed their own smile. "He looks way better than y'all two losers," she said, poking at M and M and meaning every word.

It was apparent the brothers didn't appreciate her jab. M and M were fine physical specimens, but Numbers was hands-down more attractive. It was hard to see the family resemblance.

"Fuck you, ho," the younger spat.

"Get the fuck out my house," Wynter retorted angrily, tired of the twins already. Numbers could tell she didn't care for them much.

"Come on, Numbers, let's go 'round the block to Howie's. That probably where John-John's at," Matt said as he turned and opened the door. Mel and Numbers followed.

"Don't be a stranger, Numbers." Wynter's voice changed instantly, becoming sweet as syrupy strawberries on Junior's cheesecake.

On West Twenty-eighth and DeBree, the next street up, was Howie's house. The landscape was a disaster. The two-level houses had the same exact layout as Wynter's, except this place was a mess. Howie was twenty years old and lived with his elderly grandfather, his mother, and his drunken uncle. It smelled of liquor, cigarettes, and unbathed old people.

"Howie, this is my cousin Numbers," Mel said.

Howie fit in with the surroundings—he was unkempt and sloppy. His hair was matted, and he still had cold in his eyes, even though it was well into the afternoon.

"Where's John-John?" Matt asked.

"He's in the back counting," Howie said, his southern vocals almost unintelligible to Numbers's northerner ears.

No sooner had they entered the house than someone was rapping on the screen door. Howie went to answer it. A young man maybe eighteen came in just inside the door.

"Let me get one."

Howie took his money and handed him a ball of plastic with brown stems. They were selling weed from the crib. Before Numbers could say a word, Matt assured him, "It's cool. Ain't no niggers gonna fuck with us."

How did he know what niggers Numbers was thinking of? Was he talking about the police niggers or the hood niggers? Either way, Numbers never stayed in a spot where they pumped drugs. It was against his golden rule and a sure way to get thrown in the bean, and he wasn't about to get locked down in Virginia, a commonwealth state. Nevertheless, he went against his better judgment and stayed. They went to the back room, where John-John was counting out some money, mostly ones, fives, tens, and a few twenty-dollar bills. The furnishings consisted of a queen-sized bed, a TV, a portable stereo, a dresser, and a few chairs.

John-John had the same big lips as his sister, but they looked much better on her. Other than that, there was nothing else really similar about the two. His nose was huge and flat and sat on top of his lips, making his face look smashed-in.

"So this must be the infamous Numbers? Good to meet you, bruh," he said with a big smile. "Here, light this up." He passed Numbers a rolled swisher.

"So what you think about the muscle maniacs?" John-John asked, bagging on Numbers's cousins. They did look like they were feeding on growth hormones. John-John and Numbers laughed, but M and M didn't. Numbers learned early on that the brothers didn't have much of a sense of humor.

Over the next couple of hours they bullshitted, smoked, drank, and laughed. Every so often, someone would knock on the front door to cop some smoke. They did have a steady flow of clients, Numbers noticed, but the product was subpar. He took a long toke and thought about the possibilities of coming up in this locale. *This could be a gold mine,* he thought. He quickly shook the idea from his cranium.

"So, what you think, Numbers?" Matt asked.

" 'Bout what?"

"About our little production?" Mel offered, as if he was reading Numbers's mind. "We run Park Place. Cats around here don't trip because they know we'll beat a nigger ass," Mel continued.

"I ain't got no problem busting a cap either!" Matt exclaimed.

John-John shook his head, agreeing with the brothers.

"Come on, cuz, you gotta have some connection to get some good herbs," Matt insisted.

"I ain't never dealt with that shit on no big level," Numbers lied. If they knew how deep in the game Numbers was once, they'd probably think they'd met the Messiah. He wasn't about to let them know. His main goal at present was to figure out his exit plan. The cousins' angle was revealed: they wanted to get connected.

For the next couple of months, Numbers hung out in the Park Place hood. He didn't try to get too familiar with anyone because southern boys didn't want city boys moving in on their territory. He didn't spend much time at Howie's pad—he didn't like the look and smell of it. Most of the time he went to John-John's house. John-John had a good head on his shoulders. With some schooling, he could be a good lieutenant if Numbers ever decided to get back in the game.

One evening Numbers rolled up to John-John's crib. No one was there except Wynter. He had since moved her rating up to a solid eight. She was looking hot in skin-tight jeans and a form-fitting red blouse.

"Where everybody at, Wynter?"

"Hold up, Numbers." She paused to listen. "I thought I heard the baby crying." She went to the back to check her daughter, who looked like her little twin in the crib, and came back. "I don't know where they at. I'm just glad they not here. Your cousins get on my last nerve," she huffed.

"Oh, word," Numbers replied. By now he was used to her complaining about M and M.

"And my brother's an asshole following after them. They gonna get him fucked up or something. You don't know your cousins, do you?" she asked. "Them dudes is straight fools. This guy who lived on Thirty-first and DeBree messed up their package and man . . ." She stopped.

"What?" Numbers was curious.

Wynter looked like she didn't want to say any more. "Well, this is the story I heard from them, and from all accounts, it's pretty much accurate. It's this one dude, Poppa, who lives on Thirty-first and DeBree, who owed them some money, like two hundred dollars. Poppa is a tough, hard nigger. He used to be a dealer 'round here and had the hood scared of him, but not your cousins. They'd asked Poppa many times to give them their trap, but he kept brushing them off. One thing about your cousins, they can't stand for nobody to play them like chumps." Her face showed repulsion as she continued with the story. "M and M caught up with him one day while he was walking his dog and pushing his son in the stroller by the train tracks. Mel held them at gunpoint—this is some crazy shit. Matt poured lighter fluid on all three of them and asked Poppa which one was worth his debt. Poppa didn't answer, he just stood there crying and trembling like a shaved lamb in the dead of winter, scared for his son's life, as Matt waved fire in front of them. They told Poppa they weren't heartless, so this was just a warning not to fuck with them and pay up. They gave him back his son." She paused and swallowed deeply. Numbers saw she wasn't finished yet. He waited.

"I don't know which one of them did it, 'cuz they both take credit for it, but they still set Poppa's dog on fire and burnt him alive."

A chill ran through his body. If what Wynter said was true, M and M were fucked up in the head.

First of Many

"My beautiful baby." Ms. Vasquez scooped R.C. up into her arms as soon as they came into the apartment, speaking to him in Spanish. She was determined to make sure her grandson knew the language of that half of his heritage, regardless of how little time she was able to spend with him. Numbers was cool with it; he wanted his son to be bilingual. He needed every advantage he could get in this crazy world.

"You've gotten so big! You're such a big boy," she continued, showering him with affection. R.C. giggled and laughed. "Don't be like your daddy," she jabbed, knowing that Numbers understood her.

"Mami, why you got to be like that?" Rosa spoke in English, which she knew irritated her mother. Ms. Vasquez ignored her daughter and kept playing with R.C.

"I love you too, Ms. Vasquez," Numbers said in Spanish. Ms. Vasquez cut her eyes at Numbers. She would never admit it, but she had grown fond of him because he treated her daughter so well.

"Baby, take the bags into my old room," Rosa said to Numbers, making sure her mother was watching as she kissed him on his lips. Ms. Vasquez frowned slightly. They were staying with her for the weekend. Numbers no longer had Crispy Carl's apartment, which he'd given to Jarvis. Ms. Vasquez was tolerable in small amounts. Her barbs didn't bother Numbers as much as they used to. He was just pleased she didn't treat R.C. the same way. When they touched down in BK, they went straight to his mother and spent most of the day there. She was overjoyed to see her only grandchild and to see that he had started walking.

The weekend dashed past, and it was already Monday. They needed to get back down low no later then 10 A.M. on Tuesday, since Rosa had a class to attend.

"Rose, com'ere and kiss Big Daddy," Numbers beckoned. Rosa came out of the back room in her silk pajamas. It was about a quarter to eight in the morning.

"Big Daddy? Where's Big Daddy at?" she joked lightheartedly, looking sexy as ever. Numbers watched her prance toward him. She was like fine wine, getting better with time. He couldn't wait to get her back home. He'd been able to sneak and bust a quick nut last night, but he couldn't go all out and give her the business, because Rosa was nervous about her mother hearing them. "Where you off to?" she asked.

"I gotta make that run. Stop asking a lot of questions," he teased, "and give me what I asked for." He tugged her to him gently but firmly and stuck his tongue down her throat. "I'll be back in a few hours, so have everything packed. We leaving as soon as I get here." He palmed her round rump and headed out the door.

Numbers jumped into the rental car and made a quick stop at the grocery store to purchase two big bags of coffee beans. Then he went to Mail Boxes Etc. and bought two boxes, plastic wrap, and packing tape. After getting all the supplies he needed, he took the Brooklyn Bridge to the FDR and drove uptown.

As Numbers drove he thought about what he was about to do. After nearly a year of being in Virginia and the constant badgering of his cousins, he'd agreed to get some product to distribute. His main purpose in coming north had been to visit his family, but while he was in the city, he could kill two birds with one stone. Maybe Jarvis was right: this was all he knew, and all he could do was hustle in the streets.

Getting off the 179th Street ramp, Numbers came back down to 170th Street to Sanchez's block. Although they had spoken a few times on the phone, Numbers hadn't seen Sanchez since the night Waketta was murdered. It would be good to see him. They had developed a great rapport. If they weren't in the type of business they were in, Numbers might call him friend.

Guadalupe opened the door when Numbers arrived. Numbers followed behind her fine ass carrying his bag of materials, wishing the hallway was longer so he could watch that phat rear end of hers bounce up and down some more. When he entered the living room, he saw Sanchez sitting on the sofa with another Hispanic dude. At the sight of Numbers, he popped up off the couch and greeted him with a hug and kiss on the cheek. Numbers was used to this type of greeting from Latinos.

"Numbers, my *compadre, mi amigo,* it's been too long, my man," he said in his heavy Spanish accent.

"Chez, you gaining weight, my dude?" Numbers tapped Sanchez's stomach with the back of his right hand.

"You know I love Lupe's rice and beans." He rubbed his belly and laughed heartily. "Come sit, smoke," he offered. "Numbers, this is *mi amigo* Manuel. Manuel has the best smoke in the city and the best prices." Manuel was round and looked like he was straight out the movie *Colors.* He was tatted up and down his arms and neck.

"Word, how much that exotic gonna run me?" Numbers asked Manuel.

"This higher. The other stuff lower price." Manuel spoke broken English in a Spanish accent even stronger than Sanchez's.

"Nah, they not ready for that where I'm at. What else you got?"

Manuel pulled out two small sacks of some other smoke for Numbers to sample. One was called hydro, and the marijuana was rainforest green. The other was what the streets of NYC called chocolate. It was a deep, rich, moist blend of brown weed. Both were more potent than what the down-south potheads were used to.

"Aiight, let me get three pounds of each. What can you do for me?"

Manuel mumbled to himself in Spanish as he calculated the numbers in his head. "For you, Papi . . . fifty-four."

That was a better price than Numbers expected. "Let's do it," he said.

Manuel left and came back within twenty minutes with the merchandise packaged in six individually wrapped bags. They made the exchange. Numbers double-wrapped the ganja with the packing tape and then lined the boxes with bubble wrap and poured coffee beans on the bottom. He placed the trees in the box, then covered them with more coffee beans. His load was ready for shipping now.

"Yo, Chez, where the post office at up here?"

"At a hundred sixty-fifth and Amsterdam, homie, but it's always a madhouse in there," Sanchez said, shaking his head.

"Then I may just wait to send it when I get back to BK." Numbers wanted to ship the stuff off today, so it would be in Virginia when he got back. "Listen, Chez, I'ma be out. Peace, Manuel." He embraced Chez and gave Manuel a pound, then exited the pad with his packages.

Numbers was nearing Fifty-seventh Street off the West Side Highway when 5-o's lights bounced off his rearview.

Damn. Feeling a slight tingle of dread cascade through his body, Numbers pulled over in the lane designated for traffic going to the pier. Two white cops got out of the squad car and approached the rented Pontiac Grand Am from both sides.

"Yes, Officer, how can I help you?" Numbers asked the one on the driver's side after rolling down his window.

"License and registration."

"Excuse me, what are you pulling me over for, officer?" He knew he hadn't committed any traffic violations. The other cop peered into the passenger window looking for a reason to have Numbers step out of the car. Numbers decided to forego any further questions and give the cops what they wanted. He didn't want them searching his ride. "Here you go. It's a rental." He passed the po-po his license and the car-rental agreement.

"Step out of the car," the cop directed.

"What for? I ain't done nothing. What y'all stop me for?"

"Exit the vehicle." This time the cop spoke more sternly.

"This is some bull!" But Numbers knew the routine.

"Can we check your car?" the other officer asked.

"Hell no!"

"Why? You got something to hide?" the flatfoot insinuated, while his pink partner continued investigating the car through the windows. The interior was empty other then a few packing materials in the backseat.

"Walk to the back of the car," the first cop ordered Numbers. His pink partner came around and watched Numbers, while the other officer popped the trunk.

"This is bogus. Y'all illegally searching my shit," Numbers said, agitated.

The pink flatfoot looked at his partner, smirking slightly before raising the trunk door. "You're acting like someone who's got something to hide. What you got back here?" His smirk turned to a frown as he raised the trunk hood and saw a lone pack of diapers. They had to let him go.

Numbers pulled off from the cops, happy he'd decided to ship the smoke while he was uptown. He believed that racial profiling was one of the main reasons young black men despised cops.

By the time Numbers got back to Norfolk, his batch was waiting for him. He bought little plastic pouches to distribute the smoke in ten- and twenty-dollar increments. Within two and a half weeks, they were nearly out of the potent smoke. His cousins wanted and needed more stock. The clientele did, too. The one trip to the city to score weed would be the first of many. Just like that, Numbers was back in the game.

After several trips up and down the highway, Numbers arranged to send Sanchez the money and have his boy ship it down. They were making two g's off of every pound, but it wasn't enough for all the heads that were involved. Numbers needed to bring in more bank, and as always, he had a plan to make it happen.

"I need to holla at y'all niggers for a minute," Numbers called out. Matt, Mel, and John-John were in the kitchen drinking and smoking, fucking around as usual, playing cards. Numbers was sitting in John-John's living room counting the paper. They were coming to the end of another load. Wynter was curled up on the couch, not far from him, looking like a kept woman. She no longer minded M and M being in her place as long as Numbers was present.

"What up, cuz?" Matt and Mel said, speaking almost simultaneously, as they often did. At times it was unnerving.

"I been doing some thinking, and it's time we step our game up to the next page."

A perplexed look came over the trio's mugs. As far as they were concerned, things couldn't get any better.

"What you got in mind, big homie?" John-John questioned.

"Heroin. Do you think we can move that shit out here?"

"Hell, yeah," Matt chimed.

"You ain't got to say that shit twice. Let's do it!" Mel agreed.

Numbers knew it wouldn't be hard to convince them. "There's one catch though: nobody gets paid off the next four shipments of smoke."

"Why?" M and M asked.

"Because we need every dime we can muster to cop the first brick. So y'all down or what?" It wasn't really a question.

They all agreed. He knew they wouldn't like that part of his plan, but if they wanted to make money, they had to make sacrifices.

Numbers made a call to Sanchez to let him know he would be coming up top to see him the following week. The first purchase he made was one brick at the cost of $40,000. The more he purchased, the lower the price went. A key of dope could fetch them anywhere from $100,000 to $150,000 on the streets. The challenge was getting the drugs from New York to Virginia. Numbers learned from Coney to only handle the product one time—when he picked it up from his supplier. After that, it would be moved by the mule.

That's where Wynter came in. He drove her and her daughter up with him in the middle of the night. He loved this part of the trip because she was always eager to give him head in the whip. She wasn't Rosa or Waketta, but she fit quite nicely in his stable. As soon as her daughter drifted to sleep in her car seat, Wynter was ready.

"She's asleep, Numby, you ready for me?" she asked seductively, smelling like fresh tropical fruit. She unstrapped herself from her seat belt and drew close to Numbers before taking another quick glance at her offspring sleeping snugly in the back.

"And you know it." Numbers started to rise in anticipation of her lollipop aptitude. The head she gave was savory and sensuous. She would suck on the dick all night long like it was a Willie Wonka jawbreaker. If Numbers wanted, she would put in work all the way to the Holland Tunnel. She unfastened his seat belt, then his belt, then his zipper. Numbers raised himself a little, so she could shimmy his Sean John pants down around his hips. By the time Wynter put her fingertips on his wood, it was petrified timber. She greeted the protruding Cyclops with a wet kiss.

"Hi, baby, I miss you." She spoke to it like it had a brain and personality of its own—and maybe it did—before wrapping her tongue and lips around its length; then she layered it with slobber until it was wet and slippery. Wynter had a talent for making the dick seem as though it melted in her mouth. To heighten the pleasure, she suckled, hummed, and moaned until Numbers thought he was going to lose his mind. The first time she sucked him off on the road, he almost veered into a ditch on the side of the highway. He hadn't expect it to be so good. Now, every time he was ready to cum, he pulled over on the shoulder. Better safe than sorry.

Wynter took pleasure in pleasing Numbers with her oral acrobatics because she'd never met anyone like him before. He had a way about him that made her want to do anything for him, including transport drugs across state lines with her baby. This was the fifth time she had made the trip with Numbers. The first time had been a mind-blowing experience she would never forget.

• • •

She loved the way Numbers moved. He was definitely a class act. On the initial run Numbers put her up at the W Hotel and took her and the baby shopping on Fifth Avenue. They hit the Chanel, Louie, Gucci, BCBG, and La Perla stores. For baby Wynter, who she called Winnie, Numbers hooked her up with Burberry, Ralph Lauren, Prada, and OshKosh B'Gosh. Wynter was far from a naïve little country chick. Her baby's daddy was serving time for selling drugs. She knew her position and why she was in the city with Numbers. But his generosity was above and beyond what was necessary to compensate her for her services. He wined her, dined her, and made her feel like a princess. Even after all the money he'd spent on Wynter and her baby, Numbers returned to the suite later that evening with matching sterling silver bracelets from Tiffany's for her and Winnie. Wynter was overwhelmed; she felt as though she was living a fairy tale that she never wanted to end.

"Numby, you know you didn't have to do this. I would have looked out for you for nothing. I mean it." Tears of gratitude formed in the corners of her eyes.

Numbers was pleased by her reaction. He wasn't particularly moved because of the tears, but he could see the truth in her eyes. That's why he wanted to reward her for being a down-ass broad. Although he knew he would never let her get as close to him as Rosa was or Waketta had been, he wanted to show her he appreciated her. "I'm glad you like it."

"Like it? I love it!" She beamed, picking up the baby. "Don't you love it, Winnie? Yes, I know you do, my beautiful little mommy," she cooed.

"Wynter," he said, "make yourself comfortable, order whatever you need from room service. Here's some cash." He put five hundred dollars on the coffee table. "I'll be back in a little while. I gotta make a run."

Numbers made his move to Washington Heights and was back

at the hotel in less than two hours. He needed to drive back down in the morning and wanted to make sure he got enough rest; he had a long day ahead of him.

When he returned, Wynter was getting Winnie ready for bed. She took the little one to the living room of the suite and pulled out the sofa bed, placing her in the middle of a barricade of pillows. Baby Winnie was fast on her way to sleep. The Benadryl Wynter gave her would guarantee she would sleep like the baby she was throughout the night, leaving the adults to their own devices, undisturbed.

"Numby, keep an eye out for Winnie for a minute while I take a shower. She won't be waking up no time soon, but just in case."

Before Wynter had gathered her things and headed into the bathroom to shower, Numbers stopped her. "Hold up. First help me with this." He pulled a rectangular block of high-grade heroin out of a Louis Vuitton shopping bag. "Get me the diapers from the baby's bag." He methodically divided the block into three smaller rectangles, about three inches wide, and rewrapped them in plastic. "Take one of the diapers out and open it." Wynter extended a Pampers, and Numbers placed one of the rewrapped pieces inside it. After all of the drugs were put away in the diapers, Numbers instructed her, "Make sure you use the diapers from the right package, or we gonna have a problem, you dig?" Wynter nodded.

After helping him conceal the drugs and taking her shower, Wynter came sashaying out of the bathroom with nothing on but a pair of orange La Perla boy shorts, her bare petite boobs glistening with moisture. "Are you ready for me, baby?"

Numbers watched her sexy ass as she made her way over to the bed. He was throbbing with anticipation because Wynter's pussy always stayed moist, like a sponge dipped in warm K-Y jelly. She climbed onto the king-sized bed, stood over him, and began dancing to music that was only playing in her head. She gyrated and swayed like a seasoned stripper. Numbers grew to even greater heights, stretching the front of his boxers.

"That's it, work that ass, you fine bitch," Numbers encouraged.

And she did. Slowly and seductively she slid out of the expensive bottoms. Once she was butt-naked, Numbers could see the moisture dripping from her slit. Dancing her way down to her knees, she removed his boxers. Without further ado, she began to swallow it. She took it further and further until it made her gag. Numbers moaned with pleasure; he could stay that way all night, but Wynter had other plans. As much as she loved sucking him off, she loved riding him even more. If he still had the energy, she would swallow his anaconda again after she got hers.

Before mounting, she opened the Magnum condom that was lying on the nightstand, rolled it on, then rode him like the mechanical bull in that movie *Urban Cowboy.* Her sweet spot sloshed and squirted all over his balls. Numbers grabbed her by the waist and extended himself up into her until she exploded in ecstasy.

Numbers's sperm could no longer be contained. It was time to pull over to the side of the road or risk becoming acquainted with the ditch. He had to admit this was the best part of his trip, other than the money he stood to make. And Wynter couldn't wait to get to whatever lavish hotel they would be staying at this time so they could finish getting and giving each other what they deserved.

The next morning, Numbers took Wynter and Winnie to Penn Station and put them on the express Amtrak train to Norfolk. No one would ever suspect a beautiful mother and her gorgeous toddler would be carrying enough drugs to amass a small fortune. Her instructions from him were the same as they were the first time she made the trip and every time afterward. *Keep the diaper bag in your possession at all times.*

•   •   •

Numbers set up a safe house outside of the hood in a ranch house on the outskirts of Norfolk. The property sat on five acres of land. It was perfect for a stash house because it was away from prying eyes and ears. The closest neighbor was a quarter of a mile or more in any direction. All the drugs were brought there first to be packaged for distribution. The money was then brought back there and placed in the safe. Unbeknownst to the rest of the crew, Numbers would move most the loot off the premises immediately. If the stash house got hit, he rationalized, they'd get drugs or the cash, but not both.

By packaging the heroin in emptied-out vitamin capsules, Numbers created his own brand. Matt, Mel, John-John, and Numbers sat at a big wooden dining table inside the safe house filling the empty capsules with *death*. Neither the Norfolk dealers nor the police were ready for the way Numbers was putting his thing down. They had Park Place on lockdown.

For the first year or so, business moved like clockwork. The crew Numbers put together, with the help of his cousins, was bringing in a significant tally of cash, and managed to stay under the radar while doing it. M and M made a few more contacts outside of Park Place and were now supplying the hood known as Norview as well. But the brothers weren't content with the money that was pouring in like an open fire hydrant on a sweltering summer day in Brooklyn. They wanted more. They wanted to control all of Norfolk and possibly Suffolk, too.

Numbers followed a lot of what he learned from Coney, minus the greed. He made sure to share the profits with his soldiers generously. M and M didn't agree with him about this; they reminded Numbers of Jarvis when the money started rolling in. The more paper the brothers made, the more they wanted.

Their incessant greed and bullying style generated enemies in more than a few neighborhoods. When local dealers had beef with Matt and Mel it was quickly squashed, and the brothers' reputation for destruction grew equally as fast. Most of the drug peddlers became clients by either fear or default—fear that they would be crushed by the psychopathic brothers; default because there was no one else to get grade-A product from at the cheap price they were moving it at. One of the only hustlers who didn't concede to their threats and demands was a cat from up top who went by the name Cashmere. Cash, as he was called, wasn't the type to let another person call shots on his moves.

Numbers was against the take-over-the-world attitude and warned them time and time again to slow their roll.

The temperature had fallen dramatically by November. Numbers felt the stiff evening chill as he went to put out the garbage for the Monday-morning pickup. When he came back into the house, Rosa was on the phone. Whoever was on the other end of the line had ticked her off.

"It's for you," Rosa snapped, holding out the receiver to Numbers.

He took the phone. "Yeah? . . . Yo! Why you calling my crib? . . . How you get this number? . . . You know not to call my crib. It's Sunday. That's why my cell is off," Numbers barked into the receiver. Everyone in the crew knew Numbers took Sundays off. It was his designated day to spend quality time with his family—no business, no exceptions. But that was about to change.

"Go see him for what? . . . What the fuck? Those niggers are hardheaded as shit. Aiight. Where they at? . . . Next time I could give less than a damn; don't be calling the crib, duke." He hung up abruptly.

Rosa stood nearby, staring in Numbers's mouth so hard she could see his larynx working. "What the hell was that all about, Dupree?" she asked with a tinge of jealousy.

"Nothing but business," Numbers replied, avoiding her eyes.

"What business does some chick have calling my house on

Sunday? Don't they know the rules? So what's really good, Dupree? Why is she calling our house?"

"Nothing. I mean, it's something going on, but not with her. That was Wynter."

"I know who it was, but what is she doing calling here, and why does she have our home number?"

"She told me I needed to go see her brother John-John; something 'bout my cousins bugging out again. They at the ranch house." Rosa knew all about the ranch house. She'd used her real estate license to buy the property. Along with the Colonial house they lived in, the ranch house was set up under a dummy corporation.

"So you going out, too?" Already knowing the answer to her question, Rosa got even more peeved.

"Come on, Rosa, stop acting like that."

"Keep thinking I'm stupid, Dupree," Rosa warned. Her arms were crossed and she was standing in the foyer with a don't-play-yourself look on her face. Her Latino fire made her complexion look almost cherry red. Rosa knew Numbers wasn't a saint, and Numbers knew she knew.

"Baby, I'll be right back. I'll make it up to you, I promise." He moved in and pecked her on the lips. Her lips were pursed tight; there would be no reciprocation of his affection.

He doused his lights as he pulled up into the driveway of the ranch house. Walking in through the kitchen, he could hear Matt or Mel talking loudly from the front room.

"Mane, that nigger almost shit his draws."

Laughter.

"You had that city nigger butt-naked. Ain't no way he could shit his draws."

More laughter.

John-John sat at the head of the dining room table, across from the brothers; he was unamused by their antics. Tidbit, a muscled five-foot-five grimy-ass southern nigger from Richmond, sat at the other end of the table, closest to the brothers, laughing right along with them. The brothers had recruited him straight out of prison, where he'd been doing a short bid.

"Mane, you see how that fool ran when I popped that hot lead up in his azz cheek?" Tidbit's voice was deep and low. "That mark looked like a cartoon character trying to hop his azz down that block." Tidbit got up to mimic the way their latest victim was running. The brothers were grabbing their stomachs laughing. John-John shook his head in disagreement and took a gulp from a bottle of Southern Comfort, hoping it could give him just that.

"Yo, what the deal?" Numbers entered the room amidst the hysterical exchange.

"Ain't nothin', cuz," Matt said, trying to contain his laughter.

"We had to send one of your city boys scurrying back up north," Mel added arrogantly.

"Yo, what they talking 'bout?" Numbers turned his attention to John-John.

"Mane," John-John said, looking to Numbers, "they done went over to Huntersville and abducted that Harlem boy, Cash or Cashmere, whatever they call 'im. Lumped 'im up, stripped 'im down to his balls and his socks, and then shot 'im in the ass."

"Did they dead 'im?"

"Nah, cuz," Matt and Mel replied. "He ain't that lucky." The brothers, along with Tidbit, burst out into uncontrollable laughter again. Numbers didn't smile.

"Why the fuck y'all go over there fucking with duke? Didn't I ask y'all to leave well enough alone? Y'all some hardheaded, ass-dumb niggers. Now, what if him or his boys come back at us? We supposed to be out here trying to make money. We don't have time for any unnecessary-ass bullshit. What if they go running off at the trap? These bitch-ass niggers out here are already snitching a mile a minute for nothing, and you two mu'fuckaz go and give 'em a reason. That's the type of shit that can put us at risk of losing everything." Numbers was spitting venom. He was tired of his cousins constantly doing dumb shit.

M and M may have been wild dogs to everyone else, but they knew that shit didn't fly with Numbers. They'd seen him put it on some big country nigger who got out of line at one of the local bars, and they knew he was nobody's slouch.

Tidbit sat quiet, like a puppy.

"Yo, cuz, cuz, chill out." Mel had stopped laughing after hearing the urgency in his cousin's voice.

Matt tried to downplay the situation. "That mark don't want it with us. It's cool, Numbers, man. I know them niggers over in Huntersville. They ain't rolling with dude. They don't give a damn about no Harlem."

"Plus, we told 'em we'd hit 'em off with higher-grade shit for a better price," Mel chimed in.

"Y'all gotta be smarter than that, or all our asses gonna be under the jail." Numbers sounded more at ease now. "That's it. Y'all hear me? Y'all got the nigger Cash out the way, so no more of that cowboy shit. If y'all pull another bullshit stunt like this, y'all gonna have to find your own connect. Think I'm bullshitting if you want to."

Matt and Mel sobered up real quick. "You got it, cuz," they answered.

"You better hope there's no repercussions from this shit!"

And there were none. The niggers in Huntersville didn't want trouble with the two loony brothers and their vicious pint-sized goon, Tidbit. Over the following twelve months Numbers's clientele grew 200 percent. By the end of the year his crew boasted trade in Park Place, Norview, Huntersville, and the Hole, among other places.

"Are my two favorite men hungry?" Rosa asked as she walked into the living room. R.C. was sitting on the floor in front of the forty-six-inch projection TV playing Mario Brothers on Nintendo. Numbers was on the sofa behind him coaching him.

"Yeah, baby, what you got in mind?"

"I was thinking spaghetti or—"

"Spaghetti," R.C. interrupted.

"Spaghetti it is," Numbers agreed. "Watch out, R.C. Watch out, you about to lose your man. Jump! Jump!" Numbers called to his son.

"Ooh, Daddy, you saw that?" R.C. was pressing buttons frantically, never taking his eyes off the screen.

"Yeah, I saw it, little man. That was cool." Numbers's cell phone rang. He recognized the number immediately—Sanchez. "¿Que pasa, mi amigo?" Numbers greeted him.

"My brother Numbers, I have some news for you I'm sure you be interested in," Sanchez said. "I just got word that your boy Coney was shot."

"What the fuck? Is he dead?"

"That's all the info I have. I'll give you a call back if I find out anything more. Okay." Never one to have long phone conversations, Sanchez hung up.

Numbers hadn't been in contact with Coney since coming down to Norfolk over four years ago. He'd heard many stories of Coney's antics, but that was it. On one of his visits back to New York, Numbers heard that the feds had got a whiff of Coney. One of Coney's soldiers, feeling less than appreciated, was snitching to the man. They had been trying to shut him down for years, but Coney always seemed to escape their clutches. If they had someone to finger Coney, he would be in jeopardy of losing everything. At the time, Numbers brushed the stories off his shoulders. He thought Coney was too smart to get caught up like that, but it did get him to thinking about his own situation. Numbers initially said he would only sell drugs for six months, and here it was almost ten years going on forever!

Hearing the news of niggers attempting to dead Coney, Numbers decided to try to get a read on what was going on. He promptly made a call up top to get in touch with Jarvis.

"Yo, Jar, what happened with Coney? I hear they tried to end his ass?"

"Yeah, shit is kinda crazy. Ya boy Coney took three, but he survived." Jarvis said, sounding like he enjoyed telling of Coney's near-death experience. "You know how he be flossing, right? So, the nigger shooting dice over in Little Harlem screaming at niggers, 'cuz he breaking them. He talking down to niggers like he do. I could tell dudes in the cipher were tired of his shit. Anyway, Coney running off at the trap as usual, when some little cats wearing hoodies and masks rolled up. One had a twenty-two rifle, and his boy had some other joint. They just started letting it off on his ass. Whoever the fools were, they were scared rabbit-ass niggers. If it was me, man, I woulda walked right up on his bitch ass and flat-blasted him. Them chumps was shooting and backing up. They hit 'im and all, but now that nigger think he more invincible than ever. Fucking amateurs," Jarvis finished, sounding peeved that they hadn't killed Coney.

"That's bananas," Numbers said, but he really wanted to ask Jarvis how he could be so cold.

"Nah, Numbers, that ain't all." Jarvis paused, seeming to take pleasure in making Numbers wait.

"What, Jar?"

After getting the reaction he wanted, Jarvis continued, "To add insult to injury, while Coney was in the hospital recovering, the alphabet boys swooped down on his shystie ass and arrested him for drug trafficking, money laundering, and attempted murder. His shit is fucked all around." Jarvis giggled.

Coney's empire was falling apart. Numbers remembered what Coney had told him when he first started hustling for him: *There is no longevity in this game. You got to make your score and move on.* Coney had warned that if the jealous fools on the streets or in your own camp didn't get you, the government would. A fool would rat out his momma to save his own neck, he lamented. Numbers thought to himself, *I guess a little bit of both got to Coney. He should have taken his own advice.* Numbers wondered how he would avoid the same thing happening to him.

Rosa fixed her plate and sat at the dinner table with her men. She looked at Numbers and knew something was troubling him.

After being his friend and girlfriend for nineteen years, she knew his moods like the back of her well-manicured hands. "*¿Que pasa, Papi?*" she asked.

R.C. looked at his father.

Numbers twirled his angel-hair pasta around for a moment. "It's time to move from this," he said deliberately. "I've had enough. It's too much."

R.C. didn't know what his father was speaking about and went back to eating his dinner. But Rosa was pleased to hear him come to this conclusion. "Baby, you know I got your back whatever you decide, and just so that you know, I think it's time, too. So what are you gonna do about your cousins? You know they're not trying to hear nothing about you quitting."

Rosa ain't never lied, Numbers thought. They would protest vehemently if Numbers attempted to stop their money train. "Yeah, I know."

"So what do we do?" Rosa asked.

"I'll think of something," Numbers said, now digging into his turkey spaghetti. He ate quietly for the rest of his meal, contemplating his out.

After dinner R.C. headed back to the living room while Numbers, still quiet, helped Rosa load up the dishwasher.

"I know what I'm gonna do," Numbers broke his silence. "I'm going to triple my re-up for one last run—getting thirty kilos instead of ten. I can't trust Matt and Mel to meet with Sanchez." He didn't want them to do something stupid and burn a bridge. He knew anything was possible fucking with them knuckleheads. They could blank out and try to rob Sanchez, and that would bring heat Numbers couldn't stand. "Once we get back here, we should be able to move the first ten to fifteen bricks in a week, give or take. Once I get the money from the first ten or so, I'll hit them with the next fifteen keys and we can be out. I'm gonna need for you to go to Charlotte like we discussed, Rosa."

Rosa was beaming as he discussed their plans. She'd wanted Numbers to stop dealing years ago but knew it wasn't feasible at the time. Now was different. She'd obtained her bachelor's degree in business and a real estate license. They could sell the sprawling four-bedroom, three-bath with two-car garage colonial-style home sitting on three acres for a good profit.

"Baby, I need to do something different. I just don't know what. I will be thirty in a year. And little man's getting older. He not gonna be able to take me to school for career day. What he gonna say when they ask him what his daddy do?"

"You'll figure it out, Dupree. We'll figure it out together, honey." She wrapped her arms around his waist. Her eyes met his and radiated pure love.

The last few years had been very prosperous for him and the crew. Numbers owned a couple of properties in Virginia Beach and had more cars than he could drive. He'd purchased his mother a brownstone on the good side of Fort Greene. He'd paid for his sisters' college tuition. His lady had a bachelor's degree and was a successful real estate agent. He had to admit, his life was good.

If everything went as he diagrammed, the dope would fetch over $5 million on the streets. Numbers could walk away with a little over $1.5 mil plus what he already had stashed. His cousins and the crew would be straight as well. In order for his plan to work, everyone would have to play his position. Even though he wanted to tell his cousins he was done, he thought it best that he didn't. Crispy Carl had told Numbers to never let his left hand know what his right hand was doing. Numbers took that one step further; he didn't let his index finger know what his thumb was up to. That way, no one could put him in a cross. In two weeks, Numbers would be out of the game for good.

When Numbers touched down in Brooklyn, his first stop was to go visit his mother. He pulled up to a store a couple of blocks from her house on DeKalb and Clermont to buy her a ginger ale. As he was leaving the store he was halted by a familiar voice calling his name.

He couldn't believe his eyes when he tried to match the face to the voice. "Broz?" His once overweight friend was now slimmer than him. The rumors of him being strung out on drugs must be true. Numbers hadn't seen Broz in some time, and the years hadn't been kind to his childhood running partner.

"Yo, Numbers, my man, I see you doing big things . . . livin' lovely, huh?" Broz muttered. He was noticeably high, looking from Numbers to his brand-new '03 BMW 745 .

"What up with you, Broz? How you lose all that weight?" Numbers already knew the answer but wanted to hear what Broz had to say for himself.

"Ah, man, Numbers, I was crazy sick, lost mad weight, but I'm back now," he lied. "You know your partner Coney is back on the streets? The feds had 'im and let 'im loose. Word on the streets is he gave someone up to get out." Broz paused to see how Numbers would react.

Numbers was surprised to hear that Coney was back on the streets, but he appeared unfazed. "Is that right?"

Broz continued, "Numbers, man, you better watch yourself. Word is you the one he gave up!" Now Broz had gotten Numbers's attention. Hearing his name in Coney's mix after all these years was even more unexpected. If Coney was out on the streets, he definitely had to give someone up. But Coney didn't know anything about his operation, so how could he rat him out? Broz could tell he'd struck a nerve.

"Dude, I'm glad I ran into you. I miss you and the crew. Man, we need to get back together and get money," Broz said, starting to drift into a tangent that was as delusional as it was hopeful.

"I hear you, Broz," Numbers said, not wanting to tell him that would never happen.

"Yo! Numbers, my man, I'm a little light. Can you hit ya peoples off with a little something?" Broz asked.

Numbers peeled off a few hundred bucks and cuffed it into Broz's hand as he gave him dap. "Take care of yourself, Broz. I'll see you soon." Both old friends knew that wasn't going to happen.

Numbers walked into his mother's house. It was hard to tell this family was once dirt-poor. He flopped onto the oversized plush couch and stared off into space as he usually did when he was strategizing. If Coney was trying to set him up, he would try to get in touch with him. Numbers would have to think two moves ahead of him.

His mother entered the foyer. "Dee, is that you?" she called out.

"Yes, Ma, just in here relaxing."

"Did you get my ginger ale?"

"Yeah, it's right here. I'll bring it to you." He rose from the couch and bounced to the kitchen, where his mother was putting ice in a glass. Numbers walked over and hugged and kissed his mother. He unscrewed the soda and passed it to her.

"There's some food in the oven if you're hungry," she said.

"Where's Ta-Ta and La-La?"

"Ta-Ta's out with that boy she dating, and La-La's upstairs in her room. Leave them girls alone, you not their daddy," she ordered.

"Nah, Ma. I was just wondering where they were."

"Who asking for me?" La-La bellowed, walking into the kitchen, picking up her mother's soda and drinking it while Jenny was filling the ice tray with water and putting it back.

"Get your nasty mouth off my glass, I don't know where them lips been," Jenny snapped playfully.

"Hey, big brother, I like the new car you got Mommy. What you gonna do with that old one?"

"I don't know. Give it to charity or something," Numbers answered her, his mind elsewhere. Numbers turned to walk back to the living room.

"Oh, Du, I ran into Gorilla Man. He asked about you. He gave me his number to give to you," Lakeisha reached in her back pocket, pulled out a piece of paper, and handed it to her big brother.

There it was: Coney was trying to set him up. *How did he know I was in town?* Numbers wondered. Coney wouldn't deter his plans. Numbers knew he had to be ready for anything. He called up his connect and set up the buy for the next evening. He called his cousins and had them get on point. Then he called up Coney to see what his angle was.

At the beginning of the conversation Coney was the same old Coney, boisterous and arrogant. He went into this whole big speech about how some coward-ass niggers tried to murk him and the alphabets tried to trap him off, but they had nothing on him. Then the conversation turned as Numbers expected.

"Numbers, my man, you know I put you in this game. Now I need you to return the favor."

Numbers knew where this was going and quickly interjected, "Coney, that ain't been my game for years!"

Coney became agitated. "Don't try to play me, duke! I need ya help, this is me you talking to!"

"Aiight, Coney, what you need?" Numbers asked.

"I need for you to spot me a key so I can get straight."

Numbers knew exactly what Coney wanted: a kilo of cocaine. He stopped him before he could go any further. "I got you, Coney. Tomorrow night, meet me under the El at eight-thirty and I'll bring you the key." Numbers hung up before Coney could get another word in.

Numbers was stuck. His mind reeled, but he could not get a single, solitary thought to make sense. He knew Coney was most likely trying to set him up either by robbing him or selling him to the feds—mostly likely it was the latter. Numbers was sure Coney saw him as the scapegoat, at least that's what he was betting on. If he was wrong, he could very well end up dead. Nevertheless, he was going to meet with Coney and give him what he asked for. He had to; it was the only way to get rid of him once and for all.

"I know that look, Numbers." Jenny walked into the front room seeing her son staring into nothingness, in a daze. She knew he was figuring out a problem. "Anything I can help you with, baby?" she asked. "Dee, it's time you leave all that mess alone." Numbers snapped out of his trance and looked at his mother. Jenny knew what her son had been doing off and on over the years, but she trusted him to make the right decisions for his life. She rarely, if ever, interfered, because she knew her son possessed book and street smarts and, most of all, above-average common sense. "If it's troubling you that much, maybe you should leave it alone. We'll be fine, baby, you made sure of that. It's time to move on and do something else now. Something that won't have you feeling so down and looking so lost." She bent down and kissed him on the top of his head. "I love you, son. You're a good man."

His mother's words rushed over him like a full-body massage and confirmed it was that time. His course of action was clear. He would close this chapter in his life, win, lose, or draw. "Thank you, Mommy. I love you too." He stood up and gave her a long hug.

Before she could turn and leave the room, he said, "Oh yeah. I'ma take the old car and get rid of it."

"Okay, just don't mess with my Infiniti, ya momma's balling," she laughed.

Numbers picked up the phone and called Jarvis to rework his plans.

Everything was set in motion. Matt and Mel were meeting up with Jarvis at 9 P.M. to take care of business with the drug connect. Numbers was heading to his rendezvous with Coney at eight-thirty. The meeting was set on Park Avenue, under the El of the Brooklyn-Queens Expressway. Even though there was constant traffic flowing east to west on Park Avenue, under the El where the cars were parked was relatively dark. Numbers arrived fifteen minutes early in his mom's old sedan.

Numbers listened to Hot 97 on the radio as he waited more than thirty minutes. He looked at his watch. It was now 8:47 P.M.; his cousins would be meeting up with Jarvis in a few to head uptown. Numbers planned on having his cousin pick up only fifteen birds. He didn't really trust them with all that he had planned to get, plus it was his cousin's first meet with his supplier. Once he enlisted Jarvis to assist him, he went with his original plan to cop thirty bricks. Numbers did have some reservations about putting all his eggs in one basket. He felt uncomfortable letting his cousins make the buy, but knowing Jarvis was handling it eased his mind somewhat.

Coney finally showed up, looking nowhere near as fly as he used to dress, glancing around cautiously. Numbers was leaning up against the car, surveying the area, hoping it wasn't a robbery attempt. He didn't see anything or anyone suspicious.

" 'Sup, my brother? You the top dog now," Coney said as he approached, sarcasm dripping from his voice.

"What the deal, Coney?" Numbers replied somberly.

"You know how it is, Numbers. They got a brother on foot," Coney said, alluding to the fact that he no longer owned a car. The authorities had confiscated everything. "So, Numbers, you moving big weight down low I hear? You should set me up down there, little man."

"That's not my bag, Coney. I'm strictly party promoting and real estate," Numbers insisted.

Coney pressed Numbers further. "So what you pushing, O.T.—"

"Come on, C," Numbers cut him off. "You want the key I got for you, or what? I gotta make moves."

"Yeah, boy, that's what I'm talking 'bout." Coney smiled, rubbing his hands together.

"Aiight, Coney, here's the key to the ride. Everything you need is in the glove compartment," Numbers said, dangling the car key for Coney.

Coney looked confused. "You giving me the car?" he asked.

"No doubt. I thought after all you've done for me, it's the least I could do," Numbers said before trying to turn and walk away.

Coney reached out his hand to give him a pound and pulled

Numbers close for an embrace, the kind of embrace one family member would give another if he thought he was never going to see that person again. Coney whispered, "This is a dirty game. I told you before, young buck."

Was this it? Was Coney going to try and rob him himself? Or was someone about to run up and jack him? Within moments, lights flashed, sirens shrieked, and car tires screeched from all directions. When Numbers looked up, they were surrounded by uniformed and plainclothes officers. Twenty to thirty men from various alphabet agencies, police, and other authorities drew down on them. It was a well-choreographed sting. Cars blocked off the streets—it was a gauntlet of police and task-force personnel. Numbers put his hands up in the air slowly and stood motionless as infrared beams dotted his torso.

Task-force agents swarmed, instructing Numbers and Coney to get on their knees. They complied. Numbers was clearly shaken. His previous run-ins with the law were nothing of this magnitude. They gave Coney the same treatment, even though Numbers knew Coney was their snitch. Coney was a criminal first.

At 8:55, Matt and Mel pulled up on the corner of Jay Street and Willoughby, right near the A-train station. Jarvis was at the corner waiting for them. He had gained considerable weight and was now stocky and solid. His head now looked more like a moose head than a horse's head. He was wearing all black—black leather, black Levi 501s, Black Timbs, and a pair of black biker gloves. He opened the door of the forest-green Range Rover, jumped into the backseat, and greeted the brothers. They drove north on Jay Street, heading toward the Brooklyn Bridge. The cousins had met Jarvis a couple of times when he had come to visit in Virginia. They knew Numbers had trusted him like a brother, even though

Numbers had never let on to Jarvis the full extent of his drug trade until now.

"Jar, what's cracking? You got any of that good ganja?" Mel asked.

"You know that," Jarvis said, pulling out a ready-rolled Back-wood.

"That's what popping, homie." Matt was pleased to get some of that exotic smoke from New York. Matt was driving the truck. "Which way we going?"

"Just keep driving this way; you'll see the signs to the Brooklyn Bridge. We gonna cut across Manhattan and go to the West Side Highway uptown," Jarvis directed. This was the brothers' first time in the city, and they had no knowledge of how to maneuver around the five boroughs.

"This cat T.I. is killing ya New York rappers." "Rubberband Man" banged through the car woofers. Matt mimicked the vocals and Mel chanted along.

"Yeah, but they still can't fuck with Jay-Z." Jarvis wasn't about to let these country boys talk bad about New York rappers without him putting his say in. They listened and debated the state of hip-hop all the way up the West Side Highway.

"Yo, Matt! We getting off the next exit," Jarvis instructed.

Matt veered to the right and onto the 125th Street exit ramp. They came to the stop sign and made a quick right, then a left onto Twelfth Avenue, heading farther uptown.

"Which one of you going in to get the shit with me?" Jarvis asked the brothers.

"I'ma roll with you," Mel answered.

"You got a piece, right?"

"For sure," Mel replied assuredly.

"Where the money at? Is it all counted and ready? 'Cuz I want to be in and out of that joint, you feel me?" Jarvis explained.

"The money right under your seat, nine hundred big ones," Matt said, feeling the intensity building as they got closer to the meet.

They rode under Riverside Drive on Twelfth Avenue past 130th. The area was dimly lit. The bus depot and warehouses lined the blocks on either sides.

"Yo, Matt, pull over here, my dude. I gotta take a leak. I always get a little nervous when I do these big money exchanges," Jarvis said, pointing to a dark area.

Matt pulled over on 134th Street near the structure that held up the highway. The system was bumping 50 Cent's "Many Men (Wish Death)."

Numbers sat in the back of an unmarked police vehicle, watching the authorities rip through the car. The car seats had been ripped out, and all the contents of the trunk were on the street. They had been scavenging through the car for the last thirty minutes, looking for their booty, to no avail. There was nothing to be found. No drugs. No guns. Nothing but the title and registration to the car. Coney looked at Numbers from the backseat of another unmarked vehicle, baffled. Numbers stayed motionless and stoic.

A host of agents stood near the car, including Detectives Lockhart and O'Doul. Numbers hadn't seen them since Waketta was murdered. They were speaking to a white DEA agent. Numbers couldn't hear what they were saying, but it was evident they weren't pleased. The DEA agent had his hands on his waist, shaking his head in disappointment. He paced back and forth for a moment in disgust. After an hour of searching the car and coming up with nothing, he finally gave the signal for everyone to wrap it up.

Numbers was transported downtown to central booking to be questioned.

Anything's Possible

The interrogation was wearing Numbers down. They kept moving him from the holding cell and back to the interrogation room every four hours or so. They'd now had him for thirty-nine hours, with no sign of him being cut loose. He managed to get a couple of winks in the holding pen, but every time he got comfortable they brought him back to the mirrored room. He rested his head in his arms on the steel table, secretly praying that this would be over soon.

Agent Flask entered the room with Agent Smith trailing him, holding a recording machine in his hand, looking more confident. They'd apparently had time to go home and rest and change up their wardrobe. Numbers would've paid a small fortune for a good meal, a shower, and fresh gear.

"Dupree, this is your last chance. Come clean and you may walk out of here before you're sixty," Agent Flask said.

Agent Smith placed the device on the table and plugged it in to the wall socket. He pressed Play.

Numbers listened to the taped conversation he and Coney had a day and a half earlier. Just as he suspected, there was nothing there to incriminate him. The authorities were grasping at straws. Even the wiretap from their meet revealed nothing.

"It's all right here, as clear as day," Agent Flask said, pointing at the machine. "You don't have to confess to being a drug kingpin. We got all the evidence we need. You and Nathan 'Coney' Patterson are finished." This was the first time Numbers had ever heard Coney's government name.

"Agent Helen Keller, I got no idea what you talking 'bout." Numbers rebutted Agent Flask's claim with disrespect, fueling the agents' contempt. "Y'all ain't see me do or say nothing illegal. I gave that faggot exactly what he asked for—a key. My mother will vouch that it was her car, and she gave me permission to get rid of it."

Agent Flask was hot. Partly because he knew Numbers was right and partly because of his slick lip. Flask knew Numbers was precise in his evaluation, but he continued to press, trying to make a case against him, hoping Numbers would slip up. He'd expended too many man-hours on Coney's information; somebody was going to fry. He had his sights set on Numbers's ruin.

They harassed and interrogated Numbers for almost sixty hours before he was given his one phone call. He immediately called Joshua Spitz, Coney's former lawyer. Coney could no longer afford him, but Numbers had put him on his payroll. Numbers was released a few hours after Spitz was called, with no charges levied against him. Coney, on the other hand, was stick-a-fork-

in-'im done. Numbers exited the court building welcoming freedom like a slave completing his trek through the Underground
Railroad. He had no money and no phone. He'd left his cell phone
at his mother's house. He didn't want Jake going through his contacts. That would have surely spelled trouble. They'd taken the
measly one hundred bucks he had in his pocket as evidence. The
beast would most likely have breakfast on him with that. Spitz offered him cab money, but he opted to walk home. He strolled
from downtown Brooklyn toward his mother's house. On a good
day, it would take anywhere from twenty minutes to half an hour.
Today was a good day. Numbers was free. There were a few clouds
in the sky, but it could have rained, sleeted, or snowed and Numbers would have thought it was a beautiful morning. He couldn't
wait to get to his mother's place and freshen up. He smelled like
he looked—three days old.

Numbers walked across DeKalb Avenue past Fort Greene Park
and was coming up on Carlton Avenue, barely five minutes from
his mother's brownstone, when he saw a young lady who made
him do a double take. *It couldn't be!* The girl he had his eyes glued
to looked exactly like Waketta. He continued walking toward her
as she strode effortlessly down the uneven sidewalk, seeming to
manipulate gravity's pull. Numbers kept thinking he would wake
up any moment.

"Hey, Numbers," the beautiful buxom brown honey said, smiling at him. "Long time no see. I been meaning to get at you. I got
something that I been holding for you for years." Then, as if she
just really noticed how he was dressed, "Damn, boy, you look like
you been through some shit. You all right?"

Numbers paused for a long moment, still taken aback by how
much this gorgeous young lady looked like her older sister,
Waketta. Lateesha had grown up.

"Yeah, I'm good. Nothing a shower can't handle." Numbers
embraced her like a long-lost love, all the time wishing when he

let her go that it would be Waketta, but it wasn't. She smelled like fruit, flowers, and happiness, the way all women should smell. It was a fragrance Numbers was used to his women having.

"I miss you, too," she said, as if reading his mind, slowly letting him out of her arms. She was nearly the same height as Waketta was, with the same enticing pretty browns and luscious ruby lips. She was a real stunner. "How long you in town?" she asked.

"Not long."

"Too bad. I thought we could get together and catch up."

Numbers could tell she was flirting with him. He wanted to say yes but knew he had too much to do and too much at stake.

"Maybe another time, Teesha. I gotta head back down low." He wanted to kick himself for declining.

"No problem, but listen, before you leave, come by the hood. I got something I need to give you. Promise me you will?" She wasn't going to take no for an answer. She stood there waiting for him to say the magic words.

He smiled slightly at her bossiness. It reminded him of her sister. "I promise."

"Here, take my math and call me when you're on your way, aiight?"

"Will do."

Numbers went to his mother's house, showered, ate, and slept well for the first time in over two and half days. When he awoke six hours later in the middle of the day, he called Rosa and let her know he was all right and would be home soon. Then he called Jarvis and his cousins. Neither answered. The next call he made was to Sanchez. Sanchez informed him that Jarvis and his cousins had never shown up.

Something was fishy. No one had heard from any of them. *Was Sanchez lying? Did they get stuck up for all that cash? Or did they split with the loot?* After all that Numbers had been through, he knew this was a dirty game and anything was possible. But Jarvis wouldn't cross him. He was equally confident his family wouldn't cross him either. He went back to his original thought: anything's possible, and he knew his cousins and Jarvis had the tendency for greed and power. Maybe they had their own plot—one that didn't include him.

Why?

Numbers said good-bye to his family and jumped into his triple black BMW 745 . He called Lateesha and met her on Park Avenue near building 68. She jumped into the passenger seat.

"Now, this is the Numbers I remember, looking good," she stated, sexing him with her eyes.

Numbers was equally impressed. She looked even better the second time around.

"I've been holding this letter for you since the funeral." Her demeanor changed. She spoke with a glum look on her face. "Ketta wanted you to have it." Numbers took the worn, sealed envelope from her, wondering if she knew what was in it.

"Do you know what this is?"

"Nah, but I know how she felt about you and that she wanted you to have it. It's got your name on it. I wanted to give it to you personally to make sure you got it."

"Thanks, Teesha. Good to see you. You looking well," he said, meaning she was looking very well.

"Don't be a stranger," she encouraged. She kissed him gingerly on the lips with her wet glossies. Then she opened the door and slid out, smiling seductively.

Numbers watched her move up the courtyard. She strutted just like her sister. He knew what he was thinking was wrong, but he couldn't help but fantasize about being with Lateesha. She was just as fine as her sister.

He tore open the envelope and read the enclosed letter:

Numbers,

You know I love you! I will always love you! I know this is crazy—me writing you a letter and all, especially since you're my best friend and I can talk to you about any and everything. But this is very difficult for me to say to you. I wanted to tell you before, but I was scared. I thought you might not ever want to talk to me again. I know Jar probably told you anyway, but fuck him, we'll get to that in a moment.

I went out on a date one time with Crush. I promise you nothing happened. That duck didn't get a feel off me and even though you got a girl and a kid, I still feel like you're my man regardless and I shouldn't have done that to you. I'm sorry, please forgive me. I needed to get that out the way.

Now the hard part . . . I really don't know how you're gonna take this, baby, but I will do whatever you tell me to do. I'll keep it, get rid of it, whatever you want. I'm sure you figured it out by now . . . I'm pregnant with your child.

When I found out I was so happy. Then I was so sad, because

*I didn't want to mess up anything with you and Rosa. That's
why I wrote this letter, because it was hard to say it to your face.
Just promise me when you read this you won't be mad at me
and that nothing will change between us. I couldn't stand it if
I lost your friendship, baby. I need you.*

*Now the last thing I need to tell you is about Jar. I know you
don't want to hear this, but Jar is jealous of you. I think he's
been scheming on you with Crush. That's how they knew we
weren't pumping that day in the park and that's why he was
trying to get you to split from Coney. He's been mad ever since
I chose you over him and he always says some slick shit to me
about it. Something is not right with him so watch out please.*

*Baby, please, please, please don't be mad at me. I love you
always and forever!*

Till the wheels fall off,
Ketta

"Fucking Jar," Numbers cursed, punching the horn on his ride
several times. It all started to make sense now. Jarvis set him up to
get killed, and that's why Waketta was dead now. That's why he was
able to catch Crush out there sleeping and why he murked him
before he could ask him any questions. Jarvis was probably the
one who let Rosa know about him and Waketta. *He's been plotting
against me all this time,* Numbers realized. *Why? Why would he do
me dirty like this?* Numbers was baffled. They were like brothers.
Had he really been that salty about him and Waketta all this time?
Numbers didn't want to believe his right-hand man had dogged
him.

Then again, the evidence was there. Jarvis had attempted to
undermine and destroy everything Numbers had built. There was
no limit to his deceit; he was possibly the one who'd set up Coney
as well. He'd put everything that Numbers loved in jeopardy. Rosa
and even his son could have been killed when Ketta was shot—and

he had been the real target. Had he been plotting with Crush all along?

"Nah, that nigger's dead," Numbers vented out loud, furious. He wasn't letting this shit slide. Numbers had never actually pulled the trigger on anyone in his life, but that was about to change.

He was on a mission. He parked the car where he sat, then walked to his old building. He wanted to speak to Jarvis's mother or sister or someone. He wanted answers. He knocked and knocked, but no one was home. He hit the streets. He rode around BK for the rest of the night, blowing up Jarvis and his cousins' phones trying to locate them, to no avail. At a little past one in the morning, he made up his mind to head back down low. He was tired, but the thought of Jarvis and possibly his cousins double-crossing him kept him awake and on point.

When he pulled up to his colonial home with the well-manicured landscaping next to his lady's brand-new gold 2003 Lexus RX 300 at nine that morning, he was greeted by Rosa and R.C. He walked into their nearly empty house. Rosa had done exactly as he had asked her and packed and moved almost everything for relocation.

A couple of weeks earlier when he'd laid out his plan, he had his lady go down to Charlotte, North Carolina, and find them a house. Whether things went as planned or not on this road trip, he was done with the drug game and they were moving. The last piece of the puzzle was his cousins and Jar. *Where the fuck are they?* Numbers couldn't understand it. He'd instructed his cousins to get in touch with Rosa when they got back into Virginia. He had a feeling he would be detained. He called over to his aunt's, then Wynter and John-John's, but nothing. No one had heard from either of the brothers.

Did they plan this all long? Numbers remembered when Jarvis came down to visit. He and his cousins had hit it off. Numbers remembered coming into the stash house and them huddled up, talking, until he walked in and they seemed to go hush-hush. He thought long and hard about this theory. Something was awry, but Numbers couldn't quite put his finger on it. He wished at that moment that he was as good at predicting the future as he was at predicting the cards.

The second evening after Numbers was back in Virginia, five days since he'd had any contact with his cousins or Jarvis, the phone rang. It was his mother. She was frantic and hysterical. He listened for a moment, then dropped the receiver. His face went blank. He stared off into the twilight zone. Tears began to roll down his face.

"What, Dupree? What?" Rosa queried, sensing something was terribly wrong. After a moment passed and Numbers hadn't answered, she picked up the phone and spoke.

"Oh my God!" she cried. "I'm so sorry, Momma Jenny. I'm so sorry." Tears streamed from her eyes. "I'm sorry, I'm so sorry, I'm sorry," she repeated, not knowing what else to say. "Momma Jenny, I'll have him call you back." She hung up.

Numbers looked up and saw his son looking at him. He grabbed him and his lady close, hugging them like it would be the last time he'd touch another human. He wept uncontrollably. He prayed for forgiveness as he embraced them even tighter.

Jenny had called with the news that Matt and Mel had been found dead in their truck with the backs of their heads blown off.

Several days passed. On the day of his cousins' funeral, Numbers and his family hit the road to Charlotte, leaving no forwarding address. He didn't have the heart to face his aunt. It was because of him that they were dead. He'd lost a lot in this game. More than he could ever get back. It was time for a new beginning.

He was blessed to be rid of the burden of the drug game. He'd escaped with his life and his freedom. Not many in this game could claim the same. Coney couldn't say that for sure; he was going to be doing a score or more federal time. Crispy Carl would be proud that Numbers got out when he did.

As for Jarvis, that chapter wasn't closed. He'd gotten Numbers's best friend and lover killed, plotted his demise, stolen nearly a million dollars from him and murdered his cousins in cold blood. They had been friends from boys to men, and now they were rivals to the bitter end. Numbers couldn't help but to assimilate his situation on some *New Jack City* shit. *Am I my brother's keeper?* Jarvis would have to answer for his treachery. Numbers would never underestimate any man again. Numbers had had Jarvis pegged wrong all along. He'd thought his childhood friend was more brawn than brain. He was surely much more than he appeared. Not just a reactor, as Numbers had previously believed. He'd proved to be more calculating, cunning, and devious than Numbers could have ever foreseen.

Numbers was warned early on by Crispy Carl that this was a grimy business, more grimy than the New York sewage system backed up on the hottest day of the year. But he could never have fathomed it would be like this.

Although he was out close to a million dollars, he was still okay. Sure, he didn't have enough money to live comfortably for the rest of his life. He knew he wouldn't have had that even if everything went as diagrammed, but what he did have would do until he figured out his next move. The old hustle was dead, but Numbers did have a fledgling new hustle in mind.

A brother gotta keep grinding. He ain't got enough Numbers yet!

Acknowledgments

You would think writing the acknowledgments would be the easy part after writing a novel. But this has turned out, for me, to be the most difficult part. The difficulty has been figuring out who I should thank, who I should thank first, and then how to get started. Should I praise GOD first as so many do? Or should I thank Nikki Turner for opening up this avenue for me?

After weeks, even months, of deliberation, I finally decided how I wanted to start this and who I wanted to thank first, so here it is.

I'd like to thank me . . . Dana Dane! I know you think it might sound a little arrogant and pompous, but it's not like that at all. I decided thanking myself first is appropriate because I made this happen! It started with me writing the first word, sentence, paragraph, chapter, and ultimately the book. I believed in myself when no one else would bother with me. It was my determination, drive, ambition, and focus that made this possible. It was my will to not let this be just another incomplete brilliant idea. This process was on me! Either I did it or it wouldn't have gotten done. So kudos to me for understanding that you're never too old and it's never to late to accomplish something new, to live your dream and find your passion.

Now, with that said . . . no one does anything by themselves! I would be nothing without the blessings, grace, and mercy of GOD! GOD has answered so many of my prayers and come to my rescue more times than I can count. I am truly blessed.

I have been blessed with a nurturing mother, Nora Olivia McCleese, who made it possible for me to believe the impossible was attainable. Through her hard work and dedication to me and my sister, Sheryl, I knew anything could be accomplished. I think it unimaginable to have a better mother, parent, guardian, or friend. Thank you, Mommy. I love you!

To my son Dana "Young Dane," whose own talents and abilities have inspired me to write more than rhymes. There is no limit to what you can and will accomplish. I look forward to cheering, guiding, and assisting you as you make your dreams and passions reality, whatever they may be. You have to know and believe as my mother taught me that greatness is possible.

To his mother, Sheleise, for being a great friend to me and a better mother to our son. You are truly a gem.

To my lady, Tana, for being a steady, sobering voice. Thank you for proofreading my book and making me understand that I need to brush up on my English 101. Now if I can just get organized. LOL!

And thanks to all the people I called to help me with my background information to make this story as true as possible: Theo

"Teddy" Adams, for letting me see the Norfolk, Virginia, area through your eyes. And Slick Dave aka Slick Daddyism, Thurst, Mikey Dread, Chief J-Rocker, Karief, Robo, Troy "Preme" Mott, Noodles aka Diggy, Andre "MR." Williams, and Joseph C. Grant, for your creative insight.

Craig Robinson, thank you for your time and dedication to my project. You are a phenomenal talent—can't wait to read your book. Thank you for your guidance, advice, and suggestions throughout this process. I've learned a great deal from you.

To Nikki Turner, my sister, one of the most talented and creative writers and people ever! You have given me the opportunity to expand my brand and extend my craft to those who might believe that a hip-hop artist like myself can only rap. You have become like a sister to me. Thank you for providing the talented group of people to help make my idea a reality. Thank you for all you are, have been, and will be. I truly appreciate you and I have genuine love for you!

To all the gifted and skilled writers, artists, editors, and other employees at One World/Ballantine/Random House who shaped my piece of coal into a diamond, especially Melody Guy, Porscha Burke, Beth Pearson, and Pat Mac: I thank you from the bottom of my heart!

To my friends—my support system and inspiration—you all have given me your assistance with your encouragement and prayers. You are greatly appreciated. Thank you! Thank you! Mark Boogie Brown, D-Nice, Michael "Harry-O" Harris, Leslie Wyatt, Joey, Lance Brown, Kool Alski, Wilfred "Omega" Hilton, Slick Rick and Mandy, Bido 1, Christopher "Play" Martin, Kym Smith, Mark "DJ Wiz" Eastmond, T.N. Baker, Scharee Brown-Davis, Lady B, Julie Evans, Mark Anderson, Gary, Al, Carlos, Big Dre, Lydia Harris, Red Alert, Grace/Harlem Diamonds, Dougie Dee, The Awesome 2, The Game, Big Ced, Scheketta Lawson, Dionne Randall, Jesse Itzler, Robert "Real" Nance, Regina King, Carl "C Boogillz,"

Soulgee McQueen, Buckshot, Ty Deals, Blue Flame, Chubb Rock, GMD, Whodini, Big Daddy Kane, Postive K, Elisa Askew, Stephanie Carnegie, Fred Crawford, MC Lyte, K Rock, Maha, Ice T, Queen Latifah, Melinda Williams, Chris Rock, Scott Modlin, Tonya Bird, Doug E. Fresh and the Get Fresh Crew, James "D Train" Williams, John Adams (Flashback TV), The Source, Joeski Love, Ronnie Triana, Wiz, Prowski, Francine and Champ and the Gray family, Thirstin Howl III, Kwamé and Tamekia Holland, Charles Oakley, Perry "Don P." Foster, Ash, E Boogie, Wayne Mayo, B. J. Stone, Cathy Borusso, Kenneth Spellman, Mark Jackson and Desiree Coleman-Jackson, my Sirius Satellite Radio family, DJ Kaos, Darren "D Love" Harrington, Rod Strictland, Full Force, UTFO, Mike Dean, Jermaine & Jimmy, Lilias Rodriguez, Irving Pantin, Kenny "The Jet" Smith, Scoob Lover aka Johnny Famous, Sadat X, Ike Capone, Dr. Roxanne Shanté, James Prince, Todd Westphal, Kenneth "Boo" and Wanda Williams, Ralph McDaniels, Daryl "Chill" Mitchell, and countless others!

My godchildren—Janay Wells, Bianca Graves, KJ and Khalil Williams, Julian Taylor-Brooks—and my stepson, Brandon Thompson.

Thank you, too, my legal counsel, Scott Mason and Clyde Vanel, and my business manager, Robert P. Reilly.

If I missed you, I didn't diss you, I just forgot to list you! Love, Respect, Blessings . . . Fullcircle . . . Dane

DANA DANE gained notoriety in 1985 with the release of the classic rap single "Nightmares" off his 1987 gold-selling debut album, *Dana Dane with Fame*. Known as one of the icons of hip-hop and one of its greatest storytellers, Dana has expanded his craft and entertainment outreach with his debut novel. A former Sirius Satellite Radio host, Dane tours with other hip-hop icons. Dana Dane currently resides in New York near his mother, sister, and teenage son. He is working on his next novel.